Just Say Yes

Just Say Yes

Michelle Stevens

A Half Moon Yoga Studio Romance (Book 1)

Just Say Yes

Copyright ©2023 by Michelle Stevens

All rights reserved

ISBN

Disclaimer

This is a work of fiction. Names, characters, businesses, places, events, and incidents are either the products of the author's imagination or used in a fictitious manner. Any resemblance to actual persons, living or dead, or actual events is purely coincidental.

This book is dedicated to Suzanne E Peterson, My sister who died of ovarian cancer April 5, 2023   When I was looking for a first reader I asked if she would read Just Say Yes, and she said Yes! She gave me the courage to finish Emma & Grey's story. Our hearts broke when she passed away. But her willingness to try new things and to be open to what life has to offer will live on. In one of our last conversations, she said if there's something you want to do, do it. No regrets.   You never know what life has in store for you. So here's my story of Emma and Grey, who took the happiness life unexpectedly offered them- no regrets.

"Real love doesn't die. It's the physical body that dies. Genuine, authentic love has no expectations whatsoever; it doesn't even need the physical presence of a person… Even when he is dead and buried that part of you that loves that person will always live." - Elizabeth Kubler-Ross

Table of Contents

Chapter 1

Midnight in Harlem by Tedeschi Trucks

No…no…no…. Grey Erikson's pulse was racing, sweat beginning to form on his brow. His finely tuned senses were on alert as he inched his way into the dimly lit yoga studio, unfolded his newly purchased yoga mat, and sat down. *What have I gotten myself into?* As his eyes adjusted, he scanned the room. A few candles were flickering at the front. There was a mat, some blankets, foam blocks, and a strap set out. *Wonder if I need that stuff?* He saw most people had settled in. *Arggh, should've gotten here sooner.* He hated lateness. Made a man seem lazy and disrespectful. He noticed everyone was stretching in ways that seemed impossible for his body. He crossed his legs like the woman next to him. Unfortunately, his knees were up to his shoulders, not flat on the floor like hers. Red-faced, he quickly uncrossed them. *Maybe I should leave now before I embarrass myself.*

There was a bluesy Tedeschi Trucks song playing quietly in the background. Grey recognized it as 'Midnight in Harlem.' The music soothed his anxious nerves a bit. *Well at least the teacher has good taste in music. Do I need some of those blocky things? What on earth do you do with those? I hope we don't have to do anything weird!*

Where's the teacher? he wondered. Probably some crazy woo woo chick. Celeste, his therapist, had recommended Emma Lyn's yoga class. Said she taught a gentle yoga class that included some meditation and breathing. She thought it might help him to deal with his panic attacks. Ha! Like he could ever stay still for meditation. He didn't need stillness. He needed to be active.

As former military, Grey was used to always moving. Always busy. That's why he became a personal trainer. He didn't need time to think about his life. His life had been crap. He didn't want to dwell in the past. Instead, he focused his energy on making other people's lives better and building his business, The Core Connection.

He spotted a few young women in tight leggings and tank tops, and some middle-aged women in leggings and t-shirts. His unsettledness resolved a bit when he saw a few other men in the class. *Well at least I'm not the only guy in here.* He snorted, of course none of them were Black. He felt relieved they weren't in leggings. Grey had wondered what you wear to a yoga class before finally settling on his usual attire - a pair of stretchy gym shorts and a tee shirt.

Where is the damned teacher? Lateness didn't sit well with him. Looking around, Grey noticed an attractive woman at the back of the room running her hands through her auburn, curly hair. She flipped her head forward and captured most of the curls into a bun, a few errant curls spilling out. He gulped, that was sexy. She was older – maybe late 50's he guessed. She was petite but not skinny, and a bit short. And she seemed a little anxious. She took a few deep breaths and quietly tapped her chest. He recognized the signs all too well. *Huh, funny, I'm not the only nervous one. Maybe I'll say hi on the way out. Although, I'll probably only stay for one class and then I can tell Celeste I've done it. No use in flirting when I won't be back.* He sat still, posture upright, and waited for the class to begin.

Emma knew her time as a yoga teacher was going to be over soon. She glanced at the full-length mirrors at the back of the darkly-lit studio and thought that no matter how many times she told her students to close their eyes and go deeper into the pose, they would have to open them eventually and they would notice the sags and bags of her aging body. Hard to be inspirational to people when all they saw was an old crone.

She used to be cute. Never pretty or beautiful, just cute. She accepted that years ago. Now her auburn hair was turning white. Whisps of shiny bright hair framed her face. Gah, she thought, as she ran her hands through her thick curly hair. She had started her usual routine before class. Even after all these years of teaching yoga, her social anxiety still reared its head. She gathered her hair up, checking to make sure nothing was where it shouldn't be, and- gave a few more pats to her heart. It helped calm her nerves. *I hope Crystal has time to color my hair this week!* The other day, Emma walked by a mirror and thought, who is that? before she realized it was her. *I know, I know, yoga teachers are supposed to be all spiritual and not concerned about such superficial things. Accept your body. But the reality is, we're just people, too.* Emma sighed.

She turned around and surveyed the group, noticing a new face. Darn! she forgot Celeste had referred a new person to her class. Arrghh, she didn't have time to really talk to him like she normally did with new clients. *Well, I better at least introduce myself.*

As Emma approached him, she saw he was handsome, about her age, and well-muscled, she noted with an admiring glance. Probably an athlete who thought yoga was stupid, until they started getting super tight muscles and then realized they might need to add "stretching" to their routine. She stopped by his mat. He looked nervous.

"Good morning. Welcome to class. My name's Emma. But you can call me Emma, or teacher, or guru," she laughed. Sometimes humor helped relax new students. "I promise you won't have to twist up like a pretzel or chant crazy songs." Her voice was gentle and soothing. "Do you have any questions?"

Grey gulped. The woman at the back of the room was the teacher? He started fidgeting on his mat, wondering if he should stand up. It was weird, her looming over him. Although, she was short, so she wasn't really looming. Emma squatted down next to him.

She was cute. "Ummm," he stuttered. He felt shy, a little out of his element. "Not really. Just checking out this yoga stuff." He was beginning to get anxious just looking at her. There was something about her that shook him to the core. She looked so kind and beautiful. "A friend recommended it and I felt obligated to give it a try. I'm all about physical fitness. My name's Grey." He quickly stuck out his hand and she shook it lightly.

"Well Grey, I'm glad you decided to come. Yoga is a great complement to most physical activities, but it's also good for clearing and calming the mind. A win-win." She gave him a big smile. "Let me know what you think after class."

Man, he was handsome! Emma was always glad to have new students. Yoga was her passion and she loved to share it. He did seem unusually nervous though. That's probably why Celeste referred him. Yoga's good for anxiety. *Oh well, I'll catch him after class and see how he did.*

Grey stared after her for a moment. *That's the teacher? The one who's supposed to teach me how to relax and deal with anxiety?* She was as anxious as him, for goodness' sake. This has got to be a joke. Years of experience had taught Grey to recognize another sufferer. The eyes always gave it away. *I'm going to kill Celeste.* Anxious yoga teacher. Ironic. They were supposed to be all calm and peaceful. *What's she going to teach me? Plus, I probably know all the moves. Lunges, stretches, It's a waste of time.* He sighed. Then he remembered how tight his legs were when he sat just now and how anxious he felt. He needed to deal with both issues. *Besides I did promise to give it go and I don't break promises.*

Emma walked to the front of the room, her face relaxed and confident, no indication she was nervous. She sat cross legged in front of the class and said in her soothing (some said sexy) yoga voice, "Good morning, everyone!" She scanned the room, trying to assess the group.

"Hope you're all doing well on this glorious fall day. Don't you just love the cool air? I know…I know…. some of you love the heat of our North Carolina summer, but I prefer the crispness of our autumn. We're heading towards that season where we draw inward. Reflecting on the year and preparing for the new year. Like the animals who hibernate to prepare for the coming seasons."

"Did you guys know today is the autumnal equinox? Day and night are of equal length. Everything is in balance. So that means we'll do a lot of balances today," she said with a grin.

"Keep the groans to a minimum. Sorry, you all know I can't resist a good pun," she laughed as she rolled her eyes, then resumed her more professional face.

"Okay, let's get settled into a comfortable seated position. Closing our eyes and beginning to draw our focus inward. Let's take a nice deep full breath in and a long relaxing breath out as we begin to get centered. Bringing the focus to right here, right now. Letting go of any thoughts of the past or worries for the future. In other words – don't think about what you had for breakfast or what you're having for supper tonight," she said with a quiet smile. "Just bring your attention inward to your breath."

Grey did a quiet snort. *Bring my focus to my breath? What's the point. If I wasn't breathing, I'd be dead.* He closed his eyes and gave it a try. It was hard to focus. He took a long breath in and puffed out his chest, drew his shoulders up to his ears. *Jeez, this is uncomfortable.* He tried it again, filled his lungs till he felt like bursting and let all the air out at once. *Damn this is hard.* Just then he felt a light touch on his shoulders.

"Just relax your shoulders. Let them soften," Emma whispered.

He looked up and gulped. She had beautiful brown eyes, he thought. Lots of soft wrinkles around the eyes, in a good way. Her skin was a soft ivory color. She was naturally beautiful.

"It's not a contest. Everyone breathes a little differently. Just let the air flow in and the air flow out." Grey closed his eyes and tried again.

"That's it," Emma said quietly, with a smile, as Grey relaxed his shoulders and started inhaling and exhaling a little slower.

That little smile made Grey's heart go faster. She was really nice looking, he thought.

After class, some of the students hung around quietly chatting. Emma encouraged her students to get to know one another. It made for a more relaxed atmosphere. She wasn't formal. In fact, she was pretty informal. People knew about her life. They didn't view her as a 'guru' but as a calm and engaging teacher who didn't mind laughing when she said left but meant right. Sometimes she was downright goofy.

She looked around for her new student. *Crap, what was his name?* She was terrible with names. Faces she remembered. Names not so much. She caught up with him just as he was about to exit the room. *Grey! That was it, I think.*

"Ummm, Grey," she said tentatively as she touched his shoulder lightly. Man, he was solid. "What did you think?"

Grey started. He was hoping to sneak out without Emma noticing. "Ahh," he stammered. "Hi. Eh-hem." He cleared his throat, straightened his back, and spoke a little firmer. "It was different. I'll give you that." At her questioning look, he continued, "I mean it was fine. Breathing was a little harder than I imagined." He gave her a wide grin. "And your voice was sexy as hell but still oddly calming." He couldn't believe he had said that. He guessed his anxiety really had melted away in class.

Emma blushed. "Oh goodness." She was pleased. Although she shouldn't have been. That was unprofessional and she prided herself on her professionalism. But …no one had called her sexy in a long time. "Well, fine doesn't sound very positive. Maybe you can tell me what exactly what you were looking to find?"

Grey dropped his eyes and paused. He didn't want to admit that he only came to get his therapist off his back. His anxiety had been off the scale in the last few months. He wasn't interested in more medications, but the anxious feelings were beginning to interfere with his enjoyment of his job,

He took personal training and his business very seriously. He enjoyed leading people to a better fitness level. His job was his life, and he didn't want to jeopardize it. When the anxiety started to ramp up again, he found his usual tricks weren't working as well. He already had the cardio part down. It was a natural part of his life, running or cycling every day. And they did help. When those endorphins kicked in at the end of a run, he felt high. He lifted weights and did a little stretching. He kept busy between his clients and his personal routine. But the anxiety was getting stronger, and the physical workouts weren't enough.

His therapist said by working out so much, he was literally running from his demons. And he knew she was right. After his divorce – a divorce that he knew, deep down, was his fault- he closed off his heart completely. And he was fine with that. He learned a long time ago no emotions, no pain. He only went on occasional dates now, and only with women who were looking for fun and no commitment. It was for the best. Or, maybe, he thought, it wasn't anymore. Something was missing in his life.

Celeste had given him a list of ideas to try. Acupuncture: a hard no. Needles terrified him. Yoga, next on the list, was more palatable. Celeste said the breathing and stretching might help him to slow down, get more in touch with what was causing the anxiety and give him techniques to handle it when it showed up. She recommended Half Moon Yoga studio—particularly the classes with Emma. She and Emma had a professional working relationship and a friendship, often referring clients to one another.

So, here he was. Staring into those beautiful wise eyes and trying to find a reason to weasel out of the classroom.

Emma looked up, catching his eyes staring at her intensely. "It looks like you're a little reluctant to say what you need or are looking for. And that's fine. Sometimes we don't know what we need; but by being open to new experiences, we learn. I always encourage new yoga students to not judge until they've been to several classes."

She lightly touched his arm to reassure him. "Would you be interested in committing to, say, a month of classes? Then if, after that month, you still think it's only 'fine,'" -- she grinned-- "you don't have to come back. I won't come chasing after you if I see you in the store or tie you down and not let you leave class."

Grey chuckled. He was charmed by her quiet but firm approach. And her adorable brown eyes that held a slight twinkle as she kept her gaze on his face. And that light touch on his arm had relaxed him. "Well, you have your sales pitch down. As a professional fitness trainer, I admire that. So yes, I'll sign up for a month and hold my judgement until then."

"Great! Looking forward to seeing you again. Tuesday is usually a more chill class, focusing on relaxing, gentle stretches, breathing, and learning to sit with our emotions. Now, since you are a trainer…is that right?" Grey nodded, so she continued, "You don't need the more active yoga. Perhaps you're looking to slow down a little bit and attend to your needs rather than those of others. So, I would say my Tuesday class is probably the best choice. Okay with you?"

Grey stared at her. *Oh my God what have I done.* His heart was racing and his anxiety was starting to percolate. It was like she could see into his soul. One side of his mind was telling him, no, run, run. And the rational side was saying, the class felt good, try it again. He needed help. Before he could stop himself, he nodded his head and said curtly, "Tuesdays it is. See you next week."

Emma stared after him. *Well! He's an interesting person. Very solitary. Very attractive and he said my voice was sexy.* She giggled. She watched his back as she strode out of the room. His erect posture and precise movements during class told her he must be former military. Tight and controlled with no emotions allowed in. Her husband had been military and she recognized the signs. It had ruined his life. She sighed. She probably had her work cut out for her with that one. If Celeste had referred him, it meant he was having trauma or anxiety issues. As a yoga teacher, people often came to her thinking just "doing" yoga would cure their problems. But the reality was it took work, consistent practice, and being open to changing the way they thought about their body. Emma knew the energy—the prana—in the body was powerful. It could be harnessed for good. *Hope so, for Grey's sake.*

Chapter 2

The First Time Ever I Saw Your Face by Roberta Flack

Emma got out of her car, dropping her keys, her yoga mat and almost her purse. *Damn!* It was Tuesday and she had a new group starting today. She hated being late. It always made her feel anxious and out of control. She quickly picked up everything, re-adjusted her mat bag on her shoulder, and ran through the parking lot to the front door of Half Moon Yoga studio. She was sweating like crazy and breathing heavily. *Man, I need to get in better shape! Haven't been doing much except yoga and I can feel... and see…*she ruefully thought…*my body falling apart.*

Emma used to run and cycle and do Pilates, but the last few years had been busy. Losing her accounting job had been devastating financially. Not emotionally or pride-wise – she had hated her job, but it was stable with good benefits. With four kids she had needed that. As a single parent, she'd never been able to save much money. The kids took every single cent she had. If it hadn't been for Brian's military disability, and the kids' social security payments, she'd have never survived. Now that they were adults, she'd been hoping to save more for retirement.

Then Covid hit. The company laid off half their workers, and she was one of them. Looking for a new job at her age was ridiculous. One look at her age and employers just flipped to the next resume. Next! So many people were out of work, they could choose who they wanted. And experienced people cost more. Thank goodness she had a second gig as a yoga teacher. It saved her sanity. But when her teaching job at the local gym disappeared, too, she was distraught.

Luckily for her, Half Moon Yoga, which was run by her mentor and friend Caitlyn, came to the rescue. When the pandemic struck,

Caitlyn pivoted her studio to Zoom and virtual classes. At first, there were few clients; but as the pandemic wore on, people missed their yoga and signed up. With a lot of marketing and a word-of-mouth campaign, Caitlyn built her client list back to almost normal. She hired Emma Lyn to teach seven classes a week at a decent rate of pay--better than the gym.

Emma had to adjust to being on camera though. That was anxiety producing. The new technology required a new set of skills and cueing. Thank goodness her oldest son worked for a tech start-up and was able to help her, albeit rather reluctantly. Old dog, new tricks; slow learner and impatient youth. It all worked out, though. But seeing herself on the screen was always a shock. She didn't recognize that older woman that the camera showed. She hated the way she looked. But her students didn't seem to mind. They were too busy doing their poses and meditations. Her voice was soothing. Her class was engaging. She was a good teacher. And now, actual people were back in the studio.

She ran into the studio panting. She found her room, almost smacking into the door, as she remembered she was the first class of the day, and the room was locked. *Dang it! Where are my keys?* She searched frantically through her purse and then her pockets, once again dropping her mat and yoga bag. *OMG I'm a mess!*

"Ah hem…" a deep voice came from behind. "Can I help you?" Emma turned quickly and found herself nose to chest to her newest student. Goodness he was certainly built solidly. That chest was all muscle and, as her eyes looked up, she noted, so were his shoulders.

"Oh uumm. Sorry…. Just trying to find my keys. I was running late and that gets me all…ummm…anxious. I like to get here early and set the proper atmosphere in the room. You know all calm and peaceful…." Her voice trailed off as she realized how ironic that was.

Grey grinned at her. *Oh my, he has the nicest smile!* "If I can just find my keys …."

Grey bent down and reached for a set of keys that lay on the floor. "Are these the missing keys?" His voice was solemn, but he was struggling to keep his face neutral. His lips kept twitching up like he really wanted to laugh. She was so damn cute, all rattled with her curls spilling out of her headband.

"Ohhh, yeah those are them." She wrinkled her nose. "I was just so worried about getting here. Traffic was busy, and my daughter called and was having another kid crisis. She has three kids, and someone is always causing issues. Life is hard with kids and a job. I know… and then…." She stopped for a second. *Why am I telling him this.* "Sorry, TMI. I got a late start…."

She took the keys he had extended towards her. Their hands lightly touched as he handed them to her. Emma paused for a moment to look up at him. "Thank you sooo much!" He really was handsome. Close cropped hair and beard with silver running through them.. Brown eyes, strong jaw line, beautiful brown colored skin. Rather regal nose, and those lips … *well, let's say kissing them would be amazing.* She kept staring at him.

"Should I get the door for you?" Grey asked with amusement in his voice.

"Oh! No. Thank you. I'll get it. Sorry!" Emma turned, fumbled getting the key in the lock, cursed under her breath. *I really should ask Caitlyn about getting this lock fixed.* She pulled the key out and tried again. Dang it! The lock wasn't turning.

"Let me help with that. I'm an expert at sticky locks." Grey put his hand over hers and wiggled the key back and forth until the lock finally unlatched. He kept his hand on top of hers for a second longer than necessary. Then he pulled away like he'd been burned. He felt that spark. That warmth. Looking quickly away from her gaze, he stepped back. "I guess I'll go wait in the cubby area. I'm a little early." He added coolly "If there's any oil around here, I could grease that lock, so it won't happen again."

"Thanks, but that won't be necessary. I'll tell Caitlyn-- the owner -- about it. She'll get it fixed. It's happened several times. Please make yourself comfortable. You're welcome to come in." Emma scooted into the studio and dropped her bag and coat in the closet. Grey followed her and watched as she set up her yoga mat, turned on the lights, and looked around the room.

"Guess we'll use some of our props today." Grabbing a strap, some blocks, and a blanket, she set up her spot at the front of the room. Looking at her iPhone, she found the playlist she liked to use on Tuesdays. Nice, quiet, and relaxing spa music. She plugged in her iPhone and 'Midnight in Harlem' by Tedeshi Trucks blasted through the speaker. Grey jumped and covered his ears.

"Dang it! Sorry! Sorry! The last teacher..." who, she realized guiltily, was actually her, "...must've forgotten to lower the volume."

Grey just shook his head. "It's okay. I had teenagers. Loud music I can handle. But sudden loud noises startle me. I was in the service for many years. Just wasn't expecting it here." She looked so apologetic, he commented, "Love that song though."

Emma looked ruefully at him. "That's why I try and get here early. So I can avoid all this. Students should just see the calming peaceful atmosphere with a calm and collected yogi, not the frazzled crazy old lady blasting her music. Now you'll never trust me."

She laughed and returned to setting up the room. He watched as she gently tapped her chest between her collarbones. He noticed she was pausing every once in a while to take a deep, long breath.

She saw him watching. *He must think I'm crazy.* "It's a calming technique," she explained. "EFT tapping, it's called. You gently tap certain pressure points on the body. I usually tap between my collarbones; it helps lower cortisol – a stress inducing hormone. There are other places you can tap, like the side of the eye, chin, under your arm. But that's harder to do in public. People think you're crazy if you start hitting your armpit." Emma grinned and went on with her preparations.

Grey smirked as he watched her. She was a little crazy. And maybe a little older. And certainly not calm and collected. But she was cute and entertaining and honest. Maybe he'd like this class after all.

People began drifting into class, quietly chitchatting among themselves. Emma nodded and said hi as she walked around the room. "Hi Laura, how's your mom doing?" She listened, eyes on Laura's face as Laura talked about her mom's dementia and how hard it was for her to be the main caretaker.

"This class is so helpful. I feel it's taught me how to pull back and listen to my inner voice. But I don't know how much longer I can keep this up." Laura said sadly. "I want to keep her at home. It's her home and she's comfortable there. But she's getting harder and harder to manage. Yesterday she thought she was at the ER, and they were taking too long with her x-rays. I tried telling her she was at home not the hospital, but she kept asking what's taking so long. She kept repeating they must've found something bad, getting more and more wound up. Finally, I just told her I'd go and check with the nurse. I left the room, came back, and told her everything was fine. She was free to go home. That seemed to satisfy her. But then, she started talking about my dad. She insisted he was outside pruning the roses and I needed to go keep an eye on him, so he doesn't hurt himself," Laura laughed, "Huh, he's been gone for almost 10 years."

Emma gently placed her hand on Laura's shoulder, nodded her head in empathy. "It is hard. Dementia is a terrible disease. But you have to take care of yourself. You're a caretaker and caretakers need nurturing too. It's like a plant. If you don't water and feed the plant, it can't produce food and will wither up. You need to allow yourself to do things that feed your soul. This class is one important part but don't forget to have a little fun and time away. Let me come and stay with your mom one night so you can have a break. Get out and have some fun! My mom has dementia too, so I can deal with it. She'll be safe. Pick a night and make plans. I'll be there."

Laura smiled gratefully. "That'd be great! I haven't had a chance to connect with my friends lately. Let me get back to you about that."

Grey watched her as she continued walking around the room connecting with students, quietly listening, and making sure everyone was all set. A vision of calmness and peacefulness. Quite unlike the frazzled, anxious person that he had come across earlier. *Wonder how she did that? Made herself so peaceful when she was a trainwreck fifteen minutes ago. Tapping?* He vaguely remembered his therapist mentioning that. Seemed kind of weird, though, so he didn't follow up on it. Now he thought, maybe it was not so weird? It obviously helped her. He made a mental note to follow up with his next session.

*****

Grey went up to Emma after class. "I liked the class *fine*," he joked "but I feel distracted during meditation. I want to be able to focus more." His voice trailed off. "My therapist says I'm holding in my feelings…" he stammered "…my feelings that….They want to come out and that's what is creating my anxiety; but that meditation will help me break the chains. Not sure what that means…." His voice trailed off.

"Well, asking for guidance is a wonderful first step. I noticed you had a hard time getting comfortable. Maybe we can start there. If you feel comfortable physically, that allows space for the mind to relax. When the mind is relaxed, thoughts and feelings float to the top. In meditation, we sit with our thoughts, our pain, and practice, dipping our toes into it, being okay with it. Sort of like when you go to the beach. The first touch of the water is cold. But then you slowly get used to it and you begin to relax and swim a little deeper." She glanced at Grey. "So, maybe she meant you can create a safe space in meditation to explore what's causing your anxiety. Loosening the grip your pain has over you."

"Makes sense, I guess." Grey nodded in agreement.

"So how about we try that now? Relaxing? Grab a few blankets and a block or two and we'll find a good resting position for you."

"Umm, don't you have another class? Do you have time for this?" He looked around a little anxiously.

"Yup, lots of time. This is my job. Let's start by laying back on your mat like we do at the end of class."

Grey spread out his mat and laid down. Muscles tight, shoulders up by his ears, hands tightly clenched.

Emma chuckled. "You don't look very relaxed."

"Nope, I'm damn uncomfortable."

Emma sat down beside Grey. "Let's see what we can do." Scanning his body, she took a folded blanket, lifted his head, placed the blanket underneath his neck and head. "Better?" Grey nodded. Next, she took two blocks tucked them under his thighs, so they were raised up a bit. "More comfortable?"' Again, Grey nodded. "Does your back feel ok?" Grey shook his head. "Ok, sit up for a second." She placed another folded blanket underneath his shoulders and one underneath his lower back, "How's that?"

"Better"

"Now pretend we're in savasana." She saw his confusion. "Savasana is the relaxation at the end of class. She explained, "Let yourself melt into the blankets and blocks. Unclench your hands."

Emma could see him relaxing a bit. "With practice you'll get better. So, next time you come to class, grab three blankets and two blocks. I'm going to take a picture of the set-up and send it to you. There!" She pulled her phone and took a picture. "Now you can see it for next Tuesday. What's your number?" She added his name to her contacts. His phone dinged as she sent the picture.

"Thanks Emma. I appreciate it."

"You're welcome. Let's touch bases next Tuesday and see if it helps."

Chapter 3

Everywhere by Fleetwood Mac

By the end of the day, Emma felt tired. Physically and emotionally. It had been a long day. After her morning classes, she visited her mom at the care facility. That was always draining. She felt guilt and sadness. Her mom's dementia had progressed so much that Emma and her sister were forced to put her in a memory unit. They had done all they could but caring for her now required around-the-clock attention. It was a decent place. The staff--especially the aides-- were kind and attentive. Still, it wasn't family.

Rita, her mom's main caregiver, was the best. She treated her mom like she was her own. Emma and her sister were grateful. But the guilt always claimed a space in her heart.

And now this! Emma flung down the letter that held the results of her bone density scan. Osteoporosis. She started to cry. *I'm falling apart. What a stupid year.* She paced back and forth. Fuming. *All the things I do to stay healthy, and my body is betraying me. First my eyes.* When she went for her yearly eye exam, the doctor looked at her and said she saw the beginnings of glaucoma. Emma wasn't really surprised. Both her parents had had it. It was a fairly easy fix though – just eye drops and regular checkups. *Maybe I won't go blind when I'm 90. I can deal,* she thought.

Then, at her regular yearly checkup, the PA had said, "Emma your blood pressure is high. Let's get you on BP pills."

"Nope, not for me," she had said. She hated medicine and its side effects. "Let's try more natural alternatives." Her PA had agreed to try, In the end they settled on diuretics and some supplements, which, knock on wood, had worked okay.

Her cholesterol was a joke. Though it had been high since her thirties, she had refused to take statins. The doctor had finally stopped pushing them and instead encouraged her to take fish oil, krill oil, and Cholest-off. She didn't use butter, just oil olive oil and plant-based spreads. Lots of fruit and veggies. Only fish and chicken. Not many processed foods. Well, she had the occasional fast food, but only in a pinch. No caffeine. Her bugaboo was sugar. She gave up sugar in her chamomile tea, only honey and lemon balm. But sweets were another story. Cakes, cookies, muffins, she loved them all. Mostly she baked her own stuff. It was healthier that way, but still. Oreos were hard to resist. *What's the use? I can only fight so many battles. Now this?*

Of course, her biggest fear was inheriting dementia. Her grandmother, and now her mother, both suffered from it. Her grandma had died at 90; her mom was 92. *Well, maybe I won't live that long. My BP and cholesterol will save me from broken hips and dementia.* She shook her head. *You're right, mom, getting old sucks.*

Emma googled Osteoporosis. *Hmmm,* she thought, *nope, not taking drugs, too many side effects. Maybe hormone treatment? That might kill two birds with one stone. I heard it improves skin and hair, as well as memory and sex... not that that matters.* She snorted. *My only partner has been my vibrator. But my memory could use some help.* The one thing they all recommended was weight bearing exercises and weightlifting. *I can do that. I used to run. Not sure my old knees would like that, but walking is good. Weights, yuck. They are so boring I'll need something to motivate me. Maybe I'll join a gym? I need to improve my balance and strength anyway.* Lately, she felt less and less stable in balance poses. Embarrassing that a yoga teacher couldn't balance.

She changed her google search to "gyms near me." *Oh, I like the name of this one: The Core Connection. It's near the yoga studio... convenient. They have a free trial membership. What's today? Tuesday?* Glancing at her calendar, she thought, *I'll stop by after class tomorrow.* She slumped back in her chair. A sigh escaped. *A girl's gotta do what a girl's gotta do.*

Emma got up and walked to the refrigerator. *Leftovers it shall be. I really need to go grocery shopping. Tomorrow.* She plopped herself down in front of the TV, grabbed the remote, mindlessly flipped through Netflix, and finally settled on a quick movie about love. *I do like my sappy romance movies,* she thought. She liked to count on meet cutes, unrequited attractions, realizing love was right in front of you, great sex, the breakup, and finally the reunion. She pulled her throw wrap over her and settled in.

*****

The next morning Emma bounced out the door while texting her daughters.

Emma: Anything going on today?
Lisa: Nope, just the usual, work, kids sleep.
Marie: Nope
Lisa: How about you? What's my yoga mama got going on?
Emma: Class. Then I'm joining a gym today. My Dexa scan showed I have osteoporosis. So it's weight bearing exercises for me. (sad face emoji)
Marie: Sorry mom. You've had a run of bad luck.
Emma: Yeah, feeling my age 😵
Marie: What gym? maybe I'll join with you. I'm getting so fat!! Wonder if pregnant ladies can exercise?
Lisa: You're getting fat because there's a baby growing inside you!!

Emma: Come to my studio, prenatal yoga will make you feel better.

Marie: Mom, you know I hate yoga. I need something more challenging.

Emma: 😳 I googled The Core Connection. It's near the studio. Looks decent.

Lisa: My friend goes there. She likes it. Says the owner's son is cute!

Emma: I just want someplace that will help me get stronger. Don't care about cute guys.

Marie: Mom, maybe you should. You're not getting any younger. Before you forget what sex is 😄

Lisa: As crass as Marie is, she's right. You deserve someone in your life.

Emma: Gotta go girls.

Lisa: Let us know how it goes.

Marie: Check out the guys, maybe there's a silver fox there.

Emma: OMG! Silver fox?

Those two! At least James and Steve aren't always trying to get me to date. They were very protective of her. The few times she brought guys home, they'd get all puffy and act manly. They were always asking where they were going and when he would be bringing her home. She could laugh about it now, but at the time it was annoying. They'd grown up to be good guys though. She loved all her kids. Each was unique – and each had their own unique wounds caused by Brian's death. Together, the five of them shared a special bond only loss could create.

Emma decided to walk to Core Connection. It was only a block away from Half Moon Yoga. *This'll be convenient. I won't have the excuse that it's too far away.* Emma pushed open the glass doors to the gym. *Hmm looks clean. Modern. No stinky gym smells.* As she walked up to the check-in desk .a very handsome young man behind the desk looked up and smiled at her. "Can I help you?"

He looks kind of familiar, Emma thought. "Umm. Yes. I'm interested in joining a gym."

"Well, you've come to the right place. What are your goals? We offer many options, from boot camps, to group exercise classes, to personal trainers. If I know what you want, I can guide you to the right program or person. My name is Isaac, by the way."

"Hi Isaac, pleased to meet you. My name is Emma."

"So, Emma, what made you walk in here?" Isaac had a charming smile and way of making you feel comfortable. Emma relaxed.

"I need to get stronger. I just found out I have osteoporosis. And I need to work on balance and stability." She paused. "And I'd like to build my endurance and lose a few pounds."

"We can do all that. First let me ask you a few more questions."

"Sure." Looking at him closely, she added, "You look so familiar."

He stared at her for a second. Then shook his head. "I don't think I recognize you. But people say I look like my dad. He's the owner. You'll meet him at some point."

"Guess I'm confusing you with someone else." She shrugged her shoulders. "So anyway. Before we get started. I'm not really interested in anything too crazy. I'm 62 and have my limits."

"We have plenty of choices. My dad runs a beginner boot camp that's great. Geared for those over 55."

"Yeah, don't know about that.... Boot camp seems a little extreme."

"How about we start with an evaluation. Make an appointment. You'll meet with either my dad or me. We'll run you through some tests and see where you land."

"Now that sounds great!"

"Let me see what the schedule looks like." Glancing down at the computer screen, he asked, "Are you free tomorrow at 1:00?"

Emma looked at her calendar. "Yup that should be fine. What do I wear?"

"Just comfortable workout clothes. Shorts or capris, a lightweight shirt, and sneakers. Oh, and bring a water bottle and a towel. You might get sweaty." He grinned at her.

Grimacing, Emma said, "Hope I don't regret this."

"It'll be fine. After the evaluation, we'll recommend a program for you, See you tomorrow."

Emma started to leave, but then turned back. "Isaac, forgot to ask, What's the cost?"

"Your first two weeks are free. If you decide to join, you get a discounted rate for the first three months. The evaluation is free. If you decide not to join, we'll be sad. But no pressure. We're not that kind of gym."

Reassured, Emma smiled, "See you tomorrow."

On her way back home, exhilarated from her workout, she texted her boys to check in.

Emma: How's things?

James: Busy as always.

Emma: That's good, right?

James: Keeps my bills paid and Ashley happy.

Steve: Wanna pay my bills? Girls are expensive.

Emma: LOL. kids are expensive

Emma: I joined a gym today.

Steve: Way to go mom! Which one?

Emma: Core Connection. Just down the street from the studio

James: They have a good reputation. Been looking for a new place to work out. Let me know if you like it. Maybe I'll join too.

Steve: Getting a little flabby old man? Too many late nights and fancy restaurants?

James: You're just jealous because you can't party anymore.
Steve: Am not!
James: Are too!
Emma: Boys stop fighting. I gotta go. I'll let you know if it's any good.
Steve: Bye ma. You are too getting flabby – that's for James – not you mom.
James: Am not!!! Bye mom. Go get um.

Emma shook her head. Never changes, no matter how old they are.

*****

At 1:00 on Wednesday, Emma walked into Core Connection. Isaac wasn't behind the counter. A pretty, very fit young woman was, though. "Hello, can I help you?"

"I hope so." Emma sounded a little tentative. "I have a 1:00 appointment for an evaluation with Isaac."

"Oh, you must be Emma! Isaac had to leave, but he said his dad would do it. Let me go get him."

While she waited, Emma peeked her head in the workout area. It was not too big, not too small. Obviously well maintained. Several treadmills, ellipticals, lots of weights, and weight machines. She was relieved it didn't appear to be too busy. She was a little self-conscious about being here. A lot of times, gyms were the hunting grounds of the young. But it seemed like there were all ages here.

"Ma'am?"

Emma turned around.

"Grey should be right there. He said to go ahead and look around."

"Okay." *Did she say Grey?* Her eyes widened. It couldn't be. Oh no. He said he was a personal trainer. *Please don't let it be him. Awkward. Maybe I can sneak out before....*

"Emma?"

Emma slowly turned around. It was him. *Crap, no way to escape now!* "Yup, I'm Emma"

Surprise and then recognition flickered over his face. "Emma? Yoga Emma?" He stared at her. "This is a surprise."

"Yeah, for me, too," she stammered. "I didn't realize this was your place. This is a little ... awkward. I was looking for a gym... because I need to build my strength and get in better shape, and this one was close by, and I liked the name, and my daughter said her friend comes here and loves it, so I thought I'd try it out." She took a breath. "I'll just leave and ..."

Grey chuckled at her obvious discomfort. "No...no.... Don't do that. I'm a little surprised too, but there's no reason you should feel awkward. Core Connection is a fitness place. And we can certainly help you with your goals."

"But..."

"You made me feel comfortable when I came to the studio, didn't you? I was nervous and you helped me out, right? Isn't that your job?" Emma nodded. "Let me do the same for you."

"But..."

"Are you looking to get stronger?"

"Yes. But..."

"You came for an evaluation, right?"

Emma nodded.

"Let's do that and if you feel uncomfortable at the end of it, I promise I won't go chasing after you in the store or hold you down so you can't leave."

Emma laughed as she realized those were the words she had said to him. She felt her anxiety melting away. "Okay. You got me."

"Now, tell me what prompted you to want to get stronger?"

Emma told him her tale of health woes. He nodded his head as he listened intently. When she finished, he thought for a moment before saying, "I think we can get you stronger in a way that won't feel intimidating. Osteoporosis is a common issue. With consistent weight bearing exercise, including weight machines or free weights, and walking or jogging on equipment or outside, we can slow the progress." Emma brightened up with those words. "Sometimes it can even reverse the bone density loss."

"That sounds positive. How about helping to lower my BP?"

"We can introduce more intense cardio workouts. I really think spin classes are the way to go. They get your heart rate up and they're fun. Of course, they are not weight bearing, but you should get enough of that with the other workouts."

He looked at her with a big smile. "Shall we commit to a month? And if you don't see results you can walk away."

"Can't resist a good sales pitch." She returned the smile. "Deal." She held out her hand. Grey took it and they shook, both feeling a little flicker of energy passing between them. Startled, they quickly released their hands and stepped back from each other just a bit.

"Will you be my trainer?" Emma asked curiously.

"Would you be ok with that?"

Emma nodded. "Yes."

"Good!" He smiled. "I'm thinking we'll do a combo of personal training, group classes, and maybe down the road, a boot camp. I have one for those over 55." He stopped. "You don't look old enough though. Can I ask how old you are?"

Emma blushed. "I'm turning 62 this year."

"Okay, so you qualify, although I wouldn't have guessed it."

"You would if you saw me naked," Emma murmured.

Grey smirked. "Is that a possibility? Usually we don't require that, but I'm game."

Horrified she'd said that out loud, she dropped her face into her hands. "Sorry sometimes my mouth gets a little sassy."

Stifling a laugh, Grey went behind the desk. "Do you want to start today? I have time in my schedule." *This is going to be fun*, he thought.

"Might as well. I'm here and already embarrassed myself. What have I got to lose?"

Emma followed Grey into the workout area. "What's the thing that worries you the most? "

"Weights." She wrinkled her nose. "I'm not very strong."

"Okay, then let's start with that. We'll get the worst out of the way and the rest will be a piece of cake."

"Now, I do love cake. Chocolate, vanilla, ooh, I love tres leches cake."

Grey looked at her sternly. "You know cake's not that good for you, right?"

Emma nodded.

With a sparkle in his eyes, he winked and said "but sometimes you need to balance the good with the bad. Gotta have a little fun."

"Now, let's get you off the cake train and back on the health train. I think since you're a newbie, we'll start with the machines."

He walked her through the different weight machines and wrote down the specific settings for each machine. Each time he leaned across her to fix the weights, she got a whiff of his aftershave. He smelled really good. And the view of his arms and chest as he adjusted the settings was enticing and distracting.

"Some of these don't feel quite right," Emma commented. "It's like I really have to reach. And looking at the pictures on the machines, my alignment doesn't match the way my body looks."

Grey thought for a moment. "You're kind of short. Just barely in the range of adjustment. We might have to add a pillow to make the alignment correct on some of the equipment." He went and dug a special pillow out of the closet. "Let's try this."

Emma nodded. "Much better." She flashed a grateful smile at him. "Kinda like I did for you in class."

Grey blushed remembering her gentle touch as she relaxed his shoulders and arranged the blanket and blocks around and under his body.

"Made a difference," he mumbled. "Sorry, should've thought about the pillow right away."

"No problem. How often should I do the machines?"

"Start out twice a week. As you get used to them, we'll add more weight and more repetitions."

"Will you help me out the first few times? 'Til I get more skilled?" She looked pleadingly at him.

Her brown eyes tugged at his heart. "Of course." He tipped his head. "That's my job ma'am. And if I'm not here, Isaac will be. One of us is always here."

"Good to know." Emma flashed a shy smile at him. She really liked the reassuring way he talked to her.

"Now the other part of the equation is weight bearing exercise."

"I used to run but I'm afraid my knees and hips aren't up to that anymore."

"You might be surprised. The weights build up strong muscles, which can make running easier on your joints." He walked her over to the cardio equipment. "But let's start out easy. Walking on the treadmill or elliptical works well. If that gets too easy, I'll challenge you to up the speed and jog."

Emma shrugged. "Sounds reasonable." She climbed onto the elliptical and Grey showed her how to adjust the speed and resistance.

"Think you can do thirty minutes?"

"Try my best." Emma started striding up and down.

Once Grey saw she was comfortable, he tapped on the side of the machine. "I'll leave you to it."

Thirty minutes later, a sweaty, frizzy-haired but triumphant Emma hopped off the elliptical. *I did it! Maybe this won't be so bad.*

She looked around for Grey and saw him chatting with an attractive woman. Blonde hair with highlights in a fashionable bob. Tight workout clothes, slender figure, big boobs she kept flaunting Grey's direction. *Wonder if that's his girlfriend? Or maybe he's just a big flirt.* A little part of her was jealous. Lord knows why. She gathered her stuff and headed towards the door.

"Emma. Emma." Grey came running after her. "Don't leave yet. I want to hear how you did. And we need to set another date and time for you to come back." The attractive lady followed right behind Grey. She gave Emma the once over. Raised her eyebrows, gave a little shake of the head with a *Don't bother, he's mine* look. Then she turned to Grey and said, "See you next week." With a little wink and a squeeze of his shoulder, she walked by Emma with a pleased look on her face.

Emma raised her eyebrows at Grey. "Girlfriend?" she inquired.

"Casey?" No. Just a client." He smiled ruefully, "Truthfully, she probably wants to be, but she's not my type. Besides we have rules against that anyway. You guys probably do too."

Emma, relieved, nodded "Yeah, no relationships with students. When should I come back?"

Grey looked at his schedule. "Friday afternoon work for you? I'm guessing you have classes in the morning and evenings?"

"Friday works fine. "

"Good I'll show you a few more things and write up a detailed schedule for you. Maybe plan for you to join the boot camp in a few weeks," he grinned. "The naked boot camp."

"Wow, I'm not gonna live that down, am I?"

"Nope."

"Thanks for the warning."

She turned for the door. "By the way, I enjoyed it. Well, maybe not enjoyed; but I see the benefits."

"Gotta keep my yoga teacher on track. See you Friday."

*****

This should be interesting, Emma thought as she walked back to Half Moon. *He seemed pretty competent, and he listened to me. I like that. Plus, he's very easy on the eyes.* She grinned. She hadn't been attracted to anyone in forever. Dating seems so complicated these days. When she was younger, she didn't have the time or energy for anyone. Maybe now she could make some time. Although he did say he didn't date clients. And, actually, neither did she. Rats! She laughed. *Just my luck I meet a guy and he's not available. Oh well, we'll see what the future holds.*

Grey watched Emma walk out. He liked her. She was smart, eager to learn, and oh so attractive. He hadn't been attracted to anyone in a long time. Emma wasn't his usual type. He laughed. *I haven't had a type in forever.* For a while, he'd been wild. Drinking and hanging out with people who were no good. He'd dated a few women, but only those who didn't want commitment. That got old quickly. His

30

boys needed a dad who was available and not hungover. The last few years, he'd been a homebody. Or, actually, a work body. He had been busy building Core Connection—and his relationship with his kids and grandkids. But he hungered for more, something deeper. Maybe Emma was that something.

Chapter 4

Hungry Eyes by Eric Carmen

Emma's phone buzzed as she headed out the door. She fumbled through her gym bag until she found her phone. Looking at the screen she smiled. It was Marie- her conversations were always fun.

Marie: Mmoooom, I feel fat!

Emma: You are pregnant. It's normal to gain weight. ☺

Marie: But my clothes don't fit me anymore and I'm soooo hungry…and I'm craving donuts! Of all things

Emma: ☺ Then eat a donut… You know when I was pregnant with you, they used to call me Dollie Donut because I craved donuts all the time.

Emma: What does your midwife say?

Marie: She says to go with my intuition. To eat what I want but to try and mostly eat healthy.

Emma: Sounds like good advice. You'll get through this. Only a few more weeks until the baby.

Marie: Soo much to do. Gotta get baby furniture, paint the nursery, line up a therapist to cover while I'm out…

Emma: One thing at a time. You know newborns don't need all that fancy stuff. And they don't care if they have a fancy nursery.

Marie: Sigh…..I know…but we've waited so long and I want everything to be perfect.

Emma: That baby will be so blessed to have you as a momma. I know it's scary. But between me and Lisa and your brothers and my sister you'll have all the support you and Rob will want. ☺

Marie: Thanks mom!

Emma: Gotta go. Headed to my first day at the gym.

Marie: Alright mom. Core Connection?

Emma: Yup. Went for evaluation on Wednesday. Met the owner and we set up a program for me. Kinda excites me.

Marie: Any silver foxes?

Emma: Maybe…. Kinda a weird coincidence

Marie: What?!! I need the deets.

Emma*: The owner comes to my yoga class. I didn't know. He's new. Just coincidence I chose Core Connection, But he is handsome.

Marie: Go for it mom! Do you remember how to flirt?

Emma: I'm old but not ancient! But I don't think he's interested.

Marie: Never know until you try. Wear your tightest workout clothes. And fix your hair nice.

Emma: Marie! Besides, probably unethical to flirt with your students.

Marie: Live a little mom. Take a chance!!

Emma: Go eat a donut . ☺

Marie: Hmmm maybe I will, Pumpkin with frosting is calling to me. Gah I'll be a tank before this baby is born.

*****

Emma was standing outside Core Connection. She was a few minutes late. Taking a deep breath, she walked in. Grey was waiting for her. "Sorry I'm a little late. My daughter needed some counseling."

"Seems like that was your excuse the other day." Grey looked at her, annoyed,

"Huh, uhh…. No, this is my other daughter. She's pregnant and doesn't accept the fact she's gaining weight. She says she's fat," Emma said with an eye roll.

"How many kids do you have?" Grey asked.

"Four. Two girls and two boys. The girls always text me with their issues. The boys not so much. You know. Not manly to ask for advice."

Grey nodded. "Well, sounds like you're a good mom, but you were late. Not a big fan of lateness." He grumped at her.

Emma's face turned red. "Sorry. I'll do better." Outside she looked sorry, but inside she was boiling. *That was rude! Grumpy old man. Really! Who cares if I'm five minutes late. Stuff happens. Not everything runs on time, Mr. Tight Ass.*

"Yes, well. I try to run a tight ship." Pointing in the direction of the cardio equipment, he said, "Start with a few minutes on either the treadmill or the elliptical. Okay?"

Emma nodded as she strode over to the elliptical. Anger radiated from her. *Who does he think he is?* Slapping the pedals hard, she went faster and faster.

Grey noticed Emma out of the corner of *his eye. What in the hell is she doing? She's gonna break that machine.* He walked over to her and said, "Emma slow down, this is just a warm up. No need to kill yourself. Five more minutes and we'll do some weights."

Emma curtly nodded.

"I'll be back in a few." He headed over to the front desk.

Isaac was there frowning. "Nice dad."

"Huh? Nice what?"

"You were a little gruff to that client." Isaac shook his head. "People skills, dad. People skills."

"What? She was late. I just let her know I don't tolerate that."

"Dad, she was only a few minutes late and you could've phrased that a bit better. It's not the Marines."

Grey thought it over. She did look a little upset. Reluctantly, Grey agreed. "You're right. I'll make it better. Especially since she's my yoga teacher. Don't want to aggravate her. Thanks for having my back, Isaac. We make a good team. I have the fitness skills you have the people skills." He punched Isaac's arm with affection.

"Yoga teacher?"

"From Half Moon Yoga, remember I started there last week?"

"Good one, dad. Mean to a sweet yoga teacher." He shook his head.

Huffing and puffing, Emma finished her warmup, jumped off the machine, and headed over to Grey. She felt a little less angry. He had a point. It was a little rude to be late, but no need to make her feel bad when she was only a little late. *Emma let it go. Don't get all attached to feelings of anger.* She reminded herself. It only makes it worse. She took a long exhale out.

Grey approached her, "Sorry if I was a little abrupt before. Wasn't sure if you were going to show up. Lateness makes me anxious."

"Anxious? Uh huh.. Maybe you need to do more yoga." Glancing slyly at him, she said, "I know someone who can help you with that."

"Truce? I'll be less strict about time. You try and show up on time. Deal?"

"Deal."

Isaac chortled. "Sorry Emma, my dad is a grump sometimes."

She grinned. "Old men are like that."

"Alright, alright you two. I said I was sorry. No need to kick a man when he's down. Emma, let's get started with these weights."

By the end of the thirty-minute session, Emma was tired. But a good tired. Her arms ached. Her thighs were burning, But she did better than she thought she could. Grey was a good coach. Even if he was a grump. He pushed her when she needed it and gave her hints on how to improve her form. And he let her rest when he saw she was overdoing it.

"So how did it feel, my yoga teacher friend?"

"Good. Really good. It made me feel hopeful."

"Hopeful?

"Yes, like this is something I can do." She shrugged with a wince. Her shoulders apparently ached too. "Become stronger...you know...that I don't have to accept all of the aging crap. I have some power left in my body."

Grey smiled a big, satisfied smile. "Good. Then I've done my job."

Emma was sweaty, her tee shirt was rumpled, and tendrils of her hair were falling out from her messy bun, framing her face and neck, but she radiated happiness. She had worked hard. Harder than he thought she would. There's something about her. She was special.

"I'll see you next week then. Would you be open to trying a spin class?"

"Ummm, maybe?" Emma squeaked.

"No maybe about it. I can tell you've got the energy for it. Challenge yourself."

"I'm exhausted right now. Can I tell you later? Not sure I have the wherewithal to commit."

With his firm commanding voice Grey said, "I have faith in you. Sign up on the way out for the Monday evening class. I teach it."

Too weak to fight him, she tipped her head to the side and sighed. "Okay, bossy pants."

I need a hot shower; she groaned as she left the gym. *Gonna be sore tomorrow. Why exactly did I agree to torture myself?*

Walking to the studio to get her car, Emma texted Marie and Lisa:
I survived my first workout! It was hard!

Lisa: Good for you mom. Are you sore?

Emma: I am. Can't wait to get a shower. Probably won't be able to walk tomorrow.

Lisa: Can the kids come visit on Saturday and spend the night? We need some couple time.

Emma: Think I'm free, let me check and get back to you. After my shower.

Lisa: Thanks mom! 🖤

Marie: How was the silver fox?

Lisa: ????

Emma: Grumpy and mean. Not my type.

Lisa: You met a guy?

Emma: The owner of the gym. Turns out he's one of my yoga students.

Marie: It's fate. Too many coincidences to be nothing. 😍

Lisa: Isn't that a conflict of interest? Check with James. He'll know.

Emma: I mean I don't think so. We're not dating or anything.

Marie: Yet! I have a feeling there more to this than meets the eye.

Emma: Go eat a donut. Leave me out of your romance story. All I want is a hot shower and some dinner and to veg out in front of the tv.

Marie: Yum… I do have one left from this morning, and it seems to be calling my name.

Lisa: You need to eat something healthy. How about an apple or banana?

Marie: Bleck… I need sweets.

Lisa: 😳 don't come crying to me after the baby is born because you can't fit into your clothes. I learned that lesson the hard way.

Marie: . 🙂 You were a blimp after Graydon.

Lisa: Heh!

Emma: Bye girls.

Lisa: See you Saturday. Gotta go plan my seduction outfit.

Emma: TMI. Talk to you later.

Marie: . 🙂 Have fun Lisa!

Saturday, Emma could hardly move. Every single muscle hurt. Even in places she didn't know had muscles. *Those kids better be good today.* She had originally thought they would go to the park and run around, but she'd never be able to chase after them now. Damn Grey! Him and his coaching skills.

Maybe Marie and Rob can come over and help me. Emma texted Marie and they agreed to meet her at the park later in the day. *Whew! That way they can run off some energy and then, tonight, Grandma will let them watch tv after supper.*

She grinned. Lisa wouldn't be pleased. She kept a tight watch on their screen time. But what happens at Grandma's stays at Grandma's. *I'll pop some popcorn, make a tent, throw some blankets and pillows on the floor. It'll be like the old days when I was too tired at the end of the week. Fridays were always movie night. Pizza and popcorn. Tradition!*

"Be-MA. Be-MA." The front door flew open and three energetic boys burst into the hallway. Lisa followed holding a backpack with their clothes and favorite toys. "I owe you one, Mom!"

The boys had thrown themselves at Emma, surrounding her with hugs. "Boys, I'm a little sore, be gentle please."

"What happened? You got a boo-boo?" Ayden, the youngest, asked, looking very concerned, searching for band-aids on Emma.

"Did you fall down? Mom said you had weak bones." Jayden said.

Lisa looked at Emma shrugging her shoulders. "I told them they had to be careful around you because of the osteoporosis."

Graydon looked upset at Jayden. "You dummy! You weren't supposed to say anything!"

"Sorry, Momma." Eyes downcast, he looked at Emma.

"It's fine," Emma said soothingly. "Be-ma's not going to break. She's sore because she exercised this week."

Lisa gave her mom a hug. "Glad to see you taking this seriously."

"I am. Oh, by the way, Steve's going to bring the girls later today. It'll be a full house. Marie and Rob said they'd go to the park with me to help out. But only if I promised to bake her some cookies.

"Cookies, yay!!!" the boys screeched. "Can we help make them?"

"Sure! Chocolate chip, okay? I promised Auntie Marie chocolate chip."

"But no nuts, Be-ma. We hate nuts!"

"No nuts. No nuts, no nuts," the boys chanted as they ran all around Emma.

"Bye ma! Thanks again. And good luck!" Lisa scooted out the door before the boys could stop her.

Hope I make it through the day Emma thought as she herded the boys to the backyard.

"Last one out is a rotten egg!" Graydon shouted as they pushed and shoved each other out the door.

*****

"Be-ma, I spy Ellie and Olivia in the front yard." Jayden had been peering out the bay window for an hour waiting for his cousins. He ran to open the front door. "Graydon! Ayden! They're here!"

The boys flew out the door greeting the girls. Ellie, the oldest cousin, taking charge, told the boys "Calm down. We need to hug Be-ma first. Then wanna play hide and seek?"

Ellie and Oliva skipped up to Emma giving her two big hugs.

 "How's my girls?"

"Good. Mama told us we have to be nice to you today because you have bad bones."

Emma glanced at Steve, "Boy, word sure travels fast around here,"

"I'm fine, girls. No worries. We're baking cookies in a little bit. Will you help out?"

"Chocolate chip?"

"Yup, Aunt Marie said if we baked her some cookies, she would come to the park with us."

"Yay! We love Auntie Marie. Will Uncle Rob be there too?"

Emma nodded her head, "Yup." The girls ran off to corral the boys to play hide and seek. Ellie was a stickler for rules and was already setting down the guidelines.

"Hi Mom!" Steve leaned in and gave Emma a kiss. Emma winced as she gave Steve a hug. "What's that all about? You okay?" he asked.

"Just a little sore from my first workout."

"Sorry. It does take a while to get the muscles back into shape. But once you get into the routine, you'll love the results." He flexed his arms, showed off his sculpted arms. Steve stayed in shape. For him, it was a stress reliever and an antidote for sitting all day at work. "How was the place?"

"It's nice. Small. Lots of equipment. Clean. No stinky smell. The owner, Grey, is a personal trainer. He's designed a program just for me. To make my bones stronger and give me better cardio endurance." Emma smiled proudly. "The owner has a son about your age. I think they are partners."

"Good to know. I like to support small local businesses. I'll definitely check it out."

Emma gave Steve a side hug as they watched the cousins running around. He looked so much like his dad, sometimes she did a double take. "You're a good guy, Steve. I'm so proud of you." Of all the kids, Steve had taken Brian's death the hardest. And because he was the oldest, Emma had relied on him a lot in the years following his dad's death.

The girls had set up under the big oak tree in the front yard. They were gathering acorns while the boys were ramming around.

"Gotta run, mom. Thanks for taking the girls. Emily and I needed a break. I'll pick them up first thing in the morning."

"Sounds like a plan. Did they have backpacks?"

"Whoops! In the car. Be right back." Steve was a little scatterbrained. Good thing he found Emily. She was the yin to his yang.

She was glad the girls were here. They'd help calm the boys down. Ellie, who was eleven, was a lot like her mom. Organized – she ran a tight ship. But lots of fun. Emma loved all her kids' spouses and partners, too. They'd chosen wisely. *Guess I did something right.* After Brian's death, life had been a struggle and the kids had suffered. But they turned out all right, she thought with satisfaction.

*****

Cookie baking was chaotic. But after a few arguments about who did what, they settled into a routine. Graydon, who was ten, measured. Jayden, age nine, got all the ingredients out; and Ayden, the youngest at five, dumped everything into the bowl. Eight-year-old Olivia cracked the eggs and Ellie did most of the mixing, with everyone getting a turn stirring.

Emma dropped the last of the dough onto the cookie sheets. The kids had lost interest by then and were playing quietly in the den. Ellie, Graydon, and Ayden had dragged out the old barbies and they were riding them around on top of the remote-control cars. Jayden and Olivia were playing Pokémon. Emma relaxed as the cookies were baking. She surveyed the mess. Flour everywhere, dirty spoons and bowls, chocolate chips on the floor. She smiled. Just like the old days.

Exhausting! Not sure how I did it! But we all survived. The only thing missing was a partner. She'd been alone for so long she was used to it, but the older she got the more she missed having someone to go out with, to cuddle with. To talk to.

Lately, her friend Caitlyn had been bugging her to join Match.com or one of those other dating sites. But putting herself out there was too anxiety-provoking. The thought of having to take a picture and post things about herself was daunting. Hell, she didn't even like to look in the mirror. Her body was age appropriate. Not too fat, but certainly not skinny. She didn't want to be like that lady at Core Connection. She wasn't that lady. She was Emma: mom, grandma, yoga teacher, friend. That would have to be enough. Although, she wouldn't throw a handsome man out of her bed. She laughed out loud. Like that was ever going to happen!

"Auntie Marie! Uncle Rob!"

Emma heard the exuberant squeals from the kids as Marie and Rob walked into the kitchen. Marie looked a lot like her mom. A little taller, but with Emma's wavy auburn hair and big smile. She had inherited her dad's green eyes, though. Her pregnancy was really showing now, and she was cradling her belly protectively as the kids raced to her. Only another month and a half until her due date.

"Wow, all this energy, guys slow down! Is that chocolate chip cookies I smell?"

"Yup." Jayden said proudly. "We made them for you, but we can have some too, right?"

"Hmmm. I don't know." Marie said teasingly. "I really like cookies."

"But so do we," yelled Olivia. "And sharing is caring," she said solemnly.

"Ugghhh…. you're right Olivia! Good point. I'll share." As she grabbed a cookie "But I get the first one."

"Heh!" Olivia protested. "That's not fair!"

Emma interrupted before they all rushed for the cookies. "You guys all ready for the park? Let's get our jackets and head out. Who's riding with me?"

"Me! Me!" Graydon and Ellie chorused.

"Okay, the rest of you are with Auntie Marie."

"Don't forget the cookies, Be-ma!" Ayden said as he raced to Marie and Rob's car.

It was a beautiful fall day. The park was packed. Apparently, some tournament was taking place, but the playground was fairly empty. The kids raced around and swung on the swings.

"Go rest, Mom, you look a little tired," Marie whispered. "Rob and I have got this."

"I think I will." Emma yawned. "Need to save my strength for tonight. I'll sit over there by the gazebo if that's okay."

As she walked over to the gazebo, another group of boys ran by heading towards the swing set. Graydon went running towards them.

"Look, Be-ma, its Elijah, from school!!"

"Hi Elijah." Emma smiled at him. "Is that your brother?"

Elijah nodded. "That's Noah. And my uncle Isaac and my grandpa are over there," he said pointing back towards the parking lot. "We're faster than them because they're old."

They went running towards the playground laughing at some joke Graydon was telling.

Isaac? No! It couldn't be the same… that's just too coincidental. As she reached the gazebo, she looked and, sure enough, Isaac and Grey were strolling to the playground. *You have got to be kidding me.*

Emma sat down and tried to make herself as invisible as possible. *Maybe they won't notice me. He's going to think I'm stalking him.*

She turned and walked to the back edge of the gazebo. But just then, Ellie and Olivia came running towards her.

"Be-ma, come and play. We need you! Too many boys not enough girls."

Grey and Isaac looked up from their conversation just as Emma gingerly stepped down from the gazebo.

Isaac gave her a grin. "Well, look who's here, Dad. Our newest client."

"Uhh, hi…." Emma stammered. "I'm here with my grandkids and my daughter."

Isaac piped up. "We're here for the pickleball tournament. Dad's the league champion," he said proudly. "Two years in a row!"

"Pickleball? I've heard it's the trending sport for old people. Isn't it like tennis?" Emma questioned.

Isaac snorted and elbowed his dad at the old people comment. "It is, but it has a little badminton and table tennis mixed in. It's fun. But still competitive."

Grey had smarted at being called old. But the fact was, most of the pickleball players were over 55. Some leagues were just for fun, and some were downright cutthroat. He liked cutthroat.

Grey stared at her. "You look different in civilian clothes."

"Thanks. I guess." Emma glanced down. Thank goodness she had changed before leaving. She had on jeans with a jean jacket and chiffon blouse. Her hair was loose and flowing. He didn't look so bad himself. His tight tee-shirt sleeves were rolled up, showing his strong arms, and he wore workout shorts that highlighted his muscular legs. *Those calves were to die for*, she thought. As she glanced back up, their eyes met and there was that energy, that little spark between them.

Isaac noticed it. *Hmmm.. wonder if there's something more between them*, he thought. *Lord knows dad needs someone. Might improve his mood.*

He sprinted ahead yelling back. "I'm going to go catch up with the boys. You girls want to run with me? Bet I can beat you."

Ellie and Olivia looked at Emma, and then at Isaac. Neither could turn down a challenge. "Is it okay, Be-ma?"

"Sure, go ahead. I'll be right behind you." They sprang into action. Running as fast as their legs could go.

"Nice to see you," Grey said awkwardly.

"You, too."

Ruefully, Emma said "I would run after them but…. I had a personal trainer who worked my butt off yesterday and I can barely walk." Her eyes twinkled as she spoke.

"Sorry, but I only dish out what I believe the client can handle."

Oddly pleased by that comment. Emma blushed. "Is that a compliment from the grumpy drill sergeant?"

"It is. You worked hard yesterday. I was impressed, considering it was your first time."

"Thank you." Emma looked away from Grey. "It's hard for me to do stuff like that. I was never an athlete. You know the story, chubby kid, always the last one picked for a team in gym. Never super comfortable with my body."

Grey looked puzzled. "But you teach yoga. Isn't that all about body awareness? If I recall, you said that in class."

"Ooo, you were listening!" She looked pleased. "That's one component that really drew me to yoga. I could forget about the way my body looked because I was too busy doing the poses. Feeling my body. And surprisingly, I was good at it. I'd never been good at anything sporty. I only wish I'd found yoga earlier in my life. I think it would've helped me."

Surprised, Grey commented, "Thought you'd been doing yoga all your life. You seem like a natural. When did you become a yoga teacher?"

"About twelve years ago. I was old. Probably the oldest one in my teacher training." Emma smirked. "That was an eye opener. Some of the younger ones were dancers and looked like those magazine ads you see. That was so intimidating. But my teacher recognized everyone's strengths and helped me see that I had something to offer as a teacher."

Grey was listening intently. Emma was very animated when she spoke about her yoga. He liked that intensity. It was what he'd seen the other day. Something about her tugged at his heart. She was so damn cute when she was passionate.

"So, was that why you said you wouldn't make me twist up like a pretzel?"

"Yup. People think yoga is crazy poses. And it is sometimes. But it's so much more than that. It forces you to go inward. To stay in a pose longer than you want. But when you do, it teaches you to handle adversity. That you're stronger than you think."

"That's what I do in personal training, too. We find your challenge point and ask you to go a little bit more than you want."

"We have a lot in common, even though we're on opposite ends of the spectrum," Emma commented, a warm smile lighting up her face.

Grey's heart stood still for a moment as he watched her. *She's enchanting.*

"So, Grey?"

"Yes?"

"When in meditation I tell you to go deeper... to block out the chatter in your head… that thing you find so hard to do. I'm asking the same thing you ask of me."

"And that is?"

"Find your challenge point and see if you can go a little deeper than you want."

For some reason he couldn't figure out, Grey wanted to make her happy. To see her smile. "Yes, ma'am!"

Emma stared at Grey. She wasn't sure if he was making fun of her. But the longer she watched, the more she knew he was trying to please her, not tease her. "I better go check on the kids. Marie and Rob are probably at the end of their rope. She's pregnant and gets tired easily."

"Hmm, is she the one you used as an excuse for your lateness?" He looked at her very seriously and then started to laugh. "I know. I know we have a deal. You'll be late and I won't yell at you."

Emma sniffed. "Glad you remembered."

Together they walked quietly back to the playground. Emma saw Marie giving her the look. *Oh no, I'm in for it now.* She turned to Grey, "Fair warning, my daughter has no boundaries. She may quiz you as to why we're talking and how do you know me. If you're married, do you have respectable intentions towards me, etc. Sorry."

"It's okay," he said. "I don't mind answering questions. I'm not married by the way. Divorced for many years. No girlfriend. And my intentions are honorable, so no worries".

But she could see his shoulders stiffen up just a bit. As if steeling himself for the worst. She sensed he was a very private person. *Hope Marie doesn't go too far. I really like him.* She felt protective of him. *Huh, haven't felt that way in a long time. Since Brian.* Her face saddened at the thought of what she went through with Brian. *Don't dwell in the past, Emma. The past got you here to this moment.*

"Be-ma, we missed you!" Surrounding her, they gave her hugs. Those hugs were priceless.

"Who's that guy?" Jayden pointed at Grey, looking suspiciously at him.

"Yeah, Mom, I was wondering that too," commented Marie a little sarcastically.

Emma gave Grey an *I told you so* look. Grey reached out his hand to Marie.

"Hi, I'm Grey. Isaac over there--" he pointed in the direction of the swings— "is my son. He's Elijah's uncle. And from the conversation, I gather Graydon and Elijah go to school together."

"But how do you know my mother? You two had quite a conversation going."

"Marie!" Emma gave her the you are out of line look. Of course, Marie ignored her.

"I own Core Connection gym where your mom goes. She's my newest client."

Marie's eyes widened. Her mind was racing into love connection mode. *This is good. Really good! He's handsome. Seems to be nice. Has grandkids, too.*

"Are you married?" she asked, cutting right to the chase.

"Marie! I'm sorry Grey. Apparently, her candor makes her a good counselor, but a rude daughter."

Grey looked a little ill at ease when she said counselor. Celeste had several therapists who worked at her practice. Marie looked familiar. *I bet she works there. Crap!* Tendrils of anxiety beginning to rise in Grey's body.

"I'm divorced. Isaac is my youngest son. He's in business with me. My other son, Joe, is Elijah's and Noah's dad."

"You look familiar." Marie's eyebrows knitted together as she tried to figure out where she knew him. Grey could see the recognition slowly dawning on her that he was a patient there. Thankfully, she held her thoughts and offered him a lifeline. "Maybe I've seen you at the grocery store. Do you shop at Food Lion on Stratford Road?"

Grey gratefully took it. "As a matter of fact, I do. That must be it."

Marie gave him a thoughtful look. "I think so. Anyway, nice to meet you, Grey. You made my mom pretty sore, so you must be a good trainer. She doesn't like strenuous exercise."

Just then, Isaac ran by, followed by Elijah, Noah, Graydon, Jayden, Ayden, Ellie and Olivia. "Save me!!" he mouthed.

"Good thing he's in good shape," Marie said, as she lifted her eyebrows. Then she whispered to Emma, "Like his dad".

"Time for us to get going, kids" Emma shouted. "We have a sleepover to plan."

Everyone came running back towards the adults. "Be-ma, can Elijah sleep over too?" Graydon looked hopefully at Emma.

"Not tonight. But maybe some other time. If it's alright with his parents." She looked at Grey. "So glad to see you again. I'll see you next week at yoga, and at your, umm, torture... I mean ... gym."

"Looking forward to it! I do like to make people sweat." His grin lit up his face. Grey hesitated, then added nervously, "Maybe we can have coffee sometime after yoga class. I'd like to talk more in depth about yoga and anxiety. You know, one fitness professional to another." He had enjoyed talking to her today. She seemed very knowledgeable about yoga and its effects on the nervous system. It could be useful in his personal training groups. But that wasn't the real reason. There was something about her that drew him in. He wanted more, more of Emma.

"Umm, sure. I'd like that." Emma stammered. And fidgeted. Was he asking her out? She was so out of touch with the dating rules. She did know she liked spending time with him. He was easy to talk to and she felt safe with him. "I love to talk yoga!"

"How's this Tuesday work for you? After class?" Grey pulled out his phone looking at his calendar. "I don't have any clients until noon."

"That's perfect." Emma nodded. "I usually visit my mother on Tuesdays for lunch. We can talk shop and get caffeinated, although I only drink herbal tea. But the coffee shop right near Half Moon, Café Amore, is well stocked with teas, and…" She got a mischievous look on her face, "…my favorite Italian pastries."

Grey shook his head. "So, I'll have to step it up when I see you Wednesday afternoon for some torture training?"

"Actually, I was planning on going to the gym Monday. Once I'm committed. I'm committed." Emma declared.

"Whoa. Impressive! High five?" Grey lifted his hand and Emma met it. They slapped palms lightly. A little spark flowed between them again. Grey yelled over to Isaac, "Did you hear that, Isaac?" He pointed at Emma as he did a little happy dance. "We got ourselves a committed client!"

Isaac rolled his eyes and slapped his forehead. "Smooth dad. Smooth."

They all laughed as they walked to the parking lot. Rob and Isaac were chatting about football and working out. Emma was surrounded by the kids, excitedly planning their sleepover.

Marie walked beside Grey. "Very nice to meet you, Grey. You seem like a great guy." With a meaningful look, Marie added, quietly "But don't hurt my mom."

Chapter 5

Unforgettable by Nat King Cole

"Ok people! Let's get settled." Emma clapped her hands to get everyone's attention. "We need a bolster, some blocks, blankets, and an eye bag. I know that's a lot of props, but I want you to be comfortable. We're going to sit or lay still for a while today. And, just to be clear, today's class is "Dealing with Anxiety'. It's not our usual flow class."

The ten students hustled around grabbing the props they needed and then settling onto their mats, looking expectantly at Emma. She said, "This set-up is a little complicated but once it's done, it's done for the next hour and a half. Who wants to be my model?" Several hands rose up. "Okay, Grey, you're it," Emma said enthusiastically. Grey started to protest that he hadn't raised his hand, but Emma shot him a look that said there was no getting out of it. *Shouldn't have pushed her so hard yesterday at the gym*. He sighed, waiting for Emma to come to his mat.

"All right, everyone watch how I set Grey up and then you can do your own. I'll walk around and make sure you're all comfortable." She winced a bit as she gingerly knelt down beside Grey. "Sorry folks, I'm a little stiff and sore from my workout yesterday. So, I may be moving a bit slowly today. Some trainers don't know when to call it quits." She gave Grey a withering look as she remembered him urging her to do just *one more* when her legs were about to give out. *You can do it, Grandma. You're not a weakling*. He had whispered in her ear. Damn right. She's not a weakling. But it was the "grandma" comment and the nearness of his mouth that got it done. *I am old*, she thought, *but not dead.* He was not going to get the best of her.

She had finished all the repetitions with a triumphant, "Damn you, Grey."

"So, let's go through the set-up." She had Grey up and down, lifting arms, rolling on his side, plopping blocks and blankets, then deciding that it wasn't just right, several times. Grey smirked at her. She was doing this, embarrassing him and moving him all around, on purpose. He knew it and she knew it. What she didn't know was how much he was enjoying her touching him. And when she looked at his body up and down to make sure he was comfortable, he felt the slow arousal building. *Damn it!* He thought. *She better stop now or else it's going to be more embarrassing.*

Hmmm. Emma thought. *He's enjoying this.* She saw his face turn a little red as she noticed a little bulge in his shorts. *Oh my! Guess that's my cue that he's comfortable.* She blushed. "Okay. I think that's the proper set-up. You comfortable Grey?" She smirked. Grey nodded. "Everyone, copy this." She indicated Greys positioning. "And if you need more blankets, help yourself."

Out of the corner of her eye, she saw Grey surreptitiously grab another blanket and drape it over his mid-section. She chortled. "The goal is to let our body feel supported. That's step one – the physical release. If you feel safe and supported, you can relax and focus on breathing and releasing your anxiety. That's step two - the mental release."

Emma led the class through simple breathing and relaxing poses, each bringing awareness to a different part of the body. They were meant to take time to notice where the tension and tightness were located in their body. With her soft, calming, yet still commanding, voice, she talked the group through ways to recognize the physical signs of rising anxiety.

She had everyone think back to a recent anxiety attack and notice what was going on in their body before the anxiety hit. "Maybe you clench your hands when you feel stressed. Or maybe you jiggle your legs or perhaps your shoulders hunch in like you're trying to protect yourself. Practice scanning your body and seeing, learning, the physical signs that anxiety is arising. Now that can be scary. But the more you become aware, the more control you will have. We've numbed ourselves and hidden from our feelings for so long we don't know what we really feel physically and emotionally. Because of anxiety, we find ourselves in a heightened arousal state so often it becomes normal. The tight muscles, the tension, become normal. It shouldn't though."

"But once we recognize that our body gives us warnings; signals we are in a 'dangerous' territory, we can pause and re-evaluate our situation. We can bring softness and relaxation to our body, to those tight muscles, to those physical tics, in a way that allows the anxiety to recede into the background. And then we can assess if we are really in a dangerous situation."

Grey thought back to the things that made him anxious: tight spaces, humid weather, bad rainstorms, loud unexpected noises. All the things that reminded him of his time in Vietnam. But lately, more and more things made him anxious. He worried about his business succeeding. Business was good once again, but that could change at any time. Covid taught him that. He worried about his grandkids. He worried about Isaac and Joe being happy.

All normal worries, but his thoughts often got intense and repetitive until he couldn't breathe or think straight. He'd been so irritable and grumpy lately, even at the gym, which was normally his happy place. What Emma was saying made sense. The body and the mind are connected. But the Marines had taught him not to feel. They broke that connection.

You can't succeed as a warrior if you allow yourself to feel, he had been taught. You had a job and your buddies' lives depended on you doing your job. Numbness and denial were the answer to your feelings in war. But he was no longer a warrior. He was a living, breathing man whose feelings, hidden for so long, were struggling to get out. He felt a few tears slide down his face. He needed to re-find that connection. He deserved to feel alive.

Near the end of class Emma led them in a brief savasana. When she turned the lights back on, there was a hushed silence as people moved slowly to get up and put their props away. The usual chitter chatter wasn't happening. It had been an intense session. As people filed out, each stopped to thank Emma and to ask questions. Grey waited until everyone left, just sitting and thinking about what had happened in class as Emma cleaned the room and got ready to go. "Are we still on for coffee?" he quietly asked.

"Yes, only if you're up to it. That class can be very unsettling. We deal with some pretty deep emotions. If you prefer, we can do it some other time."

"No, I'd really like to have coffee with you. You are an amazing person. I feel I can learn a lot from you," Grey said earnestly.

"Well, that's nice to hear, but it's not really true. I just share what I've learned." She flipped the lights off and gathered her mat and jacket. "Let me lock up. And we can go. It's just a short walk from here."

"Ummm… do you need help with the lock? If I recall you had issues last week?" Grey jokingly said.

"Haha. You just caught me at a bad moment. I'm perfectly capable of locking the door. Besides Caitlyn was supposed to get the locksmith in to fix it."

She gestured to Grey to lead the way out as she shut the door and put the key in the lock. "Dang it! I can't believe this." She struggled with the key, turning back and forth but not able to get it out of the lock. "Guess Caitlyn didn't get it fixed."

Grey laughed as he reached over Emma's head and jiggled the key out. "I told you I had lots of experience with locks."

Emma glared at him. "I would've gotten it eventually!!"

"Ah huh." Grey nodded his head. "But it's quicker if I do it. I need some caffeine and I think you need some sugar." Emma had to agree he was right, arrogant man that he was, as she rolled her eyes at him.

As they strolled towards Café Amore, they were fairly silent, each aware of the other's body heat. Not touching but close. Drawn towards one another. The sun was shining. The air was fall crisp, an altogether gorgeous day. Emma breathed in the fresh air as she drank in the orange, red, and yellow leaves on the trees and on the ground. It was her kind of weather.

As they neared the café, Emma broke the silence. "So, what did you think of the class?" she asked anxiously, ironically enough. She cared about—no, she mused, she felt invested in—Grey. She could see he was a kind man who had some inner demons. But to his credit, he was trying, stumbling along the path to opening up. Maybe by helping him, she could rid herself of some of the guilt about Brian.

She stopped and faced Grey. He glanced at her then cast his eyes down. *Oh, dear. He hated it* Reaching out, touching his arm. Emma continued, "It's okay to be honest. To say you hated it, you know, I won't melt into a puddle of tears or get mad." *At least not in front of you*. She did care and it might hurt if he was negative about it, but she learned a long time ago you can't please everyone all the time. Although she tried.

"Hate it?" Grey looked perplexed. "No, no, the class was …not sure how to say this." He stumbled for words "It was amazing and scary and enlightening and stressful for me. But hate it? No." He held the door to Café Amore. "Shall we? After you."

Café Amore was small and cozy, smelling enticingly like coffee. A few small tables were scattered against the wall and the front window had views of the street, just like a European bakery. The glass cases were filled with all kinds of Italian pastries. Emma walked back and forth, studying the food.

"Do you believe this place? Look at all those luscious pastries." Emma gushed. "Ohhh, its always so hard to pick just one. The cannoli are to die for, but the maritozzo is so yummy. You know, they are breakfast pastries in Italy. Do you know what a maritozzo is?" Grey shook his head. "It's a sweet brioche bun split down the middle and filled with whipped cream."

Glancing at Grey, she saw him calculating calories in his head. "You know, Europeans eat a sweet pastry and an expresso for breakfast. But the rest of the day they eat good food. They are not fat and there's a place for sweets in your diet," she lectured. "Have something with your coffee. It'll take the edge off."

She strode up to the counter. "Hi Maria, we'll take two maritozzos, a coffee…" she turned to Grey, "… black?"

"Actually, cream and one sugar," he replied, loving the shocked look on her face.

"So, a coffee with cream and sugar, and a chamomile tea with honey," she said to Maria.

"Got it. That'll be $12.50."

Grey started to hand Maria his card, but Emma waved Grey off. "I got it. It's the least I can do for stressing you out."

"Who's the handsome dude?" Maria shouted over the noise in the café. "Do you finally have a boyfriend?" She winked at Emma and Grey. "He looks like a keeper. You got yourself a good woman. Hope you know that!"

Both of them blushed, too late to set Maria straight. *Probably never hear the end of this though.* Emma shrugged her shoulders at Grey. Marie was already off gathering their order. They wandered over to the open table by the front window with a view of window boxes and planters stuffed with autumn flowers and leftover summer herbs. "Sorry about that," Emma said. "I was going to explain, but, you know, Italians love love."

Besides, Grey thought, *maybe they weren't lovers yet, but who knows? Colleagues to friends to lovers is a good story.* Grey hadn't mentioned to Emma that he read romance novels on the sly. She probably wouldn't believe him anyway. When he was at the VA hospital, sometimes the only books to read were books people left in the waiting room. He wasn't sure why, but there were a lot of romances. He found them an antidote to his anxiety. Getting lost in a crazy, funny, and sexy romance story helped soothe his nerves and forget his pain for a little while. He had enough violence and death in real life. He didn't need it in his reading too.

But it was his secret. No one knew. And this former Marine would never tell that he learned his lovemaking tricks from romance stories. He had actually become quite the connoisseur of romances. Some were sweet and funny, some were downright soft porn. But all were entertaining. He especially loved Jasmine Guillory. Her focus on well-rounded and accomplished Black men and women resonated with him. Plus, they were hot!

Maria bustled over with the coffee and pastries. "Be right back with your tea." She returned right away with a glass tea pot with the chamomile tea steeping. A floral teacup and dainty spoon along with a pot of honey made it seem special.

"Fancy!" Grey looked over the set-up. "Reminds me of my visit to Europe," he commented.

"It is. That's why I come here. Maria takes extra care with everything. The pastries and the tea, she takes pride in her work. I bet you'll find your coffee is the best you've ever had."

Grey lifted his cup and sniffed the coffee. "Mmm, if it tastes anything like it smells, you may be right." He took a quick sip. "Ahh... caffeine." He sighed with pleasure as he closed his eyes and savored the taste.

Damn, that was sexy. Emma gulped. She felt a stirring in her belly and it wasn't hunger.

"You were right. This is the best coffee I've had in a long time." Grey raised the corners of his mouth into a big, satisfied smile. "Thank you for suggesting this place."

"My pleasure." She bowed her head in acknowledgement. "I do know my cafes. Now try the maritozzo. I want to see your reaction."

Grey looked at the fluffy whipped cream and the sweet roll. "Ummm, no ma'am, not sure I can do all that sweetness. It's huge."

"Come on. Just a bite. Maria makes the best, most tender pastries in town." Challenging him, Emma took a bite of the pastry. "Oh my god that's sooo yummy!" Grey watched, fascinated. Emma's eyes closed as she let all the flavors meld in her mouth. The pleasure was evident in her face. She licked the whip cream off her lips. *Damn, that was sexy.* Her lips were full, and he could imagine them licking something else. He felt a stirring down below. He took a quick sip of coffee to distract himself.

"Now your turn."

"Emma, you're a pusher."

"One bite won't hurt. Enjoy the efforts of a master baker."

Grey looked at the maritozzo like it was poison but picked it up and took a small bite. "OMG! This is f'ing delicious!" He took another bigger bite and glared at Emma. "I will make you pay for this."

As he gobbled the maritozzo down, Emma started laughing and couldn't stop. She was laughing so hard; tears were running down her cheeks. She slapped the table and other customers began to look at her. "Oh, Grey. You are …so funny. It's a pastry. Just enjoy it."

"I did enjoy it. It was unspeakably good. I will remember the taste all day. But now I will have to run two extra miles today to balance off the calories. And you." He looked sternly at her. "You will pay for this tomorrow." Giving her an evil smile, he said, "I think it's time for you to join our boot camp."

Emma paused in midbite. "Are you kidding me?" Her eyebrows shot up. "I'm not ready for boot camp!"

"Oh, Emma" He laughed. "You are so funny. It's a boot camp. No one's ever ready. You just do it."

Emma grumbled, "Guess I deserved that. But eating a maritozzo is way more fun than sweating."

They both started laughing, their eyes meeting. Then, both paused as they felt the unspoken attraction.

"When did you go to Europe and where?' Emma asked, diffusing the charged air.

"Been through most of Europe over the years. Especially loved Italy and Switzerland. Actually, I've been thinking of going over there again this year. But I'm still a little leery of Covid."

"Yeah, I get that. Covid sucks." Emma nodded her head. "I've never been. We got married young. No time or money to travel. But before Covid hit, my daughters and I had planned a trip to Italy to see my grandmother's birthplace." Emma wistfully said, "We talked about re-scheduling the trip this year, but now Marie's pregnant and Lisa is so busy. Not gonna happen."

"So, you're Italian?" Grey asked curiously.

"On my mom's side. My grandmother came over to America when she was seventeen. She lived in the Italian Alps, right near the Swiss border."

"Funny. My mom's family is from Italy too. They came from Milan. My grandfather probably immigrated right around the same time as yours."

"Small world." Looking surprised, she paused before asking. "So, you're Italian?"

"Yes, and a mix of many races. I look a lot like my dad. My mom is Italian, Moroccan, and Algerian. My dad is African American."

"Interesting combination. Bet your mom is beautiful."

Grey looked sad. "She was. She passed away many years ago. Diabetes. My dad passed a while ago too. Heart attack."

"Sorry," Emma said quietly. "Losing a parent is hard, no matter how old you are."

"That's why I'm so careful about diet. Diabetes or heart disease are not fun to live with."

"My mom has dementia now. It's a tough disease. She's as healthy as a horse but can't remember anything."

"It seems you're either healthy physically and losing it mentally, or vice versa. Not sure which is worse," Grey said thoughtfully, and Emma nodded in agreement. Chatting about health, their kids and grandkids, and life in general, time flew by.

Emma stretched her arms and rolled her shoulder. "Sorry, sitting still isn't my thing anymore."

Grey laughed. "Mine either."

"Speaking of which…Oh my goodness! It's 11:45 - time to go have lunch with my mom."

"And I have a client at noon. We never got to speak about yoga. Maybe we can do this again?" Grey looked hopefully at Emma.

Emma nodded her head. "Yes, I'd like that."

He pulled out his phone and looked at his calendar. "How's Thursday?"

Emma ran through her schedule. "I can't do morning and I have the grandkids after school."

"How about you come to spin class at 6:00 PM and we can grab a smoothie at Joe's Juice afterwards?"

Emma wrinkled her nose and laughed, "I can't drink liquids that late at night. I'm old. I'll be up all-night peeing. How about something at Greek Guys grill? Their food is good and fresh."

"Deal. See you tomorrow for boot camp."

"Arrgh… you are so mean."

As they parted ways. Emma went right and Grey went left. Both thought, *Huh… that was interesting. Time just flew by.* Emma glanced back at Grey at the same time Grey looked back at her. They smiled.

Emma pulled out her phone which, surprisingly, she hadn't looked at all morning,

Emma: On my way to visit mom.

Emma: I just had coffee with Grey. We talked for 2 ½ hours. . ☺

Lisa: Who's Grey?

Marie: The hottie mom met at the park.

Lisa: Mom! You picked up a guy at the park?

Emma: No! He's my trainer. From Core Connection. We just happened to meet at the park this weekend and he asked me to have coffee after class so we could talk about yoga and anxiety.

Lisa: That's a good pickup line. 😄

Marie: So how was it?

Emma: Good very good.

Lisa: Did you talk yoga?

Emma: We never got around to it. He's a very interesting person.

Marie: And very easy on the eyes. . 😳

Lisa: So what's next?

Emma: Well he forced me to sign up for boot camp because I made him eat a maritozzo.

Marie: Oooo I love them! Did you go to Café Amore? And did you get one for your pregnant daughter who craves sweets?

Emma: Whoops! forgot. Sorry.

Lisa: Boot camp? Are you ready for that?

Emma: NO. Grey says you just have to jump in and do it. 😐

Marie: That's sounds kind of provocative. He must like you.

Emma: Maybe. He did ask me to go with him after spin class on Thursday to discuss the yoga we didn't discuss today,

Lisa: Sounds like he likes you. Just be careful. He might be a player.

Marie: I don't think he is. He seemed sincere. Anyway, I warned him not to hurt mom.

Emma: You what?!!!!! You did not!

Marie: I did. We got your back mom.

Emma: OMG! I'm a grown woman.

Lisa: Just be careful. Let us know where you're going. Text us after your date on Thursday. Gotta go, I have a patient in 5 minutes.

Marie: Me too. Enjoy mom. But be safe.

Emma: Love you. Although I do not enjoy this role reversal.

Emma's lunch with her mom was fun. Her younger sister Lizzy showed up too, making her mom especially pleased. The two sisters got along well and shared the care of their mom. *Mom seems to be having a good day,* Emma thought. You never know what you were going to get. She was mostly with it, although some days she was a little crazy.

Emma got her to talk about her grandmother's family immigrating from Italy and the small mountain town her family came from. It was interesting, and her mom was animated when she spoke about it. By the end of lunch, though, her mom was tired and beginning to be confused. She was ready for her usual long afternoon nap. After settling her in bed, Lizzy and Emma chatted on the way out.

"Mom was pretty good today," Lizzy commented.

"Yeah. It's a good day," Emma replied with a little secret smile. *Today had been a good day.*

"What's up with you? You look all happy. Not that you're not usually happy. But something's different." Lizzy searched Emma's face for clues.

"Umm. I kinda met a guy."

"What?!!! I don't believe it! You? Little Miss I am never going to date again. Found a guy!"

"Calm down. I'm not dating. We're just …umm… not sure what I'd call it. He takes my yoga class and I work out at his gym. And we had coffee together today to talk about yoga, but we never got around to talking about it, so, he suggested we have dinner on Thursday. But it's weird. We're colleagues and clients, but there's definitely an attraction there. I think. I've been solo for so long not sure if I know if someone is interested or not," Emma babbled.

"Hold on. He's your student? And you're his client? Isn't that kinda weird? Or unethical?" Lizzy questioned with a concerned look on her face.

"I mean, not really. I'm allowed to do things besides yoga. And we're not hooking up."

"Yet!" Lizzy said. "But you like this guy, and he likes you back? "

"I don't know," Emma moaned. "It's confusing and new. I think so. But the other thing is, he's former military and I think he's got anxiety issues."

"Emma!" Lizzy cried. "I thought after what you went through with Brian you said no more military guys."

"I know, I know. But there's something about this guy. He's funny and kind and confusing and sexy."

"Sexy, huh? Well, that trumps common sense." Lizzy shrugged her shoulders. "You haven't fooled around in forever, have you?"

"Like, not since Brian…. I've had dates but nothing intimate."

"OMG!! Emma! How can you stand it? Twenty years with no sex?? Maybe you should just jump this guy's bones today."

"I have my vibrator," Emma said with a laugh. "I even named him Fred. We're so close. So, no need to jump anybody. But I would like to explore Grey a little more," she said, wiggling her eyebrows suggestively.

"Just be careful, Emma. You're an innocent. You always see the best in people, but sometimes people aren't so good," Lizzy warned. "I don't want to see you get hurt."

"I will, little wise sister." Emma smiled. *Maybe.*

She headed home to prepare for the onslaught of grandkids. She went around cleaning up – although she wasn't sure why. Five minutes after they arrived, the house would look like a tornado had hit it. She made sure she had snacks. *Darn, almost out of milk. Guess I'll run to the grocery store. Maybe I'll have time for a short nap when I get back.*

Her thoughts wandered back to this morning. She had really enjoyed her conversation with Grey. He was easy to talk to and he made her laugh. He could dish it out and take it too. She felt a connection to him that she's never felt with anyone. Her heart felt a lightness and openness she wasn't sure what to do with. *Just enjoy the moment. Isn't that what you tell your students? Just enjoy. It's nice to have a male friend.*

*****

Grey sighed as he walked into the gym. His first client was Casey. He had tried to get Isaac to work with her, but unfortunately, she always wanted him. She was attractive in a fake kind of way, with medium length, highlighted, blonde hair, always perfectly coiffed. She had a great figure, nice boobs, a great ass, and long legs. And she was always flaunting it. Grey hated it.

He had acknowledged a few years ago that the empty spot in his heart couldn't be filled by mindless sex. He wasn't interested in hookups. So, he had a hands-off policy on clients, which he had told Casey many times. Didn't seem to sink in, he thought, annoyed at her persistence. He wondered if she was the type of woman who always needed a man. He knew from conversations she had a bitter divorce, so he tried to be kind. In his dating adventures he had met divorced women who needed validation from a man. Just last week she had 'accidentally' pushed her body up against his with a very suggestive look. He had stepped away, but she just stepped back in. "Aren't you interested?" she had whispered.

Grey had tried his best to keep the annoyance off his face as he told her, "Thanks, but no fraternizing with the clients is the rule." She had huffed away, angry; but later, on her way out, she had tried again. She thrust her boobs in his face and started acting sexy.

Thankfully, Emma was just leaving, and he had used it as an excuse to get away. He had seen the appraising look she gave Emma, like she was her competition, then dismissing her as if she didn't matter.

Casey was wrong though. Emma mattered. She was way more his style. She was real and kind and beautiful in a more natural way. *You better watch out. You have it bad for her and you don't even know her. But I want to. Friends first. Lovers later. That's how the story goes.* Staring off into space, he had a goofy grin on his face.

"Hey there Grey. I see that smile. Thinking of me?" Casey walked up to Grey and touched his arm as she preened in front of him. Showing off her best assets.

"Oh, hi Casey." Grey moved away and headed towards the weight room. "Let's get going. Why don't you start with some warm-ups, and I'll get your weights set-up." He pointed matter- of-factly to the treadmill.

Casey looked at him longingly, then turned and stomped to the workout area. *I don't know what's wrong with that man. No man turns me down. No sane man. I mean look at me!* She glanced in the mirror, fixing her hair. *I mean I'm hot. Aren't I?* She knew she looked good but needed that reassurance. Her husband had been mentally abusive, and the eventual divorce had been traumatic. Her therapist said she still had a lot to work through. She sniffed. *I'll show him. Maybe I just need to make him jealous. Yes, that's it. I'll flirt with Isaac.* Her thoughts distracted her as she finished the warmup. As she walked over towards Grey, she took a little detour to the front desk. "Hi Isaac," she said throatily. She glanced back to make sure Grey saw her.

Grey just shook his head. Poor Isaac. That woman is a piece of work. Wonder what happened to her? "All set with weights. Let's get a move on, Casey," he called out. Grey indicated the weights on the floor.

"Ten reps of biceps curls, three sets, and then move on to triceps pushbacks." When Casey's back was turned, Isaac gave Grey the thumbs up and mouthed "thank you." They managed to finish the session without incident.

When she was done, Casey, setting her sights on Isaac, sashayed over to the front area. But Isaac had seen her coming and hurried into the back office. Kayla, the other trainer, laughed at Isaac. "Chicken! I'll distract her and give you the all clear when she leaves."

"Hi Casey. You're looking good! Those sessions are really paying off," Kayla said enthusiastically. "Everything looks so sculpted!"

"Why, thank you for noticing! That's so sweet. I do try to take good care of myself. Men, you know, like a shapely woman," she said as she placed her hands on her hips and twirled around. "Too bad the men around here don't notice. Is Isaac around? I had a …a question for him."

"Oh, I'm sorry. He had a Zoom meeting this afternoon. Won't be back on the floor until later. Is it anything I can help with?"

Casey frowned. "Nope. I just needed to ask his opinion about something." She glanced around crestfallen, not seeing Grey or Isaac, or any man for that matter. She sighed.

"See you tomorrow. Tell the boys I said good-bye." Giving a little wave, she headed out the door. *I don't know why I do that. Isaac is young enough to be my son. The son I never had,* she thought sadly. *Casey you're better than that. My therapist is right. Not every man needs to think I'm sexy. I need to work on that.*

"Coast is clear, Isaac." Kayla yelled. Isaac stuck his head around the door. After checking to make sure Kayla wasn't trying to prank him, he came back to the front desk. "Whew! She's some scary person."

"That she is. That she is," Kayla agreed.

Chapter 6

Can't Take My Eyes Off of You – Frankie Valli

Emma was both nervous and excited as she got ready to go to spin class at Core Connection. She looked okay. She had fussed about what to wear. Bike shorts were not flattering on an old lady. Her spider veins and white legs were not attractive, at least in her eyes. And her flabby, though lately, notably firmer, butt was horrifying. She had gone to the sporting goods store to find some new athletic wear, but God almighty, everything was too tight and too revealing.

Just for giggles, she had tried on a biking outfit, tight compression shorts, and a super tight nylon shirt. The shorts gave her a muffin top so big it bulged out of her shirt, although the extra padding did make her butt look good. And the bra's only purpose, it seemed, was to give her a ton of cleavage, which, considering she was only a 34B, was a feat unto itself. Too bad she couldn't breathe, and the excess flab flowed over the sides. She started laughing. It was either that or cry. *Emma, girl, your sexy days are long past. You're trying to get stronger, not be a sexpot like that lady at the gym. She was a trip. Let's try on some real clothes.*

She eventually found a pair of tight capris that felt supportive but didn't make her fat overflow, and a lightweight, yellow yoga top that showed off her toned shoulders and still left room to breathe. Satisfied she looked okay, Emma hopped in the car and headed off to her cycling class. *Oh crap, I forgot to bring a change of clothes. I should probably go back, but that will make me late and lord knows what Grey will say to that.*

"Emma, what are you doing here?" Isaac greeted her with a big smile. "Come back for more torture with grumpy pants?"

"Is he in a bad mood?" Emma asked concerned. She'd hoped to burn off some stress after her afternoon with the grandkids, not get more stressed.

"Kinda. He's been super touchy lately. Running a business is a lot of work and worry, and he seems to be leaning towards the worry side."

"Sorry to hear that. Maybe he needs more yoga."

"He needs something." Isaac smirked. "He does seem better after your classes, though. You are helping him." Gratified, Emma opened her mouth to say thank you when the front door flew open, and a deep sexy female voice said, "Hey there, Isaac." Isaac looked concerned. It was the woman from the other day, the blonde.

She walked right by Emma and put her face near Isaac. "Are you teaching class tonight I hope?" Her cleavage was overflowing her bra top. It was dangerously close to Isaac. Emma was jealous, despite herself. *No muffin top on her. No side fat hanging out from her bra.* She felt frumpy.

But she had to laugh as Isaac gulped and backed away from Casey. "Nope, my dad is."

"Oooh, well that's even better." She looked towards the cycling room. "Guess I better go so I can get a good seat. And Grey can have a good view."

Emma shook her head in amazement. "Oh my! Guess I better go in too." *I want to see Grey's face when he sees the view.*

"You might want to sit near the fans. It might get hot in there." Isaac gave a knowing look as she laughed.

Emma hesitated a moment outside the cycle room while her eyes adjusted to the dark. *Dang, the music is loud in here. Wonder where I should sit?*

She saw a bike near the back row and beelined for it. Grey saw her out of the corner of his eye. He felt happy. *She came!* He had been worried she wouldn't show up.

"Emma," he shouted over the music, "let me help you with the bike settings." He started to walk over to her when Casey, standing beside a bike, spoke.

"Grey, could you come adjust my seat. It seems to be stuck." She tugged helplessly at the seat lever.

Annoyed, he looked at Casey. "Let me see what I can do." He quickly fixed it and reminded her of the settings. Before she could object, Grey scooted towards the back of the room and Emma.

"Hello there. Happy that you made it."

"Did I have a choice?" she said teasingly.

"Let's get the right settings for your bike. Why don't you hop on, and I'll see where we're at."

Emma carefully put one foot on the pedal and swung her leg over the seat. Grey sized up her position. Then he had her get off as he lowered the seat and the handlebars.

"Let's try that. There should be a slight bend in your knee and your knee should be lined up with the ankle." He lightly touched her leg. "How does that feel?"

"Fine." Actually, more than fine, she thought as she jumped slightly with his touch.

"Hmm. I don't know. Why don't you get off and let me make a few more adjustments."

Emma huffed as she jumped off the bike again. "I think it's just fine. I used to do spin classes all the time, so I know what feels right."

"Maybe, but I don't feel like I've embarrassed you enough." He gave her a look that told her this was payback for the other day.

"Fine! We're even now." She climbed back on the bike and tried to find a comfortable spot for her butt. She had forgotten how hard the bike seats were.

Grey watched in amusement as she wiggled her butt around. *She's so cute in her workout clothes. Wonder what she looks like out of her workout clothes. Don't go there yet, Grey. Friends first. That's how romance stories go.*

He walked to the front of the room, grabbed his microphone, and sat on his bike. "Good evening, everyone! Hope you're all up for a fun ride tonight. Welcome to our new rider, Emma. Always happy to have new people in class." He reached over to the speaker and changed the music. "We'll start out slow- a fairly gentle warm-up." "Just Say Yes" by Snow Patrol was the first song. Emma loved that song. As the refrain played, and the pace picked up, Grey looked at her and sang along to "Just say yes."

Emma was startled and thrilled. *He's looking right at me as he's singing that. Coincidence? Maybe. But a girl can dream.*

Just then, Casey shouted "OH! Grey you're playing our song."

He broke his gaze from Emma's face and laughed, then shook his head, "Alright everyone let's pick up the pace a bit. Almost done with the warmup and time to move to the work." Gradually bringing his gaze back to Emma, he smiled.

*****

After class Casey corralled Grey with small talk. He looked helplessly at Emma. Brusquely, he said "Excuse me Casey. I need to check in on my new riders. Thanks for coming to class."

Casey's mouth stayed open as Grey walked over to Emma. *Well, that was rude! What does a girl need to do to get attention. Wonder if Isaac is still around? Nope! Snap out it girl.*

Emma was conscientiously wiping her bike down. "Hey." Grey smiled at her. "How'd you do?

Emma looked up at him. A few sweaty tendrils of hair had slipped out during the ride. "Probably won't be able to sit comfortably for a few days. Thank you, sir!" Grey laughed and told her that would go away eventually. "It was hard. You are a task master. 'Put on more pressure,' 'go faster!' You sounded so mean. I was afraid to disobey." She stopped cleaning for a moment. "But I really liked the workout. I love the way I feel when it's done." With a sly look, she added, "I liked the song choices, too. Music is a big motivator for me."

"I do my best," he answered, tipping his head. He continued with a shy smile, "Sometimes music gets across what you can't say out loud."

"Yeah, like, 'get your lazy ass moving,'" Emma joked; but she took in what he had just said. Her heart beating just a little faster.

"Okay, I've got to clean up and lock up. Then, are you still up for talking yoga?"

She wrinkled her nose and bit her lip. "Not sure…." Grey's face flickered with disappointment, so she quickly explained. "I left my change of clothes at home and I'm kind of sweaty. And I look a mess."

"You look fine to me, and I don't mind sweat. Just rinse off in the locker room." He gestured toward it. "Do whatever you need to do to that crazy hair to make you feel better."

"Crazy hair? I'm offended!"

"Sorry. I just meant …ladies like to fix their hair.…" Embarrassed, he stammered. "Didn't mean to offend you. Your hair is beautiful."

Emma guffawed. "Just kidding. I do have crazy hair. How about I run home and get out of these wet clothes and make myself look presentable? I'll meet you there in 30 minutes."

Relieved, Grey nodded. "See you there." *Stupid idiot. Never tell a woman her hair is a mess. Luckily Emma has a sense of humor. And is so down to earth. That laugh…* He was looking forward to getting to know her better.

Grey snuck out the gym door before Casey caught sight of him. He waved goodbye to Isaac, who was trapped talking to her at the front desk. He snorted. *Poor Isaac. Taking one for the team.*

*****

Greek Guys Grill was pretty empty when he arrived. *Hope this place had decent food. I'm starving!* Grey scoped out a table and grabbed a menu. *Huh, lots of healthy choices. Good suggestion, Emma.* Anxiously drumming on the table, his left leg bouncing up and down, he was afraid she wouldn't show. He wondered if he'd gone too far with that song in class. He'd never done anything like that before. Something about that song resonated with him. Just like something about Emma resonated with him. *Gah, what a geek! My social skills leave a lot to be desired. I acted like a middle schooler doing a mix tape, or whatever they call it these days, for his crush.*

Just then, Emma came flying into the restaurant, her face lighting up as she spied Grey seated at the table. *He really is handsome. Those shoulders and arms…yum!* With those dark eyes and trim toned body, he was movie star good looking. She had changed into a floaty, dark green sweater that flattered her, and black leggings with black boots. She looked good. Freshly showered. Her hair now tamed in a tight bun with a few artfully placed tendrils framing her face and pair of gold hoop earrings. She knew this wasn't a date, but it was something. She felt compelled to look nice for Grey.

"Hi Grey," she said shyly. "Sorry I'm late." Her hand lightly brushed against his shoulder as she slid into the seat across from him.

Grey gulped at her touch. She smelled like cherry blossoms. The fresh scent lingered lightly in the air.

"You made it. I was beginning to think you stood me up."

"Hey, we had a deal. I'll be late and you won't be mad."

"Right. Thanks for the reminder."

"Have you ever been here? Have you ordered yet? This place has good food. Everything is local or organic. And the owners are really sweet. They're Greek." She laughed. "Sorry, I ramble when I'm nervous."

"I noticed. Nope, never been here. Was waiting for you to order. I'll take your word on the food."

They walked up to the counter. "Ladies first," Grey said.

"Together?" Eleni, one of the owners, asked Emma.

"Umm no, separate. I'll have the chicken souvlaki plate with the Greek salad. And a water."

"I'll have the same. And I'm paying for both," Grey said firmly.

Emma started to object. "I got it."

"Nope, you got breakfast the other day and, besides, this is a working meal. I intend to pick your brain about yoga and anxiety. It's the least I can do for making you stay out late."

Oh well, there's my answer. Not a date. Just work related. Disappointing but not unexpected. Emma you're acting like a teenager. Grow up!

They talked easily through dinner. Emma spoke about various studies that show yoga is helpful for trauma and anxiety because it teaches body awareness. Grey took some notes on books she suggested. She was in her element talking about yoga. Grey admired her passion and knowledge.

"Whew!" Emma sighed. "My brain is fried. You're making me feel like I'm giving a college lecture on yoga."

"It's been enlightening. For me, personally; but also, I have a few former military clients who might benefit from this. I may refer them to your class."

"That would be awesome." Emma was pleased. "Caitlyn would be happy for new students, too. Maybe we could even do a workshop."

"If you could get one together, I will guarantee you'll get people. There are a lot of veterans and trauma survivors out there who are curious about yoga but may be afraid of what yoga is. Kind of like I was. A one-time workshop is less threatening. I could put flyers up at the gym, and I'm connected to the local VA groups. You should do it, it's a great idea!"

Emily grinned. "Speaking of workshops, I have a workshop at the beach in a few weeks. Looking forward to getting away."

"Nice, which beach?"

"Carolina Beach. Near Wilmington. It's about finding inner peace. I think it's full. First time since the pandemic, we've had to close registration."

"Carolina Beach? What weekend?"

"October 2nd. Why?

"Funny, I have a pickleball tournament at Carolina Beach that same weekend."

"It's a small world." Emma laughed. "Tell me more about pickleball. Isaac said you were a champion."

Proudly, Grey said, "Yup, two years in a row. I started playing a few years ago when I had too much time on my hands. I was trying to build the business but didn't have a lot of clients. I figured it was a good way to make contacts. Then, I found out I was pretty good at it. And pickleball is fun. Of course, tournaments are different than the local leagues. The competition is tougher, and this one is single elimination. So, if you lose the first round, you go to a consolation bracket until you lose a second time.   Then you're out. The tournament is on a Friday."

"That's a long drive for a one-day tournament."

"It is, but I've been thinking I need a break from the gym. Some quiet time to contemplate my… well, my feelings. My life. So much pressure running a small business. Maybe do some fishing, too. Have some thinking time. Maybe meditate on the beach." He looked slyly for Emma's reaction.

"That sounds lovely! Just what you need." Emma was excited for him. She knew from her conversations with Isaac, and from watching him in class, that he was stressed. Maybe her talks about relaxing and getting in touch with his body and mind were working.

"We should go together," she said enthusiastically "As colleagues, friends, of course. Nothing more. I mean, it's just that I hate driving alone. You could stay at the Airbnb with me," The words just tumbled out of her mouth. *What on earth am I doing?* "The place has lots of room and I'll be busy with the workshop, so I won't be in your face." She hesitated as she saw the shocked look on Grey's face. "Sorry, that was presumptuous of me. I'm sure you have friends and plans for the weekend."

"Actually, I don't. Are you serious about this?" *Please be serious. A whole weekend with you. Yes!!*

Emma gulped. *What the hell. Take the risk. Just say yes.* "Yes," she said firmly.

Grey looked at her calmly, but, on the inside, his heart was doing cartwheels. *She said yes!!*

"It *would* make sense to drive together. Gas is so expensive. We can split the cost of gas and food," he said thoughtfully. "Let me see if I can cancel my hotel reservation and we can share the cost of the Airbnb."

"We can share the gas expenses, but the Airbnb doesn't cost me anything. It's part of my fee and, anyway, Melinda, my friend, owns it. She wouldn't charge me anything. Us yogis watch out for one another. Yoga is not the most lucrative career."

"Wow. Then yes, let's go to the beach together, my friend. Financially makes sense for both of us."

"Awesome! We can talk later about details."

Emma yawned. "It's been a long day between work and the grandkids and spin class. I'm exhausted"

"Me too." Grey yawned back. "We're not spring chickens anymore." He looked at his watch. "It's only 9:30 and I'm ready for bed. Not like the old days when 9:30 was when I was just headed out."

"Wild times, huh?"

Grey smiled. "For a while. Not anymore. I'm happy now with early to bed and early to rise and no drama in my life."

Emma agreed. *But I could use a little more fun in my life.*

"Thanks so much for having dinner with me. Maybe we can do it again soon. I really enjoy talking to you. It's nice to have a new friend." Grey extended his hand. "Can I call you friend?"

Emma took it, giving a little squeeze, "It was my pleasure. I'll see you at Half Moon and at Core Connection. We can talk about it and the trip." Emma paused and then added, "Friend."

*****

Lizzy: Get any action with the new guy?

Emma: Weeell, we had dinner the other day. . ☺ He asked if he could be my friend.

Lizzy: Friend? What is this elementary school?

Emma: No, it was nice. We talked about yoga. About life. And then I invited him to the beach with me.

Lizzy: You didn't!!!

Emma: I did!

Lizzy: Hussy! You go girl.

Emma: It's not like that. I have my workshop at Melinda's studio, and he has a pickleball tournament in the same town, same weekend. So I asked him if he wanted to go together.

Lizzy: Interesting angle. And he said?

Emma: He said yes. Financially it makes sense for both of us. Gas and hotel wise.

Lizzy: You invited him to share your hotel room? Who are you and what have you done with my sister?

Emma: 😃 NO. I'm staying at Melinda's Airbnb. It's a condo. Got two bedrooms. He'll be busy, I'll be busy.

Lizzy: And you trust this guy?

Emma: I do. I have a good feeling about him.

Lizzy: Keep me posted. I plan on living vicariously through your dating adventures.

Emma: So far it's not too wild . ☺ . But I am getting in shape.

Lizzy: For when you and Grey get naked?

Emma: I would like to see him naked. He's very manly. But not sure I'm ready to be naked for anyone.

Lizzy: Yet!

Lizzy: Are you teaching your chair yoga class today at Meadow Wood?

Emma: Yup. Headed there now.

Lizzy: Give mom a hug for me.

Emma: I will.

Emma had been teaching a chair yoga class for two years at Meadow Wood. She checked in and asked at the nurse's station who was up for yoga today. "I think we've got five for you today," said Anna, Emma's favorite head nurse. Anna, a petite brunette, was young, four years out of nursing school, and loved her job. She was engaging and enthusiastic and compassionate. The patients loved her. "I'll start bringing them to the exercise room. Why don't you go get your mom? I think she'll be interested in it today. She's having a good day."

The participants in the class varied from week to week, depending on their health issues. Some days were good, some were bad. It was the nature of the place. But both the patients and the nurses were always grateful for the diversion. Movement was key for the elderly.

"Hi mom. Ready for yoga today?" Emma spoke in a loud cheery voice.

"Emma? What are you doing here? Don't you have school today? How are those kids behaving for you?" She always referred to Emma's yoga classes as 'school.'

Linda, her mom, had been a schoolteacher for many years. Emma had gone to her when she was in her yoga teacher training for hints on how to handle a classroom. Her dementia hadn't been evident twelve years ago, and she'd been thrilled Emma needed her advice. Until a few years ago, she would come to Emma's senior yoga class at the Y. She was a skilled and enthusiastic student.

"Nope! I came to get you for yoga." Just then, Anna walked by, gently guiding a short, whitehaired woman and a tall slender man down the hall. They stopped and stared into the room.

"Come on Linda. Workout time."

"Hi Nancy. Hi Mark!" Emma greeted them. They were regulars in the chair yoga class. "I'll be right there. Just getting my mom. You guys ready?"

"We're not going to do headstands, are we?" Nancy asked jokingly. "Last time you said we were."

"Nope. But we might do a handstand." She laughed as Mark looked horrified. "Just kidding"

After the gentle stretch class, Anna pulled Emma aside and asked her if she knew anyone who might teach a senior cardio class. Their regular volunteer was moving, and they were having a hard time finding a replacement. "Let me think about it. I do know a few people."

Her mind immediately went to Isaac. He seemed like the kind of person who would be good with older people. He dealt with Grey, so he had experience with grumps. She made a mental note to ask him tonight at—her heart sank at the thought—her first boot camp. *Should be interesting. Better take it easy for the rest of day. I have a feeling I'm going to need all my energy.*

*****

"Good evening, ladies and gentlemen. Welcome to boot camp." Grey snickered. "As you know, I was a Marine, so I know about boot camps. No excuses." He knew his voice sounded scary, but Grey was in rare form. This was a new group and Emma was part of it. He was excited. He enjoyed teaching boot camp. It was hard work but got great results.

Grey cursed when he saw Casey had decided to sign up, too. Likely, she was talked into it by Isaac. Pay back for the other night, he thought. That meant managing her advances while being polite and giving the others equal attention. *But a paying client is a paying client*, Grey sighed inwardly. They needed all the clients they could get.

Business was doing just okay. The Planet Fitnesses of the world offered membership rates that Grey couldn't match. And the landlord had just raised the rent. Isaac had some good marketing ideas, but Grey was getting tired of always running after clients. *I should probably retire or work part-time and turn the business over to him.* He figured the stress was probably one of the causes of his ramped-up anxiety. *Retirement though? Not sure I'm ready for that quite yet. Besides, what would I do?*

"As you can see, I've set up six stations." He indicated the stations around the room. "Kettlebells, weights, TRX, ropes, Bosu ball, a bench for squats and push-ups. Everyone will get a turn at all the stations doing as many repetitions as you can. One minute on. Two minutes rest. Then move to the next station. When everyone's done all the stations once, we'll take a short break. Then we'll do it again until our 45 minutes are up. We'll start with a 5-minute warmup. Pick a machine-- treadmill, elliptical, stationary bike, rowing machine—doesn't matter which. Do it for five minutes, then meet back here. Any questions?"

Emma gulped. She was hesitant. The others looked all eager and, *oh goodness*, that crazy lady was here. Miss Skintight Top and leggings who only had eyes for Grey. She snorted; *this should be interesting. Grey's going to have his hands full. Maybe I should help him out with her. Distract her so he can do his job. Who knows, maybe she and I can be friends?*

"OK, no questions? Let's get to it. Meet me back here in five." Grey clapped his hands, and everyone dispersed, except Casey, who sidled up to Grey.

"Which machine will give me the best results?" she asked while batting her mascaraed eyes at him.

"The one that gets you moving. You're wasting your warmup time," he said curtly. He walked away and headed to the front desk. Isaac was there, grinning. "What's the matter, pops?"

"I'm gonna kill you. Why is she here?" Grey gave him the evil eye.

"Who? Emma? You signed her up. Don't you remember?"

"You know who I mean!"

Isaac shrugged, "She wanted more one-on-one time with you. But, good son that I am, told her you were booked solid. *However*, you had openings in the boot camp. We need all the paying clients we can get, Dad. And it seems money is no object for her where you are concerned. Take one for the team, like I did the other night."

Grey groaned. "Okay, I know we need the money, but please help me out if she gets too much."

"You know I got your back, man."

Grey rolled his eyes as he headed back to the group now waiting for him. He explained the different stations and assigned each person a starting point, telling them he would walk around and supervise. They headed to their designated workout stations. He could see Emma was nervous. He walked over to her. "Let's get this party started," he said and began the timer. Emma grabbed the kettlebell by her station and started her suitcase walk. "That's it, Emma. Use your core. "Don't lean to the side," he encouraged, walking alongside her.

"This is harder than it looks," she muttered.

The timer went off and they switched. After thirty minutes, Emma was wiped. Sweat was rolling down her face, her hair was frizzy, her arms were shaking, and her legs were like rubber.

Grey came over to her. "You got this. Just a few more minutes and you'll be done."

Emma glared at him and stalked off to the last station. *I'm going to kill him. Just wait.*

Grey chortled. *She's gonna make me pay for this, I bet.*

At the end of class, everyone gathered around, sweating, and breathing heavily. Casey was standing next to Emma. She leaned over and said to her, "He's some hunk, huh." She eyed Emma a little jealously. "Do you two know each other? I noticed he spent a lot of time with you."

Emma just nodded. "We're acquaintances. He's just trying to yank my chain."

Casey smirked, "I wish he'd yank my chain."

Emma giggled "You're funny. I needed a laugh after that workout."

Casey looked pleased. Usually, woman were intimidated by her; but Emma didn't seem to be. "Yeah, it was hard."

Emma chugged from her water bottle. "Well, you make it seem easy. You're not even really sweaty. My #goals are now to #be-as-strong-as-casey."

Casey pulled up her phone. "Good one for Insta. Thanks. Umm, what's your name? Come be in my selfie."

Emma looked shocked. "Emma. My name's Emma. Oh, I'm too much of a sweaty mess. I mean, look," She said waving her hand down her body, indicating her disheveled hair and sweaty clothes. With a mischievous gleam in her eyes, Emma whispered. "Why don't you get Grey to be in your selfie. Tell him I said he should. It's good for business."

"Great idea, Emma! Thanks." Gleefully, Casey ran over to Grey and pulled him into her selfie. Emma just grinned and winked at him as he reluctantly posed.

"See you in class tomorrow," Grey yelled as Emma walked by. Emma waved and smiled, leaving him to deal with Casey.

On the way out, she stopped and spoke to Isaac about volunteering at Meadow Wood. He was open to the idea but wanted to run it by his dad.

"Sounds good," she said. "I think you'd be great at it, and they really need someone. It's good PR too. Who knows, you might pick up a few clients. If not from the patients, maybe from the staff. Let me know what you decide. Also, I meant to mention, you could have Grey leave some cards at the yoga studio. We like to promote local businesses."

"Thanks, you're awesome Emma. Hope my dad realizes that."

"Me too," she said shyly.

When she got home, she was too tired to cook, so she grabbed a banana and gobbled it down. *That'll have to do,* she thought, then jumped in the shower. *I will not be able to move tomorrow. I can barely move now. Damn you, Grey.* She stood under the steaming hot water and thought about all that had happened in the last few weeks. It was a lot. It felt almost like a new page was turning over in her life. While she was toweling off her hair and body, and slathering on cream to fend off the wrinkles, as if that helped, her phone buzzed in her bedroom.

Her heart began to beat faster when she saw whose name had popped up on her screen.

Grey: That wasn't nice.
Emma: What wasn't?'

Grey: Sicing Casey on me.
Emma : . ☺ sorry.
Grey: Sure. Anyway, I wanted to tell you that you did great today.
Emma: Thanks. I tried my best.
Grey: I noticed you always try your best. It's one of things I like about you.

He likes things about me, she thought gleefully as she climbed into bed. She felt emboldened.

Emma: What else do you like about me?

Grey gulped. What should he reply? *I like the way you are so kind, I love your laugh, your sense of humor, your enthusiasm for new things, the way you relish your sweets.* That might be too much at this point.

Grey: Lots of things. Can I call you? I'm not a great texter.
Emma: Umm sure, I just got into bed though.

Grey enjoyed that visual as he dialed her number. She picked up on the first ring. "Hey friend," she said softly.

"Hey friend," he said.

"I'm really sore you know. Won't be able to move tomorrow."

"Then I'm doing my job," he said smugly. "Just wanted to make sure you were alright." *Not really, I just wanted to hear your voice.*

"I'm fine. But that was hard."

"It's all part of getting your bones healthy."

Emma smiled. She liked the way he looked after her. She wasn't used to that. Usually, she was the one doing the caretaking. It was nice.

"Thanks for watching out for me." Her voice was deep and throaty.

"My pleasure." Grey felt a heat stirring in him as he listened to her. *Damn it.*

"By the way, Casey noticed you spent some time with me. She thought maybe we had something going on." Emma smiled as she recalled the look on Casey's face as she questioned her.

"What did you tell her?"

"That we were acquaintances, and you were just yanking my chain."

"Acquaintances? I thought we were friends?" Grey sounded worried. *Acquaintances to friends and then lovers. That's the plan.*

"We are friends." She answered quietly. "New friends. Didn't want her to get jealous and rip my eyes out."

Grey laughed relieved. He loved her sense of humor.

"Actually though. She was nice to me once I got the conversation going. She's funny and direct. I have a feeling she's just insecure about her body."

"Huh, could've fooled me. She's displaying her body all the time." Grey thought about it for a second, though. Emma was probably right. He should've recognized that.

"You're a good person, Emma Griffin. You see beyond the surface. That's another reason I like you,"

"Wow. Two reasons in one night! I like it."

"Here's another one. Isaac told me about volunteering at Meadow Wood. It's a great idea. Good for Isaac, good for the business."

"Thanks! I thought about you, but you're too grumpy," she said teasingly.

"Am not!"

"Are too!" She giggled again.

"Anyway, I'm too impatient. Isaac is perfect."

Emma yawned. "I'm sorry, Grey."

He loved the way she said his name.

She yawned again, "I'm sorry, we should probably go to bed."

"What?" *Yes, we probably should, but not just yet, Friends for now.*

"I mean, I should go to bed, I didn't mean *we* should go to bed *together*. You go in your bed, and I'll go in mine," she stammered, embarrassed realizing her faux pas. "I'm tired and have a lot to do tomorrow."

"Bye, Emma." Grey grinned. She was so funny when she was flustered.

"Bye, Grey. Thanks for taking care of me." She hugged the phone to her chest. *Gaahh, you're an idiot. We should go to bed? What's wrong with you?*

Grey kept the phone by his ear, as if she was still talking to him. He really liked her. Damn.

Chapter 7

You've Got a Friend by James Taylor & Carol King

As Grey packed for the beach trip, he wondered if this was such a good idea. Sounded fine when Emma suggested it. More than fine. She had a workshop. He had a tournament. He needed a change of scenery and he hadn't been to the beach in ... well...a decade. Since his dad had passed. He and his dad had always gone fishing together. It was their way of bonding. Not many words at all. "You hungry? "That's a nice one." Laughter as one of them started trash talking when the big one on the line turned out to be seaweed.

Grey's eyes teared up a bit as he thought of his dad. *Stupid emotions!* Buried so deep for so many years. *Damn, I miss him. He was a good dad.* His father had been just a regular guy who worked hard and took care of his family. He'd served in the Navy during World War Two on a destroyer. tender. He was always proud of his service to the country. But when Grey's draft number had come up while Grey was in his senior year of college, his dad had almost begged him to drag out his education. "War changes you forever," he said. "Especially this war. Do all you can to stay out."

Grey finished his last semester and immediately had his student deferment lifted. He was scared as he thought about his dad's warning that war was hard. He knew he spoke out of love, but Grey was his own man now, a little bit of him resented his father trying to still protect him. Didn't he trust Grey to make the right choice?

Despite his father's warning eventually he enlisted in the Marines, rather than face being drafted. Basic training at Parris Island, South Carolina toughened him up for the humid jungle climate of Vietnam. But nothing could've prepared him for the brutal nature of war. Grey did and saw things no human should have to. To survive, he closed off his emotions. Numbed his brain. When he was injured in a mortar attack, the war was winding down and he was sent stateside. He returned a different person.

PTSD is what they call it today. Back then, no one spoke of it. You went through hell and when you returned, you were expected to man up. Grey buried everything and soon, he felt nothing at all. He went on with his life, but part of him was missing. To this day he jumps at unexpected, loud noises. He hides away on the fourth of July. And he hates hot, humid climates. No trips to Disney world with his kids. His honeymoon was in the mountains.

The one saving grace had been his dad. When he was first back stateside, it was just him and his dad living together. They still went fishing. They'd talk about nothing, but their small talk had a familiarity, a comradeship, to it that reminded him of what he had had with his Marine buddies. They were there for each other. His dad understood what Grey had gone through.

When he met and married Alisha, they didn't go fishing as often. But when his boys got old enough, they'd all go together on boys camping weekends to the beach. Isaac and Joe reveled in the manliness of fishing. They loved the rough and tumble, the campfires, and the peeing outdoors. Later, after he and Alisha divorced, and the boys became teenagers, there were fewer opportunities to go. The boys played sports. And teenagers don't like to hang with their dad, especially the dad who divorced their mom.

As he packed, Grey realized how much he missed those times. Maybe he'd round the boys up for a fishing weekend soon. Joe had two little boys now; they'd love it. *What did Emma say – appreciate the past but don't dwell in it?*

He smiled. *Thank you, dad. For caring. For being there when I came back. For supporting me when Alisha left me. For holding me up when I thought I wasn't going to make it. For being a great grandpa.* He let his tears flow and felt better. Huh! Emma was right when she said acknowledging feelings allows us to drain them out, kind of like poking at a wound. Once it's opened, the poison drains out and the wound begins to heal. He knew that. His therapist had been telling him that for months. But it took Emma's quiet compassion to give him the strength to do it. The push he needed. *She is a good friend. And maybe more?*

*****

Emma rushed around getting ready for the beach trip. She was leading two classes on yoga nidra, which was a type of guided meditation meant to help clients with anxiety. "Find the quiet within." She had done these classes before, so she was comfortable with the material. She just needed to review her notes. She searched through the closet for decent-looking workout clothes. Unlike other yoga teachers, Emma didn't feel comfortable wearing only a tank top and leggings. In her mind, she had too many bulges and layers of flab, especially round the belly. *Well, what do you expect after 4 pregnancies?* That little pouch just under her belly button wasn't going anywhere, no matter how many crunches, cross crawls, sit-ups boat poses, or rollups Grey had her do. She had read somewhere you should cherish your baby pooch. It was a badge of honor. A sign of fertility. *Badge of honor my ass!* she snorted.

Emma pulled out the newest addition to her workout wardrobe, a lovely, light green, loose-fitting layered top with lacy straps and no sleeves. She could put a tank top underneath, so it wasn't too revealing. She grabbed a couple of pairs of leggings. Leggings she could do if they weren't too tight around the waist. She hated that constricted feeling; it gave her a stomachache. Her legs were on the slender side, but so, *unfortunately,* she sighed, was her butt. Bootilicious she was not. But she was proud of how nice and tight it was due to yoga and those damn squats Grey made her do. She had to agree, his workouts were tough, but very effective. He always motivated her to try that one extra squat or do one more clean and press. And she absolutely loved the spin classes he led. She was always exhausted but exhilarated afterwards.

Grey had commented the other day how much stronger she had gotten. He said he was proud of how hard she worked. In her mind, she had pumped her fist and said *Yes!* To Grey she had said, "Damn right I work hard."

She noticed that her balance was much improved as well. She didn't fall out of tree pose as much or as quickly. Her ankles still wobbled but stayed upright longer. And, blessedly her arms had gotten more muscular. Still a little flabby but not nearly as much as before. She could hold plank forever it seemed. And pushups! She could do so many more of them now.

Of course, Grey was her motivator. Sometimes he lay on the gym floor beside her and counted or teased her or barked at her. He knew intuitively what she needed. A shiver went through her. She knew that they had a connection. The energy between them was palpable. She hadn't felt that energy in forever. Maybe she never had.

She had loved her husband. But they had married young and had kids right away. There hadn't been much time to find their true selves. She had met him at twenty-three, right after he had gotten out of the army. Brian was two years older than her. He was confident and brash, and he made her laugh. But she hadn't seen until later the inner scars left over from the time he had served in Vietnam. Now she realizes it was PTSD, but back then, not much was known or done about it.

He suffered from bouts of depression. Of course, going to counseling was not what military guys did. They manned up and got through. She would find him curled up in a ball in their bedroom, crying. Or he would get violently angry and throw things around. Never at her or the kids, thank goodness. She would call his military buddies and they would come to help or talk him through his rage. Eventually, he was so depressed they were able to admit him to a VA hospital for counseling. They gave him medication, but not much else. It took six months to get a follow-up appointment, and, by that time, he had backslid.

It became a vicious cycle. Depression, rage, hospitalization, meds. When he was on the upside, he was a great dad and loving husband. But when he was down, the burden for them all was great. At age forty-five, he crashed his car. His injuries so severe, he never woke up. Emma often wondered if he had crashed on purpose. He'd been so depressed …. Emma teared up.

It had been almost twenty years. But the shock, guilt, and sadness were still there. She allowed them their space along with her other feelings. It was a part of her past. She could accept and move on. She knew he had suffered, and, was almost relieved when he passed away. Relieved for him. Relieved for her. Relieved for the kids. But for them, that loss had been almost insurmountable. She had to stay strong for them. Thank God for her family and friends. They swooped in and held her life together until she could do it on her own. She got the kids the therapy they needed. Between her job, his military disability, and social security, they survived financially.

Now the kids were all grown. All married or partnered. She even had grandchildren. She was proud of them, making it through their struggles to adulthood. And she was so proud of the adults they had become. All were gainfully employed. Lisa was a physician's assistant, wildly busy with three boys and her husband, Aaron. James was a lawyer. He and his longtime girlfriend, Ashley, lived together. She wasn't sure if they'd ever get married. They were always traveling with friends and having fun. *More power to them*, she thought. Marie was a psychologist. She was married with one kid on the way. She and her husband, Rob, lived on a small farm. They had waited until a little later in life for kids and were nervous about becoming parents. Emma smiled, knowing they'd be great at it. And Steve was a computer expert, working on start-ups. He changed jobs frequently, but that was the nature of the business. He and his wife, Emily, had two beautiful little girls.

When they all got together, it was like a circus. Chaotic but fun. The kids liked to show her their new yoga moves. Schools nowadays incorporated yoga in their curriculum. Breathing and body awareness are keys to helping with anxiety, and this newer generation had a lot to be anxious about, Emma knew. Yoga had changed her life, for which she was forever grateful. She hoped it would prove helpful to her grandkids when life threw them curves.

Emma tossed the last of her clothes in the suitcase. She hoped this trip would turn out okay. She was shocked when she found herself inviting Grey to come along for the weekend trip. Where did that come from? They were developing a good friendship. But they weren't besties, as her granddaughter would say. Yet, there was some unspoken connection. Some tie that bound them together.

She knew he needed time away to think and deal with his bottled-up emotions. She would be busy most of the time. He would have time to think and relax. Grey worked so hard; so many hours were involved in running a successful business. She sensed he was a trustworthy guy, so no hanky-panky would happen. And her friend's Airbnb was a condo that had two large bedrooms, a living room, and a fabulous deck overlooking the ocean. It was large enough they would each have their own space. She smiled. *It'll be fine.*

Emma's phone dinged.

Grey: You ready? I'm outside.

She gathered her small, paisley duffle bag. Her yoga mat and props were tucked neatly inside. She grabbed her travel suitcase and her backpack and walked out the front door. *We can do this. It'll be good for both of us.* Thank goodness, this workshop paid well. *I need the extra income. And it will be a good way to get to know Grey a little better and establish firm friendship boundaries. Nothing else! If only he wasn't so hot.* Emma thought about his firm arm muscles. They were delightful to see. His muscular legs were so strong. She took a deep cleansing breath, pushed her worries aside, and headed out the door.

They had decided Grey would drive. He had a huge four-wheel drive truck. *Of course,* thought Emma as she rolled her eyes looking at the truck. *It's a manly vehicle.* She had agreed because there were bad storms predicted for Thursday night and Friday morning. The Ram 1500 was safer in the rain than her old beat-up Honda Civic.

Storms at the beach were no joke: blinding rain, hydroplaning, and flooded side roads. Emma hated driving in the rain anyway. So, she had eagerly agreed.

The time in the passenger seat would also be helpful in allowing her to go over her plan for the seminar. She was only doing three two-hour portions of the training. Two sessions on Friday, one on

Saturday. She would stay for the whole day on Friday, teaching in the morning and helping out in the afternoon. It would be busy, and she'd be tired. Saturday she would do her morning session and stay to teach an asana class. She'd be done by 12. Both meant early mornings. Emma inwardly groaned; she hated getting up early. At least on Sunday, she could sleep late. Then they could get on the road in the afternoon.

Emma gave Grey a big smile. "Thanks for offering to drive!"

"No problem, ma'am." He seemed subdued. Maybe he was nervous about going with her. Maybe it had been a mistake to ask. She'd make sure she stayed out of his way.

Emma opened the door to the huge dark gray truck. She struggled to get up the big step to the front seat with her bags and backpack pulling her down.

Grey snickered. "Hey shortie. Let me help." He quickly hopped out of the truck, grabbed her bags, and threw them easily in the back seat before she could object. Then he came back around and helped hoist her up into the seat, laughing as Emma swatted him away. "Hey, don't hurt the driver!"

"I might be short, but I could've done it myself," she grumped.

"Maybe, but I'd like to get on the road soon. Weather is supposed to be a little rough today."

Emma gave him a look of disdain. Her arms crossed. Grumbling, "I could've done it!"

Buckling her seat belt, she glanced around the truck. "Wow this is big! And so neat." She saw not a speck of dust or trash anywhere.

"Yup."

"Guess I shouldn't have expected anything else. That's one thing the military drills into you. Order and neatness." She paused as she noticed the marine logo on the back windshield.

"Yup. You all settled?"

"Yes sir!" She rearranged her purse so it was between her and Grey. She checked that her phone was in her pocket. "Let's get this show on the road. I'm excited to go. We both need a change of scenery."

Grey started the truck and headed off towards the highway. Emma glanced at Grey. "I think it should take us about 3 ½ hours to get there. Let me put the address in the GPS."

"Already done"

"Great. So have you ever been to Carolina Beach?"

"Nope."

"Well, it's lovely. I usually go twice a year for these workshops at Melinda's studio," Emma chattered. "They are usually well attended. Lots of interesting people"

"Huh. Nice."

"What are you going to do? Made any plans? The beach is beautiful and, being autumn, it should be empty. We can get a nice long walk in on Saturday if you'd like. I'm done with class by noon or so. Oh, I know! I can pack us a lunch and we can eat on the beach. The sand is usually firm. I checked the tide charts and low tide is around 11:30. Should give us plenty of time to walk and eat and explore.'

"Okay."

"Boy, you sure are quiet. Anything wrong? Am I talking too much? I tend to chatter when I'm nervous. Just tell me to be quiet if I'm annoying you."

"I will." Grey wasn't sure if he was annoyed or not. He was used to solitary driving. Emma's anxious chatter was kind of charming and kind of too much. *Maybe she'll settle down.*

Neither spoke for a few minutes. Emma was fidgeting around. This silence was making her nervous.

"Okay if I turn on the radio? Music makes the time go by faster."

"Uhh, I guess. What kind of music do you like?" Grey asked.

"Oh, all kinds," Emma said. "Except not a big fan of heavy metal or punk. But I can listen to it. My son was in an emo band for a while. So I built up a tolerance for loud head banging music… Love 70's music. Reminds me of being young. Oooo …blues are good too. Love me some Tedeschi Trucks band. That girl can sing and his guitar playing is to die for. Classic rock. Pop is good too."

Grey snorted. "Not a fan of pop," he gruffly said.

"What's your favorite, then?"

Grey sighed. "It doesn't matter. Just pick a station"

"Okie dokie. 70's it is."

Before long, Emma was humming along with James Taylor and Carol King version of 'You've Got a Friend'. She noticed Grey was, as well. Their eyes met and little frisson of something sparked between them. Both glanced away quickly. *No, Emma, no. Remember, friends only.*

"70's music brings back memories, doesn't it?"

"Yup," he said just as "American Woman" by the Guess Who began playing. "Some good and some not so good."

Emma noticed Grey was gripping the steering wheel tightly with one hand. The other was moving back and forth across the back of his neck. "I was in Vietnam when this came out. Reminds me of the war."

"Oh. I'm sorry. Let's change it. "

Emma punched another channel, "How about Motown? Some Diana Ross or maybe Al Green." She settled on a mellow jazz station.

"Those were horrendous years, I know. Do you want to talk about it?" she asked.

Grey looked over at her stoically. "I was injured in a mortar attack just before the war ended."

"Ohhh," she sighed. "How bad?"

"Enough to get me sent stateside. Chest and shoulders mostly. I was lucky. My buddies not so much. Most of them died in the attack. I've got scars from the shrapnel. And my hearing was damaged."

"I can't imagine…." She stayed silent for a moment as it sank in, what he had said. Her heart dropped. She had resolved never to get involved with another ex-soldier. Just another reason to keep Grey in the friend zone.

They drove in silence for a while. Grey was grateful she had just accepted what he said. No third degree.

"My husband, Brian, was in Vietnam too. No outward injuries." Emma's voice broke. "The damage was inward."

Grey reached over and touched her hand. "I'm sorry. That war was hell for everyone." He stared at the road, gripping the steering wheel even tighter. He hadn't meant to tell Emma about his injuries. What was wrong with him lately? Buried thoughts and feelings kept popping up every time he was with Emma.

"Yeah, Brian couldn't cope. He died in a car accident when he was 45. I think it might have been on purpose." Tears began slowly flowing down her face. Grey pulled her hand into his and gave it a reassuring squeeze.

"I didn't know. That's rough," he said gently. But his eyes were angry. So many men lost for nothing. So many scars. "Do you want to talk about it? This might be a good time for pit stop. I could use some coffee. And maybe some tea, and something sweet for you? And we can talk." He glanced at Emma. "Or not?"

"Sure, let's stop, But I've pretty much made my peace with what happened. Sometimes, though, the grief sneaks up out of nowhere. Didn't mean to cry."

"Hey, it's alright. There's a McDonald's next exit. Let's take a break."

Emma decided she needed comfort food: fries and an apple pie. Grey ordered coffee and a southwestern grilled chicken salad.

"That's some healthy snack." He harrumphed looking at her selections longingly.

"Hey, sometimes you need bad carbs so you can appreciate the good ones."

"You're right," he said as he grabbed a few of her fries, dipping them into her ketchup. Grey smiled and winked at her,

"Wait a minute." She playfully slapped his hand away. "Want some of this delicious pie too?" She split the pie and offered it to him.

"Thanks, but I really shouldn't. Need to watch the weight," he said as he patted his flat belly.

Emma snorted. "You? Come on, live a little! Take a walk on the wild side."

He shot her a quick look. *Was that a flirty comment? Probably not, just my imagination.*

He reached out taking the pie from her hand, "Thanks, I guess a few bites won't hurt."

"Now you have to share your salad though! It's only fair!"

Grey gave her a look then split the salad.

"Now we have a balance. The good and the bad. Yin and yang."

Grey nodded his head. "Guess that's good." The tension between them had eased a bit.

"Want to talk about your husband?" He looked at her face, his eyes meeting hers.

Emma cast her eyes down. "He had PTSD. But as you probably know they didn't diagnosis that. He'd get depressed and anxious and couldn't cope. Sometimes he'd get violent."

Grey's eyes flashed; his hands clenched. "He didn't hurt you, did he?"

"No." Emma said softly. "Only himself. The last few years of his life were hard though. He wasn't the man I married. I, we -- his military buddies -- did everything we could to make it better." She looked at Grey. "But we had no power against his inner demons. We lost that battle."

Grey tipped his head down, looking at the table, torn between sharing his history or keeping it locked up. Emma was so thoughtful and sympathetic, he whispered "I had PTSD too. Have it, maybe. It's what caused my divorce. Alisha, my wife, God bless her, did the best she could. But I was so wrapped up in not letting myself feel, I couldn't love her the way she needed. She left when the boys were 10 and 12. She asked me--no, she told me-- to get help, or I couldn't see the boys anymore."

"Oh Grey. That must've been devastating to hear. I'm so sorry, But truthfully, good for her. She must've loved you very much."

"She did. I just couldn't really love her back. Didn't know what love was anymore. Vietnam messed with my head."

"So, what did you do? Did you get help?"

"Nope. Not right away. I spent a few months drinking and generally trying to destroy myself. I thought my life was over. I was a shit human being. But my dad finally grabbed me by the balls and made me see the light."

"What did he say?"

"He told me I had two wonderful sons who loved their dad and missed him." Grey's voice caught. "That if I didn't straighten up, I would lose the best things I ever created. He reminded me of the bond that we had and how important a dad was to a son." Grey cleared his throat. His voice grew stronger. He looked at Emma. "Been going to therapy on and off ever since then. Celeste and I have worked through a whole lot of issues over the years."

"Celeste is great. I'm proud of you. You're courageous." Emma took both his hands, gently rubbing her thumbs over the top of his hands. "Thank you for sharing. It's never easy to admit you need help. But I bet your boys are grateful that you did."

Grey nodded. "We have a strong relationship now. A few rough years when they were teenagers, but I have to say, Alisha supported me and encouraged the boys to keep in touch with me. Wouldn't, couldn't have done it without her. She remarried a few years later to nice guy."

"How about you? No wife or girlfriend"

"No. I've had a few casual relationships, just for fun, sex." Emma blushed as he said that. "I've been a work in progress. Didn't want to hurt anyone …or myself. And you?"

Emma hesitated. "No. No one to speak of. I had four kids to raise, a job. No time. It was easier to lose myself in the day-to-day activities of my kid's lives. I've had a few dates over the years but no one serious…." Emma laughed. "Yoga has been my committed relationship for the last 12 years."

Grey nodded. "I get it. My personal training. My gym is my life. All my energy and focus have gone into building my business."

Emma laughed ruefully. "Well, aren't we a couple of sad sacks. Fulfilling careers. But no significant others. No sex lives. Well, you at least get some once in a while. None for me, except for Fred." Grey raised his eyebrows at that. "Fred's my vibrator," she grinned.

"TMI." He blushed, though he smiled as he glanced out the window. "Well, we should probably get back on the road. It's starting to rain and I'm not a big fan of rainstorms."

Once back on the road, they maintained a comfortable silence, both absorbed in their memories as the radio played quietly. The closer they got to the beach, the harder the rain fell. Strong gusts of wind alternated with downpours that made seeing two feet in front of them impossible. Grey put on his flashers and slowed way down. Emma was frightened by the intensity of the storm. She looked over at Grey for reassurance and noticed he was sweating and a had panicked look on his face. His fingers gripped tightly to the steering.

"Should we pull over and wait out the storm?" she asked tentatively. "There's an exit in a few miles."

Grey took a moment to answer. "Maybe. I'm really anxious. Thunderstorms are not my favorite. It rained a lot in Vietnam and, ever since then, strong storms bring up memories of monsoon season. Not a pleasant time of year." He took a deep breath.

"You know, I can help with the anxiety," Emma said in her smooth firm yoga voice. "Let's breathe together. We can calm each other. Deep long inhale. Really long exhale." She filled up her lungs. "Come on Grey. You know how to do this." She exhaled loudly. She continued until Grey joined in with her. "Now, bring your attention to your hands on the steering wheel. I want you to feel your fingers gripping the wheel. Can you loosen the grip just a bit? Soften the fingers with your exhale." Grey did as she suggested. "Next breath, as you loosen your fingers, can you soften your shoulders?" She was breathing loudly at a calm steady pace. Grey's shoulders finally relaxed. "Are you feeling a little better?" she asked him. Grey nodded. "Good. Let's keep it up."

After a moment, Emma, again in her calm yoga voice, said "Let's allow your forehead to soften a bit. Let your eyes, un-scrunch, open your lips just a bit and find a little bit of separation between your upper and lower teeth. Let your whole face soften…even your ears."

"How do you soften your ears?" he grunted.

"Just think about them relaxing. It'll happen"

Slowly Grey began to relax a little. His shoulders released. The panic subsided.

"Thanks, Emma"

"No problem. But can we stop at the next exit? I gotta pee."

"Yeah, me too." The corners of his mouth lifted into a small smile. "All that relaxing loosens things up."

By the time they were done at the rest stop, the storm had subsided some. The rest of the drive was quiet and uneventful.

Chapter 8

Follow You Follow Me by Genesis

When they arrived at the condo, Grey hopped out and opened the door for Emma. "This place looks nice," he commented as he stretched out and rubbed the back of his neck. Emma jumped out and did the same, rolling her shoulders up, back, and down a few times, and jumping up and down. Grey laughed at her. She looked like a little kid standing next to his truck.

"It is. It's small but nicely furnished. The view of the ocean out the bedroom windows and the living room is to die for." She pointed over to the left. "The beach entrance is right there. Just a few steps away. Tomorrow's supposed to be kind of cloudy. But Saturday is going to be picture perfect. What's that saying? After the rain comes the rainbow."

Grey nodded. "Okay, little miss sunshine. I'll look for that rainbow while I'm fishing or at pickleball," he said sarcastically. Then he gave her a big grin. He loved the beach. He took a big breath in and drew in the salt air. His mind eased a bit. He was happy to be with Emma. "I'll grab the bags." He headed up the stairs.

Emma shook her head. *That man is confusing.*

After unpacking and getting her yoga presentation together, Emma collapsed on the couch, staring at the ocean. *Ugh. We need to get some groceries. At least some breakfast stuff. Maybe I'll order online, and Grey can pick them up. I'm not sure I want to drive that monstrosity of a truck. Not even sure I can see over the steering wheel.*

Grey had disappeared into his bedroom. She got up and knocked on the door. "Grey, I'm ordering some groceries. Would you mind picking them up? Anything special you want me to get?" He didn't answer right away, so she knocked again, a little harder. "Grey?"

The door swung open "What do you want?" he said gruffly. His eyes avoiding hers. "I was trying to rest a bit. That was kind of a stressful drive."

"Sorry," a little hurt at his tone, "just ordering groceries and was wondering what you wanted. And if you would mind picking them up since I assume you don't want me to drive your truck."

Grey cleared his throat. "That's affirmative. No one drives my truck except me. Just let me know when to go. I'm going to rest some more." He quickly shut the door.

"Huh… grumpy old man," she said to the door.

Grey lay back on the bed. He didn't mean to be so gruff. She was just being thoughtful Turning onto his side, he could see the roiling waves of the ocean. Emma was right. The view was incredible. The angry waves crashed and flung foamy spray up the beach. The pounding of the waves was so strong it blocked out all other noises. What would Celeste say… ? *Is that like me? So angry I can't hear the other noises around me?* When he panicked during the rainstorm while driving, all he could think about was getting to safety. The feeling of overwhelming doom took over. It had sucked.

If Emma hadn't pulled him out of it, he's not sure what would have happened. *But she did. And I coped. It felt nice. I let her help me. I didn't shut her out. It was a good feeling. Someone cared and wanted to help me.* A small sliver of hope grew in his heart. The chains around his heart were beginning to loosen.

*****

After Grey made the grocery run, they sat peaceably together on the deck enjoying their pizza, half pepperoni and half veggie. It was windy and cool. Emma bundled up in her sweats and hoodie while Grey wore shorts and a sweatshirt.

"I'm freezing. My teeth are chattering," she said.

Grey got up and went inside without a word. Emma looked after him. *Huh? Wonder what that was about.* She could hear him rustling around in the kitchen. Hey are you alright? she texted him.

Yup, he texted back,

Strange.

He came back a few minutes later with a cup of tea and a blanket. Tucking the blanket around her legs, he handed her the tea,

"It's chamomile," he said shyly. "I think that's what you drink.

Emma's heart melted. She gave him a big grateful smile. "I think that's the sweetest thing any man ever did for me."

Grey blushed. "Can't have my favorite yoga teacher cold."

She snuggled under the blanket. "I think I'm your only yoga teacher. Unless you've been cheating on me," she teased.

He sat back down. "I'm not that kind of guy." He looked her in the eye. Again, that frission of fire arched between them.

"I know." Emma said with a nod. "You're one of the good ones."

She thinks I'm one of the good ones. Grey felt oddly pleased. His heartbeat picked up just a little. "What time do you need a ride to the studio tomorrow?"

Emma sighed. "Guess fairly early, if you don't mind. It starts at 8:30 and I'll help Melinda set-up. So maybe around 7:15?" She groaned. "I hate getting up early."

"Early? You think 7:15 is early?" Grey shook his head "That's the middle of the day! I'm going fishing at 6AM. Up at the first light of dawn. That's the best fishing time. I'll come back and round you up, and then head off to the tournament."

"OMG! You are nuts. That's way too early to be out of bed. You'd have to blast me out of bed or maybe lure me out with a doughnut." She grinned slyly. "Wake N' Bake has the best donuts on the island, and they open early. Like 5:30 early."

"I am not eating one of those greasy, fried doughs. Not good for you. Already had pie today."

"Oh, but these doughnuts are special. Unique and delicious and definitely not greasy. Pumpkin with maple frosting, topped with pecans. Snickers flavored. Chocolate with …OMG… so good."

Grey looked at her with a glare.

"I'm just saying. You don't know what you're missing."

They went back to watching the ocean, each lost in their own reveries. Finally, Emma stood up and stretched. "I'd better get ready for bed." She yawned. "Need to review my notes for the lecture one more time. Thank you so much for driving."

Grey nodded. "No problem." He cleared his throat. "Thanks for rescuing me when I was freaking out."

Emma walked over to him, lightly touching his arm. "That's what friends do. I'll see you in the morning."

Grey grinned, "Right. Bright and early."

She glanced back as she headed to her bedroom. *I really like that guy. He's confusing but maybe that's part of his charm. Wonder if he's a good kisser. Emma! Friend zone. Stay in the friend zone.*

Next morning at 5:00 am, Grey quietly gathered his fishing stuff and walked out the door. Hopping into his car, he GPS'd the Wake n' Bake donut place. *Just right around the corner. Guess I have time.* He picked out two doughnuts he thought Emma might like, paused, and then added one for him. Salted caramel. *I'll have to run three extra miles today*. He sighed. Damn woman was a temptress.

Back at the beach by 5:30, he breathed in the fresh air. Deep inhales and exhales. Emma would be proud. As he set up his two fishing poles, he thought of his dad. *Here's to you, Dad.* The waves were much quieter than yesterday. The sun was casting an orange glow over the horizon. Still lots of clouds, but that was okay. The beach was just what he needed. He felt his concerns about his business fade away. His anxiety was non-existent. The rhythm of casting and retrieving was calming. At 6:45, his alarm went off. *Better go make sure sleeping beauty gets up in time.*

He placed the donuts on the counter. He didn't hear any sounds. *I hope she's up. She needed to leave by 7:15.* He went and knocked on her door. All he heard was gentle snoring. Cute, he thought. He knocked again a little louder.

"Go away!" Emma mumbled sleepily.

"Emma, you need to get up."

"Just need a few more minutes…. Then I'll get up," she grumbled.

"Emma, it's getting late."

"Go away"

Hmmm. He grabbed the donuts, opened her door, and peeked. She was buried deep under the blankets. "Emma. It's time to get up." He waved the donuts over the bed.

Her head popped out from under the covers "What's that smell?"

"Get up and see," he teased. She threw the covers off and hopped out of bed. Dang, she looked hot. Bed head, curls all over the place, a sleepy look on her adorable face. And--he gulped—a short, very short, t-shirt. He could spy her underwear. He scooted out of the room before she could grab the bag.

"Emma, it's late. Go take your shower and get dressed. As alluring as you look in that shirt, we need to get going. Doughnuts after shower."

She gave him a nasty look and headed for the shower.

Twenty minutes later, freshly showered and dressed for her workshop with her yoga bag packed, she headed into the kitchen. "Where's my doughnut, you big meanie?"

"Meanie? I got up early to go get you those fried pieces of 200,000 calories. You would've never gotten out of bed if I hadn't. I would've been forced to rip the covers off and take you over my shoulder, strip you and dump you in the shower."

Emma's eyes widened at the visual. *Hmmm… that doesn't sound so bad she thought. Don't go there. Friend zone. Friend zone.*

"I'm sorry. Getting up early is not my thing. You were so nice to get those, even though they are against all your healthy eating principles."

Grey looked at her guiltily. She noticed a smidge of frosting on the corner of his mouth. "You hypocrite!" She glared at him. "You had one! I see the frosting on your mouth." Grey licked the corner of his mouth. Busted.

"I have to admit, they were the best donuts I ever had. Now let's get going."

Emma grabbed the bag. "I'll eat these in the truck."

"Umm, no you won't. No one eats in my truck," he stated firmly.

"Okay, Mr. Neatnik. I'll eat them when I get to the studio."

"Thank you."

As she jumped out of the truck, she turned back to Grey. "Thank you for the ride. Melinda will bring me back." Pausing for a moment, she said, "I'm sorry I was so grumpy before. I appreciate you getting me up."

"It's okay, Emma. That's what friends are for."

She gave him a long look. "Good luck at the tournament. I'll be rooting for you."

Grey headed back to the beach. His thoughts on Emma. *I'm an idiot. Why did he say he'd strip her and throw her in the shower? She must think I'm a savage.* The idea was appealing though. He pictured her naked, water sliding down her body. *Arrgh, snap out of it. You are friends. Friends only.*

*****

At the end of the day, Emma was tired. "That was great as always, Melinda. Well-organized. Great flow. Good variety of students."

"You did a wonderful job with your lectures and activities. I think they found it really enlightening."

Emma blushed. She worked hard on these workshops and was pleased to get positive feedback. "Thank you." After a brief pause, she continued, "Melinda, would you mind if I asked for a bit of advice, personal, not yoga related?" She and Melinda had been friends for many years. Emma valued her judgement.

"Sure! Do you need love advice?" Melinda squealed. "I love to give love advice! Do you have a boyfriend after all these years? You deserve some happiness!"

Emma stammered. "Yes and no. There's this guy. We're friends, but we're also colleagues and clients of each other's. It's complicated. He comes to my yoga classes, and I go to his gym. He owns the gym and also does personal training and boot camps. Both of which I do."

Melinda looked a little concerned. "Hmmm… go on."

"I'm starting to have feelings for him."

"What kind of feelings? Like… you like, like him or like you want to rip off his clothes and you know…"

"Both."

111

"Do you have individual personal training and boot camps?" Emma nodded. "And is the yoga contact in a private or group setting?"

Emma nodded again. "It's been both,"

"Oh Emma. I think it's not wise to get involved with a client, for either of you. Yoga Alliance has specific rules against that. I'm assuming his certifying agency does as well."

"Yeah, that's my thinking too. But it's been so long since I've found anyone I like. We have similar backgrounds. He motivates me to feel better about myself. I've become stronger, physically. And I think I help him. He has anxiety and I've helped him find some ways to deal with it. And to make him feel safe enough to open up his emotions. He makes me laugh. And he's fun to tease…" Emma's voice trailed off. "I know what's right." She paused. "But right feels so wrong."

"Have you actually done anything?"

"No. He's here with me on this trip, but as friends." Melinda gave her a questioning look. "Truly. He needed a little break from work. And he had a pickleball tournament in town. I needed a ride, and he was willing."

"Emma, you need to nip it in the bud now. Before either of you cross the line and jeopardize your careers."

"I know." Emma looked so sad. Melinda reached out and hugged her.

"I'm sorry."

Emma could see Melinda considering the problem. "Wait. I 'm not letting you lose out on love. You've been through too much to miss out," she said firmly. "Maybe there's another way." She thought for a moment. "I know! That's it! By George, I'm a genius!" She shouted excitedly "What if you both stopped seeing each other?"

"You mean, not see him anymore? At all? I enjoy his company. Plus, I really enjoy my workouts."

"No silly. You can see him. You can keep doing your boot camps and training, but with someone else. And you have him transfer to another yoga teacher or even another studio. Then if you decide you want to be more than friends," Melinda's wiggled her eyebrows suggestively, "you're both free of any ethical worries."

"Hmm. I could. If we decide we want more. I'm not sure how he feels, but I sense he likes me and wants more than just friendship."

"That's my girl! Get back on the old merry-go-round. Have some fun! Have some sex! Just because we're old, doesn't mean we can't enjoy what life has to offer."

Emma agreed with her. "We are old but we're not dead yet!"

"Let's finish up here. I'll drive you home… to your 'friend' and see you back here bright and early."

Emma rolled her eyes." Gaww, I hate early."

*****

When Emma arrived back at the condo, Grey was nowhere to be found. *Huh, wonder where he went.* She opened the door to the deck. Drinking in the view, she began to unwind from her day. She thought about Melinda's advice. It was sound. She couldn't risk the job she loved and worked so hard to develop. As she scanned the horizon, she saw Grey. Fishing. His back straight as he cast the rod. His arms so supple and strong as he reeled in a medium size fish. Emma watched transfixed as he took a picture of the fish, then released it back to the ocean. *Funny, he's a catch and release kind of guy.*

Grabbing a jacket, and two bottles of water, Emma headed out to the beach. "Grey!" she shouted to catch his attention. She knew he startled easily.

"Hey," she said as he handed him water. "How's the fishing?"

"Good."

The wind was picking up, whipping her hair into her face. Grey reached out and pushed the strands away. "How was the workshop?"

"Tiring."

"Yeah, I'm tired too. Just about to call it a day."

"Have you been fishing all day?"

"On and off. I took a break for the tournament, but my heart wasn't into it. It wasn't my best performance. I was eliminated pretty quickly."

Emma gave him a quick side hug. "I'm sorry. I know you were looking forward to it."

"It's okay. I needed fishing more than pickleball. Gave me a chance to think about things. And I had a short nap." A nap which included some very vivid fantasies of Emma and him taking a shower together. "And you'll be proud of me; I did some meditating too." Of course, he didn't mention he was meditating on what it would feel like to kiss her sweet lips, and neck…and more. *Stop it, you idiot. Don't ruin a good friendship*.

"Wow, a very productive day I'd say."

He nodded his head in agreement. "I did run out and get us something for dinner. I figured we'd both be too tired to cook."

"You are a very thoughtful person. I'm beat and the thought of cooking or even going out somewhere is more than I can bear." She sighed dramatically.

"Is it as bad as the thought of getting up early again?" he grinned.

She swatted his arm. "Hey! About the same level. Although I'd say getting up was much more pleasant with a handsome man holding donuts over my head."

Handsome man? Was she flirting with him? "That was a one-time only occurrence. My body's been cursing me all day. That's probably why I did so bad at the tournament. So much sugar is not good for you."

"Speak for yourself, mister. Sugar and I are good friends".

After gathering up his fishing gear, they walked back to the condo side by side, almost touching. Both aware of the energy that flowed between them.

Emma bustled around the kitchen, fixing plates and warming up the meal Grey had gotten. Chicken with wild rice and veggies.

*****

Emma sighed with satisfaction. "I love a good dinner - that I didn't have to cook."

After dinner, they settled into their chairs on the deck. The ocean was far more peaceful now that the storm was long gone. Emma covered herself with a blanket.

"I'm sorry I didn't get any wine," Emma said. "I don't drink when I'm working. Really not much at all. I'm a lightweight anyway. One glass of wine and I'm out of it."

"It's okay. I gave up drinking years ago. I might have a beer or cider occasionally if I'm out, but I wasted too much of my life drunk," Grey said quietly.

"Two old fuddy duddies…just hanging out." Emma reached out and lightly squeezed his hand. "It's nice to feel so relaxed with someone."

The sound of the waves and the breeze lulled them into a companionable silence. A few minutes later, Emma heard snoring and giggled as she saw Grey had fallen sound asleep. Old fuddy duddies indeed!

She got up and gently shook Greys shoulder. She leaned in and gave him a soft kiss on the head. Such a sweet and grumpy guy. "Grey! Grey! It's time to go to bed."

Grey startled awake. "Oh sorry" he said sleepily. He rose and bumped right into Emma. "Sorry again," he said, as they came face to face. He hesitated then wrapped his arms around her. Savoring the feel of her in his arms. Quickly backing away, he sheepishly said, "Sorry, sorry." His face turned red. "Didn't mean to do that. Tired. Not sure what I'm doing. Good night." He turned and raced to his room.

What did that mean? Maybe he does have feelings for me. Emma smiled to herself. *He hugs nice.*

Grey closed the door to his room. *You stupid fool! Why did you do that? She's going to think you're a creep. You'd better be on your best friend behavior tomorrow.* He had spent all day thinking about his life and the precious time he'd lost by being so closed off. He had resolved to be more open to life. To Emma. But she'd made it clear that they were just friends. *Hey, wait a minute.* He had vague recollection of Emma kissing his head. *Nah, that must've been a dream.* He shook it off. He took a quick shower then climbed into bed. He fell asleep to visions of Emma kissing his head, kissing his lips. *Oh man*, he thought as his eyes closed, *I have it bad.*

*****

Emma surprised Grey the next day by being up on time. "Am I seeing a mirage? Is that really you? It's 6:45 and you're up?"

"Ha ha! I can be a big girl if I need to." She made a cup of tea and a piece of peanut butter toast with blueberries and a dash of cinnamon. "And look. I'm eating healthy." She waved her toast at Greys face.

Grey glanced out the window. "Must be a full moon."

Emma wrinkled her nose at him. And then stuck out her tongue.

"Big girl, indeed." Grey rolled his eyes. "Ready to get going?"

"I am. Melinda will bring me home again. We're done by 12:00 at the latest. Still interested in going on a walk and picnic?"

"Yes. Since I'm out of the tournament. I'm going fishing again this morning. Weather forecasts a cool sunny day. Maybe mid-60's. Should be a good day."

"I'll stop and pick up some deli sandwiches after the workshop, if that's okay with you. Turkey or roast beef?"

"Roast beef. Shall we go? Don't want you to be late." He herded her out the door.

*****

"I'm home!" Emma shouted, a few hours later. "Let me change and we can get right to it."

She ran into her bedroom, shedding clothes – door still open. Grey could see her out of the corner of his eye. She whipped off her shirt, then realized the door was open. "Whoops," she said, her face all red. "Sorry, used to living by myself." And she slammed the door shut. But she was still talking, shouting through the door, "I can't wait to get my feet on the sand. Did you know I love the beach? No matter how broke I was, we always had a beach vacation. Can you grab two water bottles and, oh, I forgot to get chips, so we'll just have to suffer with sandwiches. Maybe grab a couple of apples and some grapes too. Oooo, do we have any Oreos left? Can't have a picnic without Oreos."

Grey smiled. She was too freaking cute. All excited about the beach, like a little kid. He had enjoyed that brief glimpse of her changing. No little kid there. She was all grown woman. He set about gathering water and fruit and, of course, Oreos. He shook his head. That woman didn't meet a sugar filled treat she didn't like.

"Everything's in my backpack. I grabbed a towel we can sit on. Ready?" Grey looked at Emma. "Let's get a move on woman. It's a beautiful day."

"Ready! Oh, don't forget sunscreen and sunglasses." She put the glasses on her head and grabbed the sunscreen off the table. "Now I'm ready!" She stopped again, "Oh crap, let me pee before we go. My bladder's not like it used to be."

Grey sat back down. "Anytime today would be good," he muttered, drumming his fingers on the table. He'd had another thought-filled morning fishing. His anxiety level low, he'd allowed thoughts of his life and experiences to rise up. He'd been able to stay detached, like Celeste had suggested, and examine all that had happened. As he came to terms with how he had screwed up his marriage, he had cried a bit. The tears had been cathartic. He felt lighter, less tense. Alisha didn't deserve the way he treated her. He would apologize to her when they got home. She'd been a good wife and mother, and he stomped all over her. Refusing to share what he was going through with her. He'd been an all-round jerk.

It's time for a new start.

Emma pranced out of the bathroom. "Really ready this time."

They strolled slowly along the shore. The waves were gentler than they were the day before, and there were lots of shells. The sun was warm. Emma lifted her face to it and smiled deeply. "This is perfect. The sun, the sand, the beautiful blue sky." And, looking shyly at Grey, she added, "And a good friend." They picked up the pace a bit. Emma walking slightly ahead of Grey, who stopped once in a while to reach for a shell.

The next section of beach was deserted. Emma stopped and yelled to Grey, "Let's have lunch here. I'm starving."

They settled on to their towel, shoulders almost touching. Each keenly aware of the other. Emma handed Grey his sandwich and a water. "Roast beef as requested, sir."

"Thanks. How was your workshop today?"

"Good. Glad it's over. It's so intense sometimes. I'm not an extrovert and it takes a lot for me to get up and speak in front of people."

"But you seem so confident up there."

"We all have our tricks. I love yoga so much I was willing to overcome my fears. It took lots of practice. And it still happens. Sometimes my mind goes blank when I realize that I'm up in front of people. My anxiety just overtakes everything. So, I prep for my class, writing down what I'm going to do, sometimes even what I'm going to say. I've learned to always have notes with me. I can glance down and that helps me get my focus back. When I first started teaching, I had a routine I had to follow or else I would freak out. You know, like baseball players do. But after a few times of things messing up, like mics or music not working, I learned I could handle it. Still makes me anxious, but I can deal."

"You'd never know. You have that calming, throaty voice when you're in class."

"You told me it was sexy," she teased.

"It is sexy." *I'd like to hear that voice as I lay in bed with you.*

"It's weird. It's a voice that comes out only in yoga, only when I'm doing something I love. I mean, you hear my voice now. It's not the same, is it?"

He shook his head. "Weird."

They began packing up the remains of their lunch. Emma stood up and decided she needed a picture of the sun and the ocean and dunes. Taking her phone out, she snapped a few. But none of them looked right. *Maybe I need something to focus on.* "Grey, can you come and be in this picture? I need something to break up the scenery."

"Over there," she said, pointing to a spot in the sand. As she took a few shots, she laughed, realizing Grey was posing like a model. "What are you doing?" she asked.

"Livening up your pictures."

While they continued goofing around, a woman with blonde hair, long legs, and bright red jacket strode by. She started to walk past them, then stopped and turned around. "Want me to take a picture with both of you?'

"Um, no thanks," Emma replied.

"Yes," said Grey at the same time. "Come on Emma. We need a memento."

She handed her phone to the woman and reluctantly stood next to Grey.

"No, no, no! That's all wrong. Move closer," the woman instructed. Emma moved a little closer. "Relax," the woman called out. "That's too stiff."

Grey reached out, whispering, "Let's just do it her way. She reminds me of Casey, bossy and blonde. Doesn't take no for an answer." He grinned as he put his arm around her.

"That's better, but still not quite right," she shouted. "What's your name sir?"

"Grey," he answered.

"Grey, turn towards…" she paused. "What's your name?

"Emma"

"Emma, lean into Grey."

Grey whispered again, "If we don't do it, she'll keep us here all day. Just do it."

Emma slowly turned towards Grey.

"Now, Grey, rest your chin on her head or maybe her forehead."

He held still for a moment and then gently did as the woman asked. Emma sighed with pleasure. Moving in a little closer, they were both aware of the heat between them.

"Emma, put your arm around Grey."

Emma carefully wrapped her arms around his waist. Her whole body was tingling.

"No, no, no, his shoulders."

Grey nodded his head. "It's okay." She moved her hands higher, and he sighed. His body was on fire.

"Perfect!" the woman shouted as she took a few more pictures. She handed Emma her phone back and strode away.

"Thank you," Emma stammered, her hands still around Grey's shoulders, Grey's chin resting in her hair. He dropped his forehead to hers. The energy was palpable between them. He lightly kissed her forehead. Both surprised by the kiss, they slowly eased away.

What just happened? Emma wondered. *We're friends and clients.* But she had felt that pull towards him. When he dipped his head and let it rest on her, she felt the power. Like electricity. Sparks. Whatever it was, it was powerful.

Grey broke the silence. "Let's head in that direction." He pointed towards a curve along the dunes.

They continued their walk, each absorbed in their thoughts. Emma was walking fairly fast, trying to puzzle out what was going on between them. *I really like Grey. As a friend. As a client.* But was there more here? *I don't want to cross that line between professional and personal. But in some ways, I already have. Arrgh… what's wrong with you old woman!*

Grey was strolling. Looking at all the myriad of shells and rocks on the beach. He loved the beach. The air, the smell, the sound of the ocean pounding. *What the hell had happened with that lady? She must've thought we were husband and wife.* The way she had them pose into each other. *Not gonna lie, it felt good. Emma's hair – all curly and wild.* She had been obviously uncomfortable with him touching her, but then something changed. He could feel Emma's slow melt in his arms. It was hot. *But she's a client and I'm a client and there are boundaries. Some of which we might possibly have just crossed.* He continued looking at the sand for seashells, occasionally glancing up to see where Emma was. *Man, she walks fast.*

"Look Emma!" he called out. "I found a sand dollar!"

Emma walked towards the water line, feet crunching on all the little clusters of shells. Watching his excitement warmed her heart. *He's like a little kid. It's a whole other side of the closed off Grey.* This trip was worth it, she realized.

Grey gave a big grin as he showed her the sand dollar. It was whole. "It's a solid find. Loved those sand dollars since I was a little kid."

Laughing with him, she gave him a high five. "Congratulations! Maybe there's more out there."

"Nah. I'm happy with the one I have. It's like an unexpected treasure. Not the only one I've found on this trip." He gave her a long look and continued his amble along the water's edge.

Emma stared after him. She picked up her pace and kept walking towards the little cove in the distance.

The dunes curved slightly to the left. As she followed the dune line, it became quieter and quieter. The ocean's constant roar was muffled. The sand was flat and pristine. No people, just beautiful blue sky and puffy white clouds. Dark green trees and vegetation in the distance. The sea oats on the dune danced with the gentle breeze.

Emma stopped and drank it all in. It was like a hidden paradise. She closed her eyes and just listened. She heard the gentle lapping of the waves in the cove. And that was it. Nope, she listened harder. The breeze was quiet but there. She took a deep, full breath and lifted her arms to the sky. As she exhaled, she opened her eyes. It was heaven.

Emma looked back to see where Grey was. She waved excitedly and called to him, "Grey! Grey!" *He needs to see this. To feel this.*

He still hadn't seen her. Summoning up her loudest 'the class is too busy socializing and it's time to start class' voice, Emma yelled, "Grey!"

He heard her this time. He looked up, saw her waving wildly, his heart in his throat. "What's wrong Emma?" he shouted. He sprinted towards her, closing the distance as fast as he could. *Hope she didn't get hurt. Maybe she stepped on sharp shell. Or a jellyfish. Don't have a first aid kit, but I could use my shirt to stop the bleeding. If it's a jellyfish, I could pee on the sting. Good God, I hope it's not that.* "What's wrong Emma? Are you ok? Bleeding? Jellyfish sting?" Grey panted as he finally reached her.

She looked confused. "Ummm, no! I'm fine. Take a breath ….in and out…" She softly touched his shoulder. "I'm okay. Just wanted you to witness, to feel this beautiful spot."

Grey huffed. "The way you were waving and yelling I thought something bad had happened to you."

"I'm sorry. Didn't mean to scare you." She lowered her head, embarrassed. She had forgotten anxious people always fear the worst. "It's just this place was so quiet and peaceful and beautiful. It reminds me of the way a true meditation should feel."

"Sheesh, as long as you're alright." Grey's heart rate and breath were getting back to normal. His mind slowly came out of panic mode. *Dang, why do I always expect the worst to happen?* Emma's words began to filter through. He noticed the stillness. No noises except the lapping of the waves and the occasional wind. It was weird. Huh…. He felt a sense of calmness flow over him.

"Close your eyes, Grey." Emma said softly.

"Why?" Grey asked, hands on hip.

"Grey, close your eyes!" she said firmly.

Afraid to disobey the tone in her voice, he closed his eyes. The tone reminded him of his mom when she was telling him something he needed to hear.

"Okay, now what?"

"Just listen and feel."

"What am I listening for? Give me a hint." Grey whined.

"Just listen and feel."

Grey focused all his attention on listening. He heard the quiet waves. He heard Emma's inhale and her exhale. He heard his own breath coming into sync with hers. He felt the breeze dance across his skin. He felt the sand under his feet. He noticed the warmth and the coolness blended in the pebbly sand. It felt good. He felt grounded. Rooted. He started to relax. Emma was fine. He was safe. He'd made peace with his dad's death yesterday. Accepted his part of the divorce from Alisha. Grey noticed he felt lighter. His heart was feeling things today. He felt like he was one with this universe. He'd never felt this way before. In sync.

Emma held her breath. *Grey is doing it!!* He was letting go and enjoying this moment. Emma carefully kept her breath in rhythm with his. Steady, even breath, in and out. She reached out and took ahold of his hand. Grey started, and then began to open his eyes. "Grey," she said quietly, "keep your eyes closed for just another second. Breathe with me. Inhale and exhale. Notice how you feel. Burn this feeling into your memory."

After a few moments, she let go of his hand. "Now, slowly open your eyes. Take a long, lazy look around and drink in the beauty. The solitude."

"Arms by your side," she said in her soft yoga voice. "Palms out. Gaze forward. Together let's take a nice deep inhale as we raise our arms up to the sky. Feel the sunshine wash over your face gently exhaling hands to heart." She paused, glancing at Grey. "The light in me honors the light in you. Namaste."

"Namaste," he repeated.

Both were quiet for a moment. Taking it all in. Grey turned to Emma. "Thank you. That was the most peaceful I've ever felt."

Emma bowed her head, "Your welcome. I'm so proud of you. You let go enough to let it happen. No fear."

"It's because I trust you Emma," Grey said seriously. "And you're a great teacher!"

She grinned, "I am a good teacher".

He gave her a quick hug. "Shall we head back?"

They resumed their walking pace. Emma hustling ahead, Grey lagging behind looking for shells. But Emma knew something had deepened between them. Their connection had grown stronger. She wasn't sure if that was such a good thing.

Chapter 9

True Colors by Phil Collins

On Sunday, they had a no plans. Grey got up again and went fishing. Emma watched him from the balcony as she drank her chamomile tea. Things felt easy and relaxed between them, but she couldn't help but wonder where this was heading. She wanted more. More intimacy. But did Grey? She wasn't sure. He had kissed her forehead yesterday and hugged her the other night. It had been nice -- better than nice; it left her wanting more. But he seemed hesitant about anything more. In fact, he made a point about being friends. Hadn't he told her he had avoided relationships? Just looked for fun, no commitment, he always said. Was he afraid of opening up? Of being hurt? She knew he had PTSD, but was working on it. That would never go away, but it could be managed with therapy, medications, and yoga. He had anxiety, but was that related to his past or to the business stresses? Maybe he'd been so scarred from his divorce that he was too afraid of getting hurt again. She wasn't sure.

Emma wasn't a one-night stand girl. Sex meant more to her than the physical act. She hadn't been attracted to anyone since Brian. Although she'd had men approach her, she just wasn't interested. And life was too busy. Grey, though, interested her. He was attractive and funny and smart and driven. They had a lot of common experiences. But he kept most of his feelings hidden. *Maybe I need to take the first step*. She really wasn't the aggressive type, though. The idea scared her. She thought of Casey from the gym with a smile. *Nope! Not like that. Maybe some subtle hints. Like what though?* Perhaps Lizzy would have an idea. Probably Marie would, too, though she was not sure her advice would be the best. She'd probably tell Emma to dress sexy and seduce him. *Not gonna happen*. Emma sighed. Why do men have to be so complicated?

Grey looked back and gave a wave when he saw her watching him. *Wonder what she's thinking about?* They needed to get on the road by noon since they both had a busy Monday. He'd felt so comfortable around her this weekend, despite his attraction to her. Not just to her body, although that was great; it was her attitude, and willingness to express her feelings and wants that attracted him. Like those damn donuts. She conned him into getting those cholesterol killers. He laughed as he remembered waving them over her head to get her out of bed. He wondered what she would've done if he had climbed into bed with her and kissed her senseless, a thought that had flown through his mind in the moment. She looked so funny in the morning, with bedhead and no pants. He felt a stirring in his body. *Wonder if she wants me the way I want her*. He had enjoyed that brief hug and gentle kiss on the forehead. She felt so good in his arms. He'd have to settle for that he guessed, for now. The romance formula was clear: acquaintances, check. Friends, check. Next, lovers. He wanted that next step soon.

When they were all packed up to head home, Grey walked out onto the balcony and surveyed the ocean. The waves were peaceful today. The sky clear blue. It was perfect. He took a deep breath. Maybe it was time to make a small move, a step towards his goal. He quieted his nerves with a deep breath – 4 breaths in, 6 breaths out– and called Emma out to the balcony.

"Emma, come say goodbye to the ocean. It's beautiful."

Emma walked out and stood beside him. She sighed. "I don't want to leave. It's been wonderful."

Grey put his arm around her and tugged her in close. "Indeed it has." He hesitated. "Emma..".

"Yes?" Emma turned towards him. *It's now or never,* she thought and kissed him sweetly on his mouth. He froze for a second. *Did that actually happen? Did she kiss me?* She glanced up at him. "Is that okay?" she asked nervously.

He wrapped his arms around her and kissed her back, gently at first, then more fervently. The world around them dissolved. It was just the two of them. Their lips touching was the only thing they were aware of. "You don't know how much I've wanted to do that," he said as he released her lips. He quickly moved back for another kiss. She tasted so good. Just as he had imagined. Sweet and soft. Delicious.

"Oh my," Emma sighed, placing her hands on his chest, moving in just a bit closer to him. What had she just done? His kiss was even better than she had dreamed. She was a goner. She wanted more. Evidently, so did he. But she heard Melinda's voice in her head warning her to be careful.

She pushed away. "We better get going. We have a long ride." She searched his face for his reaction. She saw longing and desire and fear and maybe disappointment at her words. "That was …nice," she said, gazing into his eyes. "But, maybe we need to take it slow, because as much as I want to go further, we have some professional issues to think through."

"Nice? You thought that kiss was just nice?" His tone was shocked. "I felt that spark and so did you! You are amazing and I want more."

"It was …everything you said," she whispered as she laid her head on his chest. Hearing his heartbeat. "But we need to think about the consequences. We both need our jobs. Our reputations. And getting involved with a student isn't wise."

Grey considered her words. Slowly releasing her, he said, "Okay, you're right." he said sadly as he stepped away. But know that I will do whatever it takes to make this work. I want you, Emma."

Emma reached her hand to his face, gently stroked her thumb over his jaw and cheek. "Thank you. Let's take some time to think and talk about it."

"Whatever you want." Grey turned and went back in, grabbing the suitcases as he headed to the truck. Looking back at her, he asked, "You coming?"

Emma nodded, grabbed her yoga mat and bag, and followed Grey out. As she locked the condo, she touched the door. *Thank you for this precious time. Let's see what the future holds.*

On the ride home, Emma sat next to Grey. His hand was resting near her. She took it and lifted it up and kissed his fingers. Grey smiled. Their hands intertwined; she turned on the radio. It was so easy, she thought, singing and listening and talking about nothing. His hand found its way to her thigh. Both started. "Sorry!" he said. "Don't know what came over me. It just seemed so natural." She agreed it did and left it there. They stopped for a quick dinner, but both avoided talking about what happened at the beach. They needed to absorb it all.

*****

Pulling into her driveway, he shut off the truck. "Emma. Thank you for a wonderful weekend." He reached for her and kissed her.

She sighed. "It was."

He helped her with her stuff. As she fumbled with the keys, he laughed. "You have an issue with keys." He took the keys out of her hand, reached over her head, and unlocked the door. "Maybe you should consider getting a keypad lock."

"Maybe, but then I won't have an excuse to have you so near to me."

"You don't need an excuse." He kissed her forehead, then stepped away making sure she got in safely. Emma watched through the window as he drove away. She grabbed her phone. She had to tell someone what happened.

Emma: I kissed him!

Lizzy: Huh? Kissed who?

Emma: Grey, workout guy. Guy I went to the beach with.

Lizzy: OMG! No way!

Lizzy: You kissed him or he kissed you?

Emma: Both. .

Emma: It was amazing.

Lizzy: Good for you. Did you do more than kiss .

Emma: No. I had second thoughts. Told him we needed to think about it.

Lizzy: Think about what? Kissing?

Emma: No. If we should be together. The whole client teacher thingie.

Lizzy: Ohhh..what did he say

Emma: He agreed. Kinda. Said he wanted to be with me and would do whatever he needed to do that.

Lizzy: So romantic.

Emma: We held hands all the way home.

Lizzy: Nice

Emma: It was.

Emma: He's really nice but he does have a past.

Lizzy: At our age we all have a past.

Emma: Well… he's divorced and has PTSD and works a lot.

Lizzy: Hmmm….divorced isn't a big deal. Unless he was an abuser.

Emma: No. He said he was messed up by the war and couldn't work through it. He has two kids. His wife told him to get his act together, but he couldn't, so she divorced him.

Lizzy: Hmmm.. Does have his act together now?

Emma: Mostly. I think. He's done, and still does, therapy. Has a good relationship with his sons and he says he and his ex-wife are friendly.

Lizzy: Well that's all good.

Emma: He does have anxiety though. But I seem to calm him.

Lizzy: That's good. I guess. What's the holdup?

Emma: Not sure he's ready for a relationship. He seems scared of his feelings.

Lizzy: So, go slow. You haven't had sex for 20 years what's a little more time

Emma: But I'm soooo ready.

Lizzy: Be careful. Your body may be ready but are you ready for a relationship? You've lived alone on your own terms for a long time. Being with someone means compromise.

Emma: I know. But I think I'm ready.

Lizzy: Then go for it! Even if it doesn't work out at least you relieved your sex drought . 😄

Emma: Well I haven't yet. Gotta get there first.

Lizzy: Make a plan. Invite him to dinner or to the movies. Spend a little time getting to know him better. Then…let it happen naturally. Who could resist my sister for long?

Emma: Thanks Lizzy. I knew you'd be supportive. Love you!

٭٭٭٭٭

Grey got home and texted Isaac to let him know he was home and to find out how it went while he was away. Isaac assured him everything had gone well. Isaac didn't know it, but this had been a test. He had been pondering cutting back a bit and letting Isaac take on more responsibilities. He wasn't ready for retirement yet. But if

Isaac did a good job, he could work less and enjoy his life, especially now that Emma was in it. *Maybe I'll broach the subject this week. See how he feels about it. He's a smart and motivated guy, and the clients love him.*

Isaac: How did the romance go?

Grey: Romance?

Isaac: Come on dad. With Emma. It's obvious how much you like her.

Grey: Yeah… I do like her. She's fun and smart and she makes me feel good.

Isaac: Scoop her up! Anyone who can make you less grumpy is worth her weight in gold. Does she like you?

Grey: What is this, middle school?

Grey: Although, she kissed me.

Isaac: Oh man. That's big! Did you guys sleep together?

Grey: Isaac! That's not something a son should ask his dad.

Isaac: Well did you?

Grey: No. Not yet. She's afraid.

Isaac: Of what?

Grey: There's this little complication of student-teacher. And she knows about my PTSD. Her husband had it as well.

Isaac: Yet she still kissed you. Did you tell her you go to therapy? And you can fix the client teacher thing by stopping being each other's students.

Grey: Yes and yes. Just not sure we're there yet. She wants to go slow.

Isaac: So, go slow. Ask her to dinner. To a movie. And then seduce her. Man- when's the last time you've had sex? Can you even do it anymore?

Grey: Boundaries son, boundaries. But for your information I'm fully functional. I'm old, not dead.

Isaac: Good to know! Seriously dad. Take her out and go slow. Give her time to see the real you.

Isaac: I can't wait to tell Joe!

Grey: Can we keep this our secret for now? It may not go anywhere.

Isaac: Oh and I can tell Casey. That might keep her off your back.
Grey: Isaac. No one!
Isaac: Fine. Good luck and keep me posted.
Grey: Will do. And thanks again for covering this weekend.

Grey unpacked and thought about the weekend. It had been one of the best weekends of his life. He picked up the phone to text Emma but thought better of it. *Maybe she doesn't want to hear from me.* Just then his phone buzzed. It was Emma. His heart warmed.

Emma: Can I call you or you call me?
Grey: Yup. Are you in bed?
Emma: Not yet. But I can be in a minute
Grey: That's not what I meant.
Emma: Awww.
Grey: On second thought…
Emma: Yes?
Grey: Let me take a shower and call you in a few minutes.
Emma: Ok.

Emma grabbed the phone as soon as it rang. "Hi friend!" she sang happily into the phone.

"Hi friend. Are you in bed?" He spoke suggestively.

"Yes," she answered shyly. "Are you?"

"Yes," he said huskily. "Are you naked?"

"No! Are you?"

"I always sleep naked."

Emma gulped as she pictured him resting against the pillows. "Good to know." She quickly changed the direction of the conversation. She had never had phone sex and wasn't even sure how you had sex with a phone, anyway. "It's been a long day. I'm really tired." She yawned, covering her mouth.

"Me too. It was a long drive. But the company was nice."

She smiled. "Yeah, it was." She nestled down among her pillows. Her small frame was dwarfed by the comforter. "I wish you were here."

"Me too," he said softly, pulling the covers up and settling in. "If I was there, what would we be doing?"

"Ummm…" Emma swallowed. "Talking?"

"What else?" Grey's voice deepened as he imagined lying next to her.

"Kissing? Making out like two teenagers?"

"I like that. Would you have clothes on?"

"If I did, would you take them off?" she teased.

"In one minute flat, you'd be naked as the day you were born."

"Oh my! Would you throw my clothes on the floor? Or fold them? You seem like the neatnick type."

Grey paused, a smile playing at his lips. "You got me there," he conceded "I'd probably fold them and put them on a chair next to mine. And then hop in next to you."

 "So, you'd be naked beside me?"

"Yeah…Or on top of you. How would you feel about that?"

"I'll allow it. Although I do like to be on top." She said breathily.

"Emma, you're killing me." He pictured her naked straddling him. "What else do you like?" He was getting aroused.

"Grey, stop. You're making me all excited. I'm too old for phone sex. And too shy."

 "So, you'd rather have in-person sex? I can arrange that." His voice was thick.

Emma paused. She did want in-person sex. But she still wasn't sure about the ethics of it. "We need to talk about it."

"About ethics or about sex?" His voice was hopeful.

"Both." Emma spoke firmly.

"Fine. How about this Friday? I'll make dinner and we can talk."

"Do you cook?" Emma sounded surprised. "I figured you to be a takeout kind of guy."

"I'll have you know I'm an excellent cook. Can't afford to eat out all the time."

"Huh...do you bake, too?" she asked hopefully.

"No, Miss-I-can't-live-without-dessert. I don't bake. How about if I cook dinner and you bring a dessert?"

"Disappointing."

"What is, my dinner invitation?" He sounded unhappy. Was she turning him down?

"Nope. That you don't bake." She laughed heartily. "Just kidding. I'll bring a healthy dessert and you cook a healthy meal, and we'll talk."

"Deal! Can I see you before then? Like maybe for lunch? Tomorrow?"

"Aren't you sick of me?"

"Not yet." She could sense the smile in his voice. "So, lunch tomorrow?"

"I can't do lunch. It's my day to visit my mom. I eat lunch with her."

"Why don't I come with you? I need to talk to Meadow Wood anyway about Isaac volunteering. I could meet your mother and while you visit, I'll work out the details with their activity director."

"You want to meet my mom?" she sounded surprised and pleased.

"I do."

"Okay then, let's do it. Meet me at the studio and we can drive there together."

"It's a date. Ohh…. and Emma."

"Yes?"

"On Friday…" he said cheekily. "Bring a change of clothes."

"Confident, are we?"

"Hopeful."

"Good night, Grey. Have a good night's sleep."

"Good night, Emma. See you tomorrow."

*****

Emma was nervous about Grey meeting her mom. She wasn't sure why she had agreed to it. Linda could be a loose cannon sometimes—actually, she reminded her a lot of Marie given the lack of filter. Of course, that was part of her charm. Her openness was disarming and brutal at the same time. And now with the dementia, there were even fewer filters. Good luck to Grey. *It'll be fine*, she sighed. *He's a big boy.* She rolled over, closed her eyes, and eventually fell asleep.

The next day, Grey was at the studio right on time. "Are you sure you're ready to meet my mom? She's kinda crazy."

"I'm sure. I'll just say hello."

"She may give you the third degree. She's got no filters."

"I can handle a 90-year-old woman. If she's anything like her daughter, she'll find me immensely charming."

Emma raised her eyebrows. "Okay. We'll see, Mr. Charming."

Meadow Wood was just a few minutes away from the studio. As they pulled into the shaded driveway and found a parking spot, Grey turned to Emma. "Hope she likes me."

Emma laughed, "Is Mr. Charming worried?"

"No. But you're important to me, and if your mom doesn't like me, how will you feel?"

"The same as I do now. She has dementia. She won't remember meeting you tomorrow or even five minutes after she meets you."

Emma led Grey to the memory care unit. Luckily Anna was the head nurse again. Smiling at Emma, the petite brunette let her know her mom had just come back from her music therapy session and was a little tired.

"Thanks, Anna, I'll make lunch quick then."

Anna looked questioningly at Grey.

"Oh, sorry. Anna, this is Grey Erikson. He's a…friend. Also, he's a personal trainer and owns Core Connection. I believe he talked to Marissa, the activity director, about providing a cardio instructor."

Grey nodded. "Nice to meet you," he said, holding out his hand to Anna. "My son Isaac has agreed to teach a senior cardio and movement class. And also, if you want a strength and stability or balance class, we'd be willing to do that as well."

Anna's face lit up. Their regular instructor had left unexpectedly. "Oh my goodness, that would be great! Not to be pushy, but when can you start?"

"I'll have Isaac get in touch with you once I work out the details with Marissa. Talked to her this morning and she said she'd be around today at lunchtime."

"Pretty sure she stays in for lunch on Mondays. I'll page her and let her know you're here. She'll be so excited!" Anna scooted over to the nursing station and paged Marissa. Emma looked at Grey, "Ready to meet mom? Her first name is Linda, by the way."

"And her last name? I don't want to call her Linda. I was taught to respect our elders."

Emma smiled. He was so serious. "Perilli."

As they strolled down the hallway, Emma greeted several of the patients and nurse's aides by name. It was a warm, welcoming place without a lot of staff turnover. Grey got a couple of admiring glances from some of the women.

"Seems they like you." Emma laughed.

Grey nodded. "As always."

She stopped in front of an open doorway about halfway down the hall. Emma peeked her head around the entryway. "Hi, Mom! I bought a friend to meet you. Okay if we come in?"

Linda was seated at the edge of her bed with a small tray table in front of her. "Is that you, Emma?" she squinted. "Don't have my glasses on. Come on in!"

Emma gave her mom a quick hug. "Mom. I'd like you to meet Grey. He's a friend of mine."

Grey stepped forward and held his hand out to Linda. "Delighted to meet you, Mrs. Perilli. I've heard a lot about you from your lovely daughter."

Linda grabbed his hand placing her other hand on his. "Well, well, well. You sure are handsome. Emma, you didn't tell me you had such a good-looking boyfriend." Grey blushed but kept his hand in Linda's.

"We're just friends. Emma teaches me yoga and I teach her to be stronger. I own Core Connection. It's a gym."

Linda eyed him carefully. "You are in love with my daughter, aren't you? Are you sleeping with her?"

"Mom!" Emma said loudly before Grey had a chance to answer her. "Please behave. Grey is just a friend. His company is going to provide some exercise teachers and, since we were both coming here, he wanted to meet you."

"Mrs. Perelli," he smiled. He was still holding her hand. "I do like your daughter very much, but I respect her as well. Before we get further involved, I needed to make sure that her family approved of me."

Linda looked him squarely in the eye. "That's very wise of you. Did you know she has four children, and she was married before?"

"Mom!" Emma squeaked.

"Yes. We've talked about that. She knows I have two sons and an ex-wife. I was in the Marines during Vietnam."

"Brian was in the service, that was her husband. He had mental health issues. Do you?"

Grey gulped. She was very direct. Didn't seem too confused to him. "I had…have some anxiety about the time I was in Vietnam. But I go to therapy and, actually, that's how I met your daughter. My therapist recommended her."

Linda smiled and nodded her head. "She is a good teacher. I used to go to her classes. That was a long time ago. Now I can't do that up and down stuff anymore." She looked off into space. "Can't remember, can't do anything like I used to."

"Well, I think you're a good mom. That'll never change." Grey squatted down, so he was eye level with Linda. "You raised Emma and she's fantastic. She said you supported her and kids after her husband died. That means something. My dad was there to help me when I needed it. He probably saved my life. And I'll do the same for my boys."

Linda was silent for a moment. She seemed to be searching for words. "Family is very important. I can tell you're good man. Hope Emma keeps you around. Lord knows she hasn't had a man in decades."

"Mom!" Emma groaned.

Grey laughed. "Maybe I can change that."

Just then, Anna entered with Linda's lunch tray. "Lunch is here, Miss Linda." She placed the tray down and turned to Grey. "Marissa is in her office. She said to come on down." Grey stood up as Linda released his hand. "I'd better go. Very nice meeting you. Enjoy your lunch, Mrs. Perelli."

"Emma, I'll come by when we're done." She nodded and mouthed, "Sorry." As he headed out the door, he heard Linda ask Emma "Who was that handsome man?"

"Just a friend, mom." Emma replied.

While her mom ate her lunch, Emma texted Lizzy.

Emma: Mom gave Grey the third degree. It was embarrassing.

Lizzy: You brought him to meet mom?

Emma: He invited himself.

Emma: Mom asked him if he was sleeping with me!

Lizzy: .😄   OMG! What did he say?

Emma: That he wasn't and that he respected me. Wanted her approval before going any further.

Lizzy: OMG. That is so sweet.

Emma: He was rather charming, considering. she asked him if he had mental health issues.

Lizzy: Mom must be in rare form today.

Emma: She seems pretty with it. Although right after Grey left she asked who he was 😀

"Emma. I'm finished. Can you move this darn tray and help me get back into bed. I'm tired." Linda looked pointedly at Emma.

Emma noticed she hadn't eaten much of her lunch. She made a note to mention it to Anna. Linda's appetite had diminished lately, and she was looking frailer. And although the food was decent, it wasn't like homemade. *We need to bring in more meals. I'll talk to Lizzy.* She was the cook in the family.

"Sure, Mom! Although…I did bring you a cannoli from Café Amore. Maria made it special for you."

Linda's face perked up. She loved sweets. "Did you say cannoli?"

"I did mom. Fresh from the bakery."

"Well in that case, I'll postpone my nap." She grinned as Emma gave her a small bite. "Hey, give me a bigger piece than that. You know I love them."

Linda gobbled the whole cannoli and then made a satisfied sigh. "You're a good daughter."

Emma thought, Well, maybe not so much. Cannolis weren't very healthy, but sometimes you need to feed the soul. Who knows how much more time they had together. *I'd rather she enjoys than be healthy at this point.* She settled Linda back into her bed, nestled a pillow beside her and pulled the covers up to her chin.

Looking Emma straight on, she grinned, "And give that man a chance."

"Yes ma'am. See you on Wednesday, Mom."

She kissed her with a sad sigh and went to the lobby to wait for Grey.

He was still in with Marisa, so she stuck her head in the office. "Hey Marissa, sorry to interrupt. Grey, I'll wait in the lobby."

"We were just finishing up. Thank you so much for recommending Grey's company, and Isaac. You guys are a good team." Glancing from Grey to Emma, she smiled devilishly. "Are you two a team? Like boyfriend girlfriend? That would be so cute! Yoga girl and exercise guy. What's that in yoga? Yin and Yang."

Emma just shook her head. "Bye, Marissa. See you Wednesday."

As they walked out of Meadow Wood, Grey turned to Emma and winked, "Everyone seems to think we're together. Hope they're right."

*****

For both of them, the rest of the week was pretty busy with clients. Emma had picked up a few private clients. They always paid well, and she needed the money. But she still made time to go to boot camp. She was determined to get stronger. After class, Grey reminded her with a cheeky look they had dinner plans on Friday.

"I'm looking forward to it." She blushed and kissed him on the cheek before heading out the door.

He turned back around and ran smack into Casey. "You two got something going on? I thought Emma said you were just friends."

Grey sighed, irritated with her. In boot camp, she had tried to corner him several times. It annoyed him. But he had to admit, she was very athletic. She killed those drills they ran. And she was a hard worker, once she got her mind off Grey. He tried to remind himself of what Emma had said about Casey feeling insecure.

"We are friends." Then, quickly changing the subject, he added, "You did excellent in boot camp today. You are a strong person. Did you play sports when you were in college?"

Over the last few weeks, he recognized there was more to Casey than appearances. She had a quick wit and he felt maybe there was something in her past that drove her actions. He regretted being so callous. He of all people was familiar with trauma affecting behavior.

Casey looked pleased he had noticed. "As a matter of fact, I did. I played tennis and swam. Our swim team made it to the state championship one year."

"You're so athletic, I figured. Since you're here all the time, have you considered getting your group fitness certification? We've been looking to expand and could use another instructor. How are your dance skills?'

"I'm a really good dancer," she said eagerly. "I danced all through school."

"Wonderful! We could add a Zumba or Cardio Dance class if you were willing to get certified. You'd get paid for doing something you're good at."

"Hmmm… I never thought about it. But it does sound like fun. Since my husband and I divorced, I've been looking for a new outlet."

"Let me talk to Isaac. He can hook you up with the right workshops so you can get certified."

"Wow." She seemed stunned that Grey hadn't brushed her off. "That's so nice of you. I do love group workouts. Thank you for picking up on that. This gives me something to look forward to." She turned and strutted off.

Hmmm, Emma was right. Casey did need some reassurance. Once he stopped focusing on her irritating advances, he could see that she actually was a pretty good athlete, and a good motivator in his class. He really could use an instructor. *Could be a win-win. She'd have lots of other people to listen to her and admire her. And she'd be too busy to bother him. Emma's so perceptive.*

⁎⁎⁎⁎⁎

By the time Friday night rolled around, Emma was a mess. She had already decided to bring a change of clothes, just in case. She knew her resistance to Grey's charm wouldn't last long. If he said the right words, she was his. But she needed to make sure he knew she was serious about keeping her reputation intact. Her job was her passion, and she had no intention of jeopardizing it. If he didn't agree, then maybe a relationship wasn't in the picture. But she really wanted him and all his messiness. He was sexy and sweet, and he had charmed her mother. What did mom say? "Give that man a chance." *Okay mom tonight's the night. He'll get his chance.*

She picked up her phone and texted Lizzy:

Emma: Heading over to Grey's for dinner.

Lizzy: Nice! Is tonight the night?

Emma: For what?

Lizzy: You know. The end of the drought. ☺

Emma: Possibly. I'm bringing a change of clothes.

Lizzy: That's my girl!

Emma: I'm worried.

Lizzy: About what? Sex? Hasn't changed. The mechanics are the same . ☺

Emma: Not that!

Emma: Well, a little about that. But more of what his expectations are. If we have a relationship, we need to protect our jobs. And a little afraid of getting hurt.

Lizzy: There's no guarantees in life. Sometimes you have to risk it. What's that Dr Seuss quote? About smiling because it happened?

Emma: Don't cry because it's over, smile because it happened?

Lizzy: Take a chance big sister. We'll be here to support you if it doesn't work out.

Emma: Also, could you drive me over there? That way you'll know where I am.

Lizzy: Sure thing! Can I meet him?

Emma: Not yet. Maybe later. Wish me luck.

Lizzy: Aww…Good luck. Text me.

*****

Grey started as the doorbell rang. He wiped his hands on his apron and rushed to open the door. Emma stood shyly on the porch. He noticed she had an overnight bag with her. *Yes!* He fist-pumped in his head. *Things are looking good for taking the next step in romance.* He'd been a good friend, even though the restraint was killing him. It was high time to move on.

"Come on in. Let me take your coat. Where's your car?" He looked around outside as a car drove off.

"Oh," she said casually. "I had my sister drop me off. We were out shopping, and it was getting late." She blushed.

He grinned knowingly. "And, is that an overnight bag?"

"It might be, or it could be my newest pocketbook. Big is trendy this year." Emma stepped into the hallway and lowered her bag to the floor. Sliding out of her coat, she handed it to Grey's outstretched hand. Their fingers accidentally brushed. Again, the spark was there. She shivered in anticipation of the evening. She glanced into the immaculate living room. "Nice house."

"Thank you. Not very big, but just right for my needs. Can I get you a drink? I have wine or beer or water."

"Water's fine."

"Lemon in it?"

"Yes, that would be nice." She followed him to the kitchen. It was small but comfortable. The table was set for two, with candles and a low vase filled with colorful flowers. She was impressed with his efforts. "Why Grey, you surprise me. I didn't know you were so fancy."

"There's lots you don't know about me."

"Like what?"

"That I've taken lots of cooking classes because it's fun and relaxing. That I hate messes." Emma looked around. Everything was neat and orderly. Not an item out of place. No piles of clutter.

"I can see that."

"Now tell me something I don't know about you?"

"Umm, well, I don't like to cook so much. I like to bake. And I'm a messy person."

Grey handed her the water with lemon. She sipped it as she looked at the stove. "What's for dinner? It smells delicious."

"I'm making a mushroom risotto and a salad."

"I haven't had risotto in years. My mother used to make it. It's a northern Italy specialty."

"Yup. I know. Remember, my mother's family is from Milan."

She stood next to him as he stirred the risotto. Watching him add the wine little slugs at a time. It was arousing to see this man cooking. She leaned over and gave him a kiss on the cheek. "So sexy."

He paused stirring for a second. Gave her a quick kiss on the lips. "Don't disturb the cook. Any distraction and it could be ruined."

"Sorry." She backed away. "Anything I can do?"

"Nope. Got it under control. Did you bring dessert?"

"Whoops. Left it in the other room. I'll just go get it."

"So, you remembered your overnight bag but not dessert? That's shocking. I know how big a sweet tooth you have. Does that mean you're excited about tonight?"

"No. It means I'm old and forgetful. Although I am looking forward to dinner and our talk."

Emma went and rescued her rustic apple tart from the other room. When she came back, Grey had turned on some slow, bluesy music.

"You're in full seduction mode, aren't you?"

"I just wanted to let you know you were special. Is it working?"

Emma laughed a full throaty laugh. "Possibly."

"Good. Dinner's ready. Are you?"

They sat at the table. Grey dished out the risotto and Emma added the salad to their plates. Lifting his water glass, he said, "Here's to more evenings like this." They softly clinked their glasses together. Emma took a bite of the risotto, and then another, and groaned with pleasure. "This is delicious. So glad you can cook!"

"It's one of my many talents," he said meaningfully, staring at Emma. The tension between them deepened. The heat was palpable.

Emma averted her gaze, not quite ready to open the deeper conversation. "So, how are the grandkids, Noah and Elijah?"

"They're good. Joe has his hands full with them."

"Lisa too. Boys are wild. Girls are too, but in a different way. Boys are so physical. Rough and tumble."

Subject successfully changed, they chatted amiably during dinner. The energy between them was bubbling just below the surface. Afterward, Emma cleared the table and Grey took care of the dishes. "That was the best meal I've had in forever!" Emma said as they strolled into the living room, his arm around her shoulder. The mellow music relaxed and excited them at the same time, setting the mood.

Grey cleared his throat, "So you want to talk about us."

"Yes." She turned to face Grey. "I do".

Chapter 10

All of Me by John Legend

Emma stared up at Grey. Their bodies were so close. She could feel the heat, the want, flowing from his body. Her body and her eyes were full of desire too. Her mind was racing, spiraling between fear and longing. *What are you doing? He's a student. You're a teacher. There are professional ethics. A code to uphold.* Yet she could feel the attraction overwhelming the rational part of her brain. The connection, the energy, that flowed every time they were together was so strong.

He was everything she was not. Strong. Challenging. Funny. Unafraid of the physical. She inched a little closer.

Grey could see her struggle. He wanted her, there was no doubt. He could sense she wanted him. She was everything he was not: kind to a fault, open to feelings, beautiful in her soul, beautiful in her body. But she was a client and there were rules for this. Grey moved a little closer.

Emma reached a hand to Grey's jaw. Grey caressed the back of her neck. He pulled her closer, wrapping his arms around her, resting his forehead to the top of her head. She smelled like flowers, a heady mix of vanilla, roses and lilacs. He wanted to protect her. He wanted to be with her. He felt safe with her. *Damn I have strong feelings for this woman. I want to be with her, in her ....*

She breathed in his scent, so clean and masculine. He smelled like outdoors, fresh and clear. She had never wanted a man like this before.

Emma whispered, "What are we going to do about this? I have feelings for you. I think you have some for me. But...."

Grey swallowed. "I know," he said as he pulled her in tighter. He whispered, "What if, for tonight, we pretend we're just Emma and Grey? Two lonely souls who need each other. Forget the world and its rules?" He kissed her forehead lightly. "Just say yes," he said quietly. She sighed. He kissed her eyes. An energy center, he remembered from her class. Light tender kisses. He gently cupped her face as he lowered his lips to hers. It was a soft kiss. She tasted so good. And he was so hungry for her touch. Emma pulled away for a second and then dove right back in. She put her lips to his in a passionate kiss. Her lips opened up to him, inviting him in. Grey stopped for a moment to look at her. "Is this, okay?"

Emma smiled, "Yes."

They were gently swaying to the music, being seduced by the song in the background. Grey whispered in her ear. "The first time I saw your face, I knew." Emma's body was on fire. His breath, his voice …Grey placed soft kisses along her jaw and down her neck. His hands roamed across her shoulders and down her arms, sliding along the edges of her body. Emma started and stiffened. "What's wrong?"

Emma looked up at Grey, "You know I'm uncomfortable with my old lady body. Lots of lumps and bumps. I'm not a slender spring chicken. Or built like Casey." Her eyes teared up. Grey's hand stopped at her waist.

He said, "I want *you* Emma. With all your soft curves and strong muscles. The ones we made together. Remember?" He kissed her again. "You are a beautiful person. I love your mind. The deepness of your soul. I love the way you are so kind to everyone. And I especially love the way you are to this old, damaged man."

Emma wrapped her arms around Grey. "Just give me time to become braver," she whispered into his chest. Grey ran his hands up and down her back, caressing her shoulders, her middle back, her love handles. Easy gentle touches. He whispered sweetly in her ear, "You are beautiful, and soft, and so sexy." He felt her relaxing and softening. She looked up and kissed him again. Deeper. Stronger.

"Do you want me, Emma?" She nodded her head. "We've been working together. I know how you look. How hard you've been working. How strong you've become. Enjoy all your hard work. Let me admire your body. Tell me in your sexy voice that you want this. If you do. Just say yes."

Emma pushed away from Grey. Meeting his eyes with hers. She began to unbutton her shirt. Grey moved closer. Emma held out her arm. "No, wait. Let me do this. I'm saying yes in my own way." Grey watched, fascinated, as she finished unbuttoning her shirt, letting it slide off her shoulders. She reached around and unfastened her bra, letting it drop a little. Grey groaned. They were finally going to do this. His eyes locked with hers. She reached out to Grey and pulled him in. Emma reached to the hem of his T-shirt and began to lift it up. "Ummm… I'm a little too short to get this over your head. And my bra is falling down." She giggled. "Can you do it?"

Grey growled out, "Yes," as he ripped his shirt all the way off. She looked at the scars that ran across his chest. Tears formed in her eyes.

"Oh, I'm so sorry" she said, as she ran one hand along the scars, kissing them lightly. "You've been through so much. Seen so much."

He pulled at her shirt, so it dropped all the way off. His breath was heavy and deep. Hands on the straps of her bra, he slowly slid them down her arms. "You are so lovely." Her hands clutched the bra close to her chest. His eyes met Emma's. "Okay to let this go too?" Emma hesitated, took a deep breath, and let her bra fall to the floor. Grey reached for her and hugged her tightly.

Her breasts pressed to his chest, skin to skin, heart to heart, and she sighed. "OMG, this feels like heaven." Her hands roamed up and down his back and then let them drop further.

He groaned. "Oh, Emma."

She grinned and said, "Is this okay? Just say yes."

"YES. Oh Yes"

"Good because I've wanted to squeeze this firm ass for a long time."

Grey pressed closer. Her hips pushed up against him. "You mean you've had inappropriate feelings for me?" he asked smiling.

"Very inappropriate, I'd say." Emma let her hand slide up to his chest again, grazing his nipples. He groaned. Her hands kept roaming shyly, touching here and there. "It's been so long since I've been with a man. Well," she giggled. "There is Fred."

Grey growled, "I'm better than Fred." Emma had to agree.

She let her hands move down to his waistband. He groaned as she paused. "Please don't stop," he whispered.

"Sooo, I guess you have some inappropriate feelings yourself?" She let her hand slide across the front of his pants, gently moving her hand up and down his hardness.

"That would be an affirmative, ma'am."

She giggled and he could feel her inhibitions begin to lift. Her breath caught as his hands slid under the waistband of her leggings. He began slowly sliding them down. "Let me do it," she said as she grabbed Grey's waist and cautiously began stepping out of them one foot at time. Almost falling backwards, she said, "Guess I need to work on my balance and stability more."

"I can help with that, you know."

Grey picked her up and carried her to his bedroom. He carefully laid her down on his bed. Emma glanced around. *Good thing we're at his house, mine is the usual disaster. Everything in here is neat.* His king size bed was big and neatly made up. The comforter a dark cerulean blue, with yellow and green pillows. *Huh,* Emma thought, *Marine colors. No clothes on the floor. No crazy knick knacks. Actually, not much of anything. A lamp, a desk, and a bureau. A few books....Are those romance novels on the desk? Hmmm. Nah...my eyesight's not so good. Must be mistaken.* Except, Emma's eyes widened as she noticed a collection of seashells on his nightstand. Right in the center was the sand dollar he had found on their beach trip. Her heart melted.

Catching Emma's eye, he unbuttoned his jeans and stepped out of them. Emma gaped at the bulge in his boxer briefs. "Wow," she gasped. "Let me help," she whispered, her hand reaching up to the waistband and slowly sliding them down. "I'm impressed Grey."

"That's what you do to me," he stated hotly.

Grey climbed up next to her and gathered her up in his arms. Kissing her face, her neck, working his way down to her breasts. Emma sighed with pleasure. His hands gently cupped her, his thumb caressing her nipples. "OMG, that feels so...." She melted under his touch.

"So what?" he teased.

"So... inappropriate..." she groaned. "Please keep it up.

His hands continued roaming down her body, kissing her belly. "So... soft and delicious." He kissed her hips. She stiffened a bit as he got closer to her center. "It's okay, baby girl. I won't do anything you don't want."

Emma thrilled when he said baby. His voice was warm and gravelly and full of desire. He let his hand wander down her legs, caressing and squeezing, moving down the outer edge of thighs and then back up the inner thigh. She sighed with pleasure. Her hand gently touched him. He gasped with pleasure. His hand meandered between her legs. "Is this okay?"

"Ahh. Yes. Yes," she huffed. Her desire was growing with each caress. His hands reached up and tentatively touched her center. "Ohhh… god, that feels so good." She sighed as she melted into a pool of sensation. He kept softly exploring, watching how she reacted to each touch. Small circling motions brought her hips up to meet his touch. Keeping his hand where it was, he scooted up and began to kiss her. Gently at first, but then, as she moaned with his touch, he couldn't contain himself. Strong, needy, passionate kisses came next. He lowered his head to her nipples, drawing one into his mouth. Greedily sucking and biting. Her hips began moving with more need. "Oh Grey," she moaned. He slid one finger into her, and she sucked in her breath.

"Is this, ok?"

"More than ok!" she whispered. "Please don't stop." Grey slid another finger in and began moving them in and out, gently at first, then with more force. She pushed her hips into his hand. "Oh...my… God," she moaned as he softly rubbed her center. "I think I'm going to come. Oh god, oh god. That feels so good. Yes! Keep going." One last stroke and she came. Shattering, she felt like she was falling over a cliff, pulling Grey into her. Breathing deeply, muscles relaxing, the feeling of release flowing from head to toe, she opened her eyes and stroked Greys face. "I never felt so….That was amazing!"

"Better than Fred?" he teased. *A million times better*, she thought as she nestled into his warm body, facing him, her head under his chin, his hands pulling her closer. She could feel his hardness pressing into her belly. Inflaming her desire once again,

She rose up and pushed Grey onto his back. "Your turn." Her hands wandered. Her lips kissed and tasted. Grey, groaned. "Oh Emma … so good." His breath was ragged. His hands massaged her shoulders and arms. Her lips worked their way down to his naval. Her hands gently moved lower and lower until they encircled his hardness. "Is this, okay?" His hands gripped her hair.

"YES," he moaned. As her lips kissed the tip of him, he groaned with desire. She enticingly moved her hand up and down his shaft. "Show me how you like it," she commanded. Grey placed a hand on top of hers and guided her hand, stoking up and down. Leaning down, she took him into her mouth, alternating kissing and licking, focusing on the tip. "That's it, Emma." He groaned with pleasure. He released his hand as Emma took over. She drew him deeper into her mouth. Faster and faster, they moved together. Creating a rhythm that was their own. In tune with one another. The energy flowing. He shouted as he gave one last deep thrust and then came in her mouth.

Emma collapsed on top of Grey. "That was amazing. You tasted so good."

Grey ran his finger through her curls. "It was more than amazing. It was astounding." Pulling her up so her head rested under his chin, he noticed that she fit perfectly, like they were two puzzle pieces. Her leg draped over his. She could hear his heartbeat. He stroked her back, drawing little patterns up and down and around.

She sighed deeply, fingers resting in his chest hair. "What have we done Grey? Was this wrong?"

"Did it feel wrong?"

Emma shook her head. "No. It felt like it was meant to be. It was perfect."

"We'll figure it out.   Tonight, let's just enjoy." He hugged her and lifted her lips to his as he tenderly kissed her. "Besides this old man is still feeling frisky. Not often I have beautiful yoga teacher in my bed." Grinning, he continued, "Give me a few minutes to recover and we can do some more exploring."

"Oh really?" she said huskily. "Are you up for more? Because I got some needs that haven't been met yet." She lazily stretched out, exposing her breasts and belly. Immediately realizing what she had done, she curled up back into Grey, pulling the covers over her.

"Emma, are you ashamed of your body? It's beautiful. Show it off. Let me see those lovely breasts." She shyly rolled onto her back; arms draped across her chest. "Emma, let go." He pushed her hands away and admired her.

"I'm so old and crinkly and flabby."

"No, your skin is soft and sensuous. Like velvet." His hands pressed into her belly. "You have six pack abs under there." Rising up, he kissed her arms. "Your arms are strong and amazingly sexy. And those legs...curvy and sensuous and delicious." His fingers gently caressed her legs. He released her and then rolled her onto her belly. Kissing her back, he licked his tongue down her spine. His hands curved over her bottom. "And your ass is so tight and firm." He kissed his way down the back of her legs, stopping at the back of her knees. "I think I heard … in one of your classes…you mentioned sexual energy centers. And … I believe…back of the knees was one of them." He licked. She moaned with pleasure. "Huh. Who woulda thought..?"

He continued kissing them as Emma softly moaned and nodded her head, grunting, "I believe that's correct. The neurovascular points are stimulated." He worked his way all the way down to her ankles, massaging the calves and soles of her feet.

Rolling her back over, he kissed her eyelids, one by one, and then let his kisses trail down to her cheeks. "I believe those are the other two...neurovascular points."

By now, Emma had melted into a puddle of need and want. "You, sir, are a good listener."

"I aim to please, ma'am."

Emma reached down and felt his growing erection. "Hmmm... maybe we can work with this." She quickly straddled him, knees on either side of his hips. Slowly and sensuously, she rubbed up and down, gliding over his firmness. Grey's eyes widened, "Where's my shy girl now?" he grinned. Placing his hands on her breasts, squeezing lightly as she moved back and forth.

"She left about six kisses ago. She's been replaced." But, stopping for a moment, she said, "Umm Grey I'm afraid I may be a little dry... would you have any...?"

Grey reached over to his bedside table, opened the drawer, and pulled out a small bottle of lubricant. With a grin he asked, "Will this do?"

"Well, actually, I like something more natural." She blushed. "Would you have any coconut oil? It works well."

"Coconut oil? That's first for me." Grey hopped up, ran into the kitchen, and grabbed the coconut oil. He was back in a flash.

"How's that for service?" Emma gave him a big smile and scooped a little of the solidified oil. Grey watched as the oil began to soften and liquefy in her hand. She touched him again and ran it down his shaft. Grey gulped. "Wow, that feels fabulous. And it smells good too." Emma kept softly stroking him. "Here, Grey, take some and put it on me". He felt the oil melt into her tender skin, making her wetter and smoother.

"Well, as much as I liked shy Emma, this new girl is way more fun." He pulled her down and suckled on her nipples. He could feel her get wetter and wetter. His dick growing bigger and harder as she slid up, and, then slowly down his length with her wetness.

Adjusting her hips, she let the tip of him touch her entrance. Staying as still as she could, she asked, "Is this okay? Or do we need a condom?" Smiling shyly, she added, "I can't get pregnant. But I haven't had sex in twenty years. I don't know the rules anymore."

"I haven't been with anyone in several years. And I always used a condom. I think we're good."

She sighed in relief, lowering herself a little deeper onto him.

"Emma...Emma...." His breath hitched as the sensations overwhelmed him. She was so warm.

"Grey..." she gasped. "I didn't know it could feel this good." Tears of pleasure sprang to her eyes.   She drew him in some more. He responded, rocking his hips to her.

Emma stilled her movements. "Let's enjoy this moment."

Grey looked wildly at her. "Ummm I am *thoroughly* enjoying this moment," he growled.   Hands to her face, he said, "I thought you were too. We can stop if you want."

"No Grey," she exclaimed. "I'm loving this moment. Just want to pause and savor." She looked soulfully at him. Grey harumphed, his shoulders sagging under her gaze. "Okay," he sighed as he mumbled. "But I was savoring just fine."

"Thank you," she said in that very sexy commanding yoga voice that turned him on so much. "Now close your eyes. Tell me what you feel. How you feel."

"I feel your warmth." He murmured. "...So delicious, the softness of your pussy surrounding me. It's like velvet." He struggled to talk, his breath was so thick and heavy. He struggled to keep still. "I feel your breath on my skin. I feel like we're connected through some invisible force." He groaned. "It's just you and me, Emma." His hands were running along the edges of her body, pulling her deeper into him. His voice deepening, he said, "Oh, baby, that's it, please." He begged. "Have I savored enough? I can't stay still. I need you." He began to move his hips slowly.

Emma met his movements, breathing heavy, faster and faster until they were moving as one. "I've never felt this way," she said, her voice ragged with need. "Almost there." She frantically pressed up and down.

"Come on baby." Grey's hands on her hips took charge, slowing her, moving her smoothly up and down. He wasn't sure how much longer he could hold off. "Come for me. Fuck! I need you to come." The sound of his voice was desperate with need, encouraging her, pushing her over the edge. Emma exploded with soft, mewling sounds of pleasure as she came.

Catching her breath, she looked at Grey. Watching his face with intensity, she whispered devilishly, in her commanding voice, "Fuck me Grey. Fuck me. I want to feel you let go inside me." She kept her hips moving. Grey's eyes darkened. Need and desire taking over. Thrusting fast and hard. Emma keeping pace with him. "You are a witch," he grunted. "A wonderful, magical witch." Her hips dancing with his faster and faster. "Ohh... Emma, love, I need you," he shouted as he came.

Emma collapsed on his chest. Both breathed heavily. Waves of pleasure flowed over both of them. Both were sated.

"Wow." Grey looked at her in amazement. "You went from hiding your body to commanding mine. Wow! Wow wow!" She started to release him. "Please don't. Not yet..." Grey whispered as he gently stoked her hair.

Emma sighed with pleasure and nestled in a little closer. She giggled. "You called me a witch, a magical witch."

"Seriously, you are. You've cast a spell over me."

"Grey, I feel such a connection to you. I can't begin to describe it."

"Then don't," he said as he wrapped his arms around her tightly. "I feel it too. Let's just enjoy it."

"But I'm scared." she mumbled into his chest.

"So am I, Emma. So am I, my little witch," he said as they both closed their eyes and fell asleep.

*****

The next morning Emma awoke to Grey crooning, "Good morning sleepyhead." She was tucked into him. His arms wrapped around her, hands cupping her breasts. She flipped over and curled alongside him, her head resting on his chest and her fingers wrapped in the fur on his chest.

Raising her head, she mumbled, "I'm not awake yet." Dropping her head back down quickly, she snuggled a little closer, peering at Grey through strands of hair that covered her eyes. Grey let his fingers run through her curls. "Man! You have some crazy hair." He laughed and kissed her forehead. "I know you're under there somewhere."

"At least I have some hair," she teased. Smiling contentedly and lifting her hand to cup his jaw, she said, "I feel so peaceful and full. I feel like purring."

"Well, I'm a dog person. You can purr, but I prefer to rub my back in the grass with my legs in the air." Both started laughing uproariously.

She rubbed his belly. "Good doggy."

"Seriously Emma." With a tremor in his voice, he said, "It's good. What we had. What we have. Isn't it?" His hands played lightly with her hair. "I haven't felt so alive in years. Maybe forever. You know I'm not very open with my feelings and emotions. But you, you little enchantress,"—he tapped her nose lightly–"make me want to feel. But I'm not sure how much I can. I don't want ever to hurt you."

"It's not easy opening up your heart. It's okay to be afraid." She took his hands and wove their fingers together. "I'm afraid too. Brian's death was devastating. I tried to save him, but I couldn't. I swore I'd never get involved again with a man who was military."

Emma looked at Grey. His face was guarded, his muscles tense, steeling himself for the inevitable rejection. His heart was already closing up. "But,"—Grey's heart was beating so fast, Emma could feel it – "you're different. I feel safe with you. You are helping yourself, something Brian never did. You've been honest with me. You've been a good friend. Never pushing me; well, except for those damn pushups." She grinned. "I think we should give this… whatever this is … a try."

She felt him relax. "I don't want to lose you Emma."

"You won't unless you're a real ass."

He kissed her tenderly. "Thank you, I'll try not to be."

"And speaking of ass," she said as she grabbed his and pressed herself to him.

"Man, Emma you are the most surprising woman I've ever met. Strong and gentle. Not afraid of speaking your truth, and… way sexy."

*****

Later that afternoon, Grey drove Emma home. He kissed her tenderly on her eyes, her cheeks and mouth. "Can I see you tomorrow?"

"I think we can work that out." Looking at her calendar, she said, "I have 9:30 and 11 am yoga classes. Oh, and, also, I signed up for a spin class at your gym." She looked sternly at him," Are you teaching it?"

"I am."

"Maybe I should reschedule with another teacher? We need to think carefully of the consequences of our relationship."

"Well, it's a group class. No personal contact. And I would miss a certain cute little yoga teacher who really tries hard. Plus, she's hot in those shorts."

"Grey! We need to take this seriously. I don't want to damage either of our reputations. We both love and need our jobs."

"You're right," Grey conceded. "But I think spin class would be fine. Let's re-think the personal training and boot camps."

Emma's face fell. "You motivate me to try harder. Not sure anyone else can," she said sadly. "But that's the ethical thing to do. I'm going to check with Caityln as well. I'm sure you'll have to find another yoga teacher. Unless ….you want to re-think us? We can go back to friends."

"I do not," Grey said fiercely. "We'll figure it out. If it means I have to give up yoga, I will."

Emma got out of the truck and turned back to Grey, "I'll see you tomorrow in my sexy bike shorts. Maybe I won't wear a bra."

Grey groaned. "That was uncalled for. Now all I'm going to think about today is you, braless."

"Bye." She sashayed up the sidewalk into the house.

*****

The next day she spoke to Caitlyn about her new relationship. Caitlyn agreed that Grey should go to a different yoga teacher so there was no conflict of interest or claims of sexual harassment. Emma asked Gwen, a yoga teacher at Half Moon who specialized in meditation, to add Grey to her class. Gwen agreed with a little wink. "So glad to see you getting out there finally!" Emma knew Gwen would take good care of Grey.

She was sad about it, but it was for the best. At least she would see him around the studio. And it meant they were free to be Emma and Grey.

Later in the day, she met Grey before spin class to discuss what Caitlyn had said. He pulled her into the office and kissed her. "Grey!" she squealed. "We need to talk first."

"Nope, first things first." He kissed her again. "Now we can talk."

Emma told him about her discussion with Caitlyn. "Gwen is really good. You'll like her."

"She's not you." He pouted. "You know me best."

"Maybe it's good, she's not involved. She can have a fresh eye on what works for you."

Grey reluctantly agreed. "I spoke to Isaac about us. He agrees it best not to have me as your coach. Spin class is okay though. He's going to take over this session boot camp. And next session, you can sign up for Kayla's. She's going to start a new one for women only. That way I don't have to worry about you flirting with the other guys." He smiled as he said it, but Emma could tell he was a little anxious.

"You'll never have to worry about me and other guys. I'm pretty loyal. And you're pretty special."

"Same here." Grey reached out and gave her a quick hug.

"I bet Isaac gave you a hard time." She laughed. "Especially now that he'll have to coach Casey."

"Yeah… he did. But he seemed pleased that it worked out between us. He said he knew we were meant to be together. And he was willing to take one for the team, again."

"He's a good young man. You should be proud."

Grey nodded. "Both the boys turned out well in spite of me." Looking at Emma, he said, "Which reminds me, I owe Alisha an apology. I promised myself at the beach I would make amends for what I did. I'm going to ask her out for coffee, if that's okay with you."

"Of course! I'm glad you're at that point in your journey." She added with a little trepidation, "I don't have anything to be jealous about, do I?"

Astonished, Grey looked at her. "Jealous? Is Miss Live-and-let-live jealous? No, you don't. Alisha and I are friendly co-parents. Her husband is great, and he's been a good stepdad to the boys. I just feel like I've never apologized to her for what I put her through. She deserves to hear that I regret it and that I'm working through my past. I owe her that."

Emma agreed. Grey was making amends to the people he hurt. It was a very good sign.

After spin class, they both showered at the gym and then went back to Grey's house for dinner. He was indeed a good cook of simple, fresh meals that were delicious. He knew his way around a spice rack. Emma brought a dessert. Lately, she was using more fruits in her baking, which made Grey happy. "Can you spend the night?" he asked as they cuddled on the couch watching *Young Sheldon*. He kissed her deeply. "I can't get enough of you," he gasped as he came up for air.

Emma herself was breathless. "I know what you mean. It's like a hunger that can't be satisfied."

He tugged at her shirt. "Let's take this off."

"I should go home. My house is a mess and I have an early class tomorrow. Can't stay up all night. I'm old!" She whined as she pulled her shirt off and hungrily tugged at his sweatpants.

"Okay, a quickie it is. I'll get you home in less than an hour."

Three hours later, they woke up in each other's arms. Emma sat up mumbling, "I need to go home and clean my house."

Grey mumbled right back, "in a minute," and then groggily fell back asleep, hugging her tightly into his chest. She gave up. *I'll have to make the walk of shame tomorrow. Hopefully the neighbors won't be around.*

Chapter 11

Can't Get Enough of Your Love by Barry White

They were acting like teenagers who had discovered sex for the first time. Except they were more skilled. They had spent several nights together, alternating houses. The one night they couldn't be together, they talked until midnight on the phone. They hadn't told anyone about how far their relationship had come. It was their secret to treasure before life got in the way. He went to yoga. She went to Core Connection.

Emma's refrain all week was "Oh my God!" as Grey played with her body. She didn't know old people could come so many times with so much passion and desire, each and every damn time. "Aren't you getting tired of me saying that? I have to think of some other way to shout out my feelings."

Grey nuzzled her. "Nope, it's perfect. Makes me feel powerful… godlike."

"Well then, we're good, because in my mind you are godlike." She ran her hands across his scarred shoulders and back, thinking of all he had been through and how damaged he'd been. But also, how strong and determined he was to heal himself, like a phoenix rising out of the ashes.

"And you, my dear, are my goddess."

"Oh…. like Apollo and Aphrodite?"

"Sure," he mumbled distractedly as he traced the outline of her breasts with his tongue.

"Apollo is the good of the sun, music and healing, you know. Hot, like you," she giggled. "And strong and able to heal wounds. That describes you to a tee."

"Uh huh...." His tongue was licking and tasting her neck and ears. "And Aphrodite?"

"She's the goddess of love, sex, and beauty."

Grey lifted his head and his gaze raked down her body. "That describes you to a tee."

"Love," he said he kissed her forehead.

"Sex," he whispered. His hand dipped down and ran through her wetness. Emma stilled.

"Beauty," he groaned as he gently followed the outline of her body with his hands. "So beautiful, lush, and velvety." He paused for a second, his desire obvious. "I need you, Emma," he growled.

"Oh my god!" Emma gasped. Grey rolled on top of her, supporting himself and surrounding her. "I can't believe we're going to do this again! I'm gonna be so sore."

"I believe, Aphrodite, my name is Apollo. And healing is one of my powers. I'll help with that that soreness later," Grey mumbled as he slowly entered her, tenderly kissing her lips. Their hips moved together in unison, melting into each other, finding that connection, rising and sinking until they both found their release. Breathless and satiated, they clung to one another.

"Oh Grey, that was, I have no words! Each time gets better and better. You are so good."

"Yup. I'm a god alright." He grinned. "So much better than Fred." Carefully rolling off her, Grey turned her to face him and drew her in close. Her head nestled into his chest, his arms cradling her, his heart full of emotion. He felt the chains around his heart breaking one by one. With a wave of feeling so strong, he thought, *I love this woman with all my heart. She fills that empty space in me.* He was not quite sure he was ready to handle all that it entailed, but he needed to try.

Emma kissed his chest and closed her eyes, beginning to doze. He dipped his head into her hair and kissed her so lovingly it brought tears to his eyes. *I love her.* The feeling washed over him again. Emma, asleep, rolled away from him, landing on her belly beside him. Her arms stretched above her head. Her hair was all wild and curly, falling over her face. Grey slid his hand possessively to her back, resting it just below the curve in her back. *Mine*, he thought. *She's mine.* Emma's eyes opened lazily, looking sleepily at him. She whispered, "Yes. I'm yours. I'm saying yes."

Grey started. *Did I say that out loud? I don't think I did. Damn woman is a mind reader. A witch. An enchantress. My Aphrodite.* Grey pulled her in towards him. She flipped over, her backside cuddled up to him. He laid his arm over her just above her waist, protecting her, needing her. Emma sighed deeply and pushed in a little closer, feeling safe and desired. They both fell asleep.

Grey woke up to Emma urgently shaking his shoulder and prodding. "Get-up! Get-up! The doorbell's ringing. I forgot I'd told Lisa I'd watch her boys this morning."

"Huh? What?"

"You have to get up! Lisa's here with boys." Emma scrambled out of bed, grabbing a sweatshirt and some pants. She stumbled to the door, yelling at Grey to get dressed.

The front door opened as Lisa stepped in, "Mom! You okay?" she shouted. "I'm here with the kids."

Emma raced out of the bedroom to face her daughter.

"Mom?" Lisa gaped at her mother. *Damn, she looked like she'd been having wild and crazy sex.* "You okay?"

"Yup, just overslept. Forgot about babysitting," Emma said brightly, glancing nervously towards her bedroom.

Just then, Grey, shirtless and clad only in boxer briefs, stepped into the hallway. "What were you saying? About getting up?"

"Mom!" Lisa looked at them both, shocked. Glancing from one to the other, she started to laugh. "Sorry, didn't mean to interrupt."

The boys caught sight of Grey and shouted, "Look Grey is here! And he's in his underwear." Giggling and running around the living room, they chanted, "Underwear. Underwear. Grey is in his underwear."

"Boys, head out to the backyard," Lisa said firmly.

Emma's face was bright red. "Sorry, Lisa. I'm so embarrassed."

Lisa smiled. "Nothing to be embarrassed of. You're a gown woman. Glad to see you have a little fun." Looking at Grey, she said, "He's the one who should be worried. The boys are never going to let him live the underwear thing down." Looking meaningfully at his crotch, she giggled and added, "Although doesn't seem to be anything embarrassing there."

"Guess I need to get dressed," he mumbled slowly, backing into Emma's bedroom. *Damn it,* he cursed. *That was humiliating!* Thank goodness he thought to put on his briefs. He pulled his sweatpants and shirt on and walked back out into the living room. "Sorry about that."

"It's okay. I see half naked people all day. I'm a PA. Although they're *not* usually in my mother's hallway." She giggled. "So, you two are an item now?"

Emma and Grey exchanged glances, feeling like two teenagers caught fooling around. "I'd say yes," Grey said firmly. Emma nodded. "Your mom is something special."

Emma reached out and took Grey's hand. "And so are you."

"Well, well, well, looks like we got ourselves a little romance. Can't wait until I tell Marie. This is going to be fun." She chortled.

"Can you give us until Monday, please?" Emma pleaded. "You know Marie will be relentless."

"Aww, Mom. What fun is that? Can I at least tell James and Steve? They'll leave you alone. I gotta tell someone."

"Tell your husband," Emma said firmly. "And give us a little time to prepare for the onslaught."

Fine." Lisa backed off. "But fair warning, your phone is going to be buzzing off the hook on Monday."

Emma looked gratefully at Lisa. "Thanks. Now don't you have a hairdresser appointment?"

Lisa jumped. "Oh no! I'm going to be late," she wailed. "Crystal will kill me. I'll be back in a few hours. Hope you two lovebirds can keep your hands off each other while the boys are here."

"We'll be good," Emma promised. "See you in a bit."

Emma collapsed against Grey. She couldn't believe she'd forgotten about babysitting. Their quiet weekend was going to be a lot noisier. "I'll go check on the boys. Do you want to grab some breakfast? I've got eggs, frozen muffins, fruit for smoothies…."

"Sure, although, I had planned on having you for breakfast." He pulled her into him, giving her a big hug and gentle kiss. "But I can wait until lunch."

"I'm sorry to spoil the weekend. My family takes a lot of my time. Might need to set some boundaries." She tilted her head up for a kiss.

"Be-ma and Grey sitting in a tree. K-I-S-S-I-N-G. First comes love then comes marriage then comes Be-Ma with the baby carriage." Three pairs of eyes were peering in the kitchen window. Giggling. "Be-ma's got a boyfriend," Ayden said. "Does that mean he's our grandpa now?"

Emma sighed. "I'd better go nip this in the bud. Thanks for understanding."

"No problem. Family is important. I regret the time I didn't spend with my boys. Maybe we can take them to the park. I can call Joe and see if his boys want to join us."

With a grateful smile, Emma nodded. "Perfect! Lisa should be back by noon. Then we can rest."

Grey wiggled his eyebrows. "Resting is not what I had in mind."

Emma rolled her eyes as she walked to the door. "Insatiable."

*****

But rest they did. After Lisa picked up the boys and Grey dropped his grandkids off, they were exhausted. Emma looked at Grey. "We need a nap and no funny stuff! I'm tired." Grey could only nod in agreement. Five wild boys and not much sleep added up to naptime. Grabbing his hand, she led him into the bedroom and they laid down together. Within two minutes, both were sound asleep, her hand still resting in his.

Emma's snoring woke them both up an hour later. "I do not snore!" Emma huffed, outraged.

"I beg to differ with you. "You're lucky the neighbors haven't complained," Grey grumped.

"Humph… well you do too! And you drool!"

"But it was your snoring that woke us up. And I don't drool," Grey argued.

Emma pointed to the wet spot on her shoulder. "Oh yes, you do!" They looked at each other for a second and burst out laughing. "Aren't we the romantic couple." Emma said between snorts, "I've been alone so long who knows what I do in my sleep."

"Me too." Grey touched Emma's face. "It's nice to have someone to show you your faults."

Emma begrudgingly agreed. She sniffed, "I need to take a shower. Sex and sweaty little boys don't make for pleasant perfume."

"How about I join you? Sex in the shower can be hot." *At least, it is in romance books.* He pictured water sluicing down Emma's shoulder, between her breasts. Pinning her to the shower wall and ravaging her. *God he was getting hard just thinking of it.*

Emma hesitated. "Ummm...I'm not so sure old man. We're not young anymore." She was a little sore from all their activity and her shower was small, not one of those fancy, step-in showers. It might be awkward. Or even dangerous. Don't need any broken bones. Plus, she wanted to clean up, not get messy; and she could use a little alone time. She wasn't used to all this togetherness.

"Come on babe. Let's do this." He was overcome with visions of her riding him while the water ran down her back.

Emma reluctantly nodded her head. She started the shower and then looked shyly at Grey. He had stripped down, all ready to go, in more ways than one. But she was not excited about taking a shower with him, or anyone for that matter. "Why don't you start, and I'll join you?"

Eagerly, Grey jumped in the shower. "Jesus," he screamed. "The water is freezing." He scrambled around searching for the shower handle. Finally, he found it and gave the lever a turn, only to find it was too hot. "Damn!" he screamed. *This is a fucking disaster he thought. My dick will never recover.* "Emma!" he shouted. What's the trick to this shower?"

Emma, still fully clothed, slid the shower door open and reached in. "It's a little old and finicky." Her shirt was getting soaking wet, and her hair was dripping. She turned the faucet to the correct setting. "Sorry," she said turning to slide out and running smack into

Grey's limp penis. Grey looked at her, all thoughts of hot shower sex gone.

"Maybe this was a bad idea," he conceded. "I'll take a quick shower. Then it'll be your turn."

Emma backed out of the shower door, smacking her forehead on the edge of the door. "Ouch!" she cried, her hand flying up to her forehead. *That'll need ice.* She grabbed a towel to dry her hair. *Dang it, now my hair's going to be all frizzy.* She usually used a shower cap when she took her daily shower. Annoyed, she stripped off her wet shirt, creating a water puddle on the floor. *Crap! That was the last towel.* Grey needed one and now she had to wipe up the puddle on the floor. *Arrggh.* Topless, she ran down the hall to the dryer where a load of towels waited to be folded. Grabbing a couple, she made back to the bathroom just in time to hear Grey swearing as he slipped in the water, landing smack dab on his butt. "Oh my god, Grey, are you alright?"

He glared at her, "Do I look like I'm alright?"

"Umm …no?" She extended her hand and tried to pull him to his feet. "Let me help you up." He grasped her hand as she tugged, trying to get him up. Her weight was no match for his, though, and she tumbled down on top of him. Grey looked up at her in disgust.

"Guess we need to work on your weightlifting skills."

Stung by his tone, she looked down at Grey, tears in the corner of her eyes. "You don't have to be so mean! I'm doing the best I can! You're six feet tall. I'm 5'1" Besides I didn't want to take a damn shower with you anyway! I needed some alone time."

Grey glared up at her. "You should've just told me!"

"I guess I should've of! I didn't want to hurt your feelings. This is all new to me," she huffed as she started to get up.

But the sight of his handsome naked body splayed unceremoniously on her bathroom floor and her wet half naked torso hovering over him was too much. Emma burst into laughter. Her boobs bouncing up and down on Greys wet chest. "So much for hot shower sex.," She gasped trying to catch her breath. "You look so wet and mad, and not in a sexy way." Tears poured from her eyes as she rocked with laughter.

Grey glared at her. "It's not funny."

"Oh yes, it is. Look at us!"

Grey glanced down at his wet naked body. He took in her naked torso, boobs shaking all over the place, her wet hair hanging around her shoulders and dripping on to him. The corners of his mouth began to lift up. "Well maybe it is kind of funny." He guffawed. "Hilarious." He let out a deep belly laugh. "Apollo and Aphrodite. At their finest."

She choked as the laughs continued to stream out of both of them. "Your boobs, they are just bouncing away." He grinned, reaching up to still them. "Afraid they're going to knock me out." Their laughter gradually died down. Emma eased her way off of him and offered her hand once again to help him up. He gingerly stood up, rubbing his butt. "Don't think anything's broken but my pride."

Emma handed him a towel and backed out of the bathroom. "I'll let you and your wounded pride have a moment."

Grey looked at her. "I'm sorry I was so grumpy. This," he gestured back and forth to her him, "us, is, all new to me too. Guess I got carried away."

"Yes, you did," she firmly. "You hurt my feelings."

"I'm so sorry. I'll try not to hurt you again," he said as he reached out to Emma for a hug. His anxiety ramping up a bit. *I hope I don't*

*hurt her… Breathe Grey breathe. Emma will love you no matter what…..
I hope.* He pushed his fear deep down for now.

*****

Emma felt much better after she showered and dried her hair.
Grey had settled in front of the tv, watching the UNC-Duke football
game. She grinned as he cheered for UNC. Thank goodness he's not
rooting for Duke! That could be a game breaker for her boys…and
she wanted her family to like him as much as she did.

"How's your butt?" Emma asked, dropping down beside him on
the comfortable beige sectional that had seen better years. She had
always wanted a cream-colored couch with fancy decorations around;
but truthfully, that wasn't her. The room was cozy, with light sage
walls and splashes of jewel-toned colors in the pictures on the wall
and the knickknacks scattered about. Emma's vibe was comfortable.
It was a little cluttered, but warm. No point in white sofa or walls
when the house was so often filled with kids. She sighed. She liked
her messy bookcase stacked with all kinds of magazines and books
for kids and adults. She liked the baskets stuffed with crayons and
markers and coloring books. She even liked the section of the living
room devoted to kids' crafts. Which, she thought ruefully, the boys
had torn through earlier.

"It's fine, probably a little bruised." He blushed. He wrapped his
arm around her and pulled her in closer. She rested her head on his
shoulder. "Glad no one was here to witness that debacle. No more
shower sex in real life. Maybe just in my dreams."

Emma had to agree. Sometimes imagination was better than
reality. She was glad they were spending time together. He saw her
messy life: her messy house, her kids and grandkids always around.

And he hadn't flinched yet. *Wonder what he thinks.* She had spent some time at his house as well. His was a much quieter, more organized house. Everything was in its place. It was very masculine, except for his collection of romance books. She had meant to ask him about those. Maybe left over from an old girlfriend. She felt a flash of jealously as she thought of him making love to someone else. *Stop it, Emma. We both have a past. He's here with you now.*

Over the course of the last few weeks, she had seen how busy he was with running the gym, his personal training and his pickleball. He was a hard worker. Maybe too much so, she thought. She knew from their conversations that his therapist felt he worked overtime to avoid his feelings. She agreed.

They had talked a little about his anxiety; but lately, it seemed it had been under control. She felt proud about that. But she also knew those feelings came with complications. They didn't just surface and disappear. They needed to be worked through; and who knew what snags Grey could hit in the process. He might run away from any deep involvement with her. *Best to be prepared*, she thought. *Maybe don't get too attached yet. There could be a storm approaching.*

"Hey, Emma. Where are you? I asked you a question." Grey waved his hand in front of her face.

"Oh. Sorry. Just thinking. What did you ask?"

"If you wanted to watch a movie. Been flipping through Netflix and saw this Hallmark movie."

Emma stared at him incredulously. "You want to watch a Hallmark movie?"

"If you do, I do." He said tentatively.

"Wait a minute," she said slowly. "I saw all those romance books in your bedroom. Do you like romance novels?"

Grey's face reddened. "Yes," he said shyly.

"Huh.   That's …interesting. Mr. Manly Man! I love a good romance, but don't know too many men who do."

"When I was in the VA hospital, there wasn't too much to do but read, and books were in short supply. I'd go into the waiting area and look for any books people left behind. Mostly found romance stories. You know, Harlequin and historical fiction and all of that. I got hooked. It was soothing compared to the usual spy or war stories. And I needed soothing." He searched Emma's face for her reaction, his shoulders tense. He'd never told anyone about it. *She probably thinks I'm weird.* But he saw no judgement. Only compassion.

"Huh." Emma's heart broke at the thought of Grey suffering and needing an escape from his pain. "You continue to amaze me Grey Erikson." She kissed his cheek lightly. "Let's watch it. Want some popcorn? All I have is Smart Pop, though. The healthy one. That okay?"

"Perfect!"

✳✳✳✳✳

After the movie, they made dinner together. Grey grilled some salmon fillets while Emma made a kale salad and sauteed some carrots and zucchini. She pulled a tray of mini baguettes out from the freezer and put them in the oven to bake. Emma snuck up behind Grey and put her arms around him. He started at first, then relaxed into the hug.

"This is nice. Having you around," she whispered. Emma felt contented. She was self-sufficient. She'd survived. She had a family who loved her and a house that was almost paid. Having a man around wasn't necessary, but it sure was enjoyable. She loved him with an intensity she wouldn't have thought possible. Yet, if it didn't

177

work out with Grey, she knew she'd be okay; sad, but ok. *Remember we only have the present moment; the past is gone, and the future is not assured.* Her yoga had taught her that. *I can't guarantee Grey will stay, but I can enjoy each moment he's here.*

"We have only one more day before my family finds out about us. Then we're in for it. Let's enjoy it while we can." There was a tinge of sadness in her voice. Emma didn't want this peaceful time to end. They were in their own little cocoon, protected from the pandemonium her family could create. They were loud and loved to tease. There were so many of them, someone always needed her. She loved it. She just hoped Grey could handle it. She kissed his back and then headed to the kitchen to set the table.

Grey wanted to scoop Emma up and take her away, somewhere far away from family and jobs. Somewhere they could be themselves, with no stress or anxieties. These last few weeks had been the best of his life. He never felt so satisfied. Emma eased his pain and made him laugh. She challenged him to feel. But deeply buried feelings were sneaking out and surrounding him. He found himself getting really angry at the things he shouldn't. Some he could handle, but some were scary. Like when he slipped in the shower. It was annoying and embarrassing for sure, but he lashed out at Emma. He knew he was wrong to yell at her, but he had no control over it.

He was starting to have nightmares again. The night Emma wasn't with him, he dreamed he was back in the jungles of Vietnam. He was whimpering and shaking, curled into a ball. It was dark and he thought the enemy was surrounding him. He had the urge to hunker down and not shoot, but Grey knew if he didn't, he or his bunkmates would die. As he raised his gun to shoot, he woke up in cold sweat. "No more killing, no more killing," he muttered. He was afraid of what Emma would think if he told her about the nightmares. What if he hurt her when he had a nightmare? Would she hate the man he had been? The man he was now?

He was glad he had an appointment with Celeste this week. She knew he was breaking though his tough shell and was working with him to cope. But was he worthy of Emma? He wasn't sure. Maybe he should back out now before they got too involved, and she got hurt. *Who are you kidding? You're in so deep you'll be the one hurt.* Emma was strong. She'd bounce back. He might not. But he had promised Marie he wouldn't hurt her mom. Had he lied?

Grey was quiet during dinner. "Anything wrong?" Emma asked as he played with his napkin.

"No. Dinner was delicious. Thank you. Just tired. We've had a busy day. I was thinking I'd go for a run. Sometimes that perks me up." He could feel his anxiety percolating. Running helped tamp it down. All he kept thinking was that he was going to hurt Emma if he wasn't careful. "I think I'll head home and get my running shoes."

Emma looked confused. "Oh. Okay. See you later tonight? I got strawberries and whipped cream. We can have strawberry shortcake for dessert."

"I was thinking maybe I should stay at my house tonight. Aren't you a little sick of me?" This weekend had been so good. *Too good. It was scary.* He'd been happy. But he didn't deserve happiness. He loved Emma. He hadn't loved anyone except his boys, and he had abandoned them. He sensed his anxiety taking hold. He really needed to go. *Get away from Emma before you hurt her* was repeating over and over in his head. He thought of the hurt look on her face when he lashed out at her when he fell on the shower. He was scared that more of that anger about the war, what he had done and what was done to him would manifest itself in more sudden bursts of anger. His field of vision narrowed, and he was starting to sweat. "I've got to go," he said as he sprinted towards the door.

"Grey, what's wrong?" Emma ran after him. "Grey, can we talk?" She wasn't sure what had caused it, but she could see he was panicking. She ran to catch up with him. Putting her hand gently on his arm, she said, "Grey, breathe. Deep breath in, Deep breath out."

He slowed down as she walked beside him. He could hear her voice. It was soothing and calming.

"Grey, listen to my voice. Can you breathe in again and then out slowly?" Grey nodded. "Good. Just keep your focus on your breath and my voice. In and out. Can you feel my hand touching you?" Grey nodded. "OK. now breath in and breath out. Make that out breath long, really long." Grey did as she asked. He could feel the repetitive thoughts slowing. The fear receding. Her voice was steady and calm as she guided him back to her house. She sat him down on the sofa.

"I'm getting you a drink of water. Will you be okay if I go to the kitchen?'

Grey nodded. His breathing began to settle down. He was still feeling shaky, but no longer overwhelmed by the need to run away.

"Thanks." He took the glass of water and gulped it down.

Emma sat next to him, placing her hand on his shoulder. "Okay if I hug you?"

"I'd like that," he said quietly. She pulled Grey into her, her arms encircling his shoulders. He rested his head on her chest.

"I'm so sorry. I'm such a mess," he whispered, tears in his eyes.

She tenderly stroked the back of his neck. "It's okay, baby. Just let me hold you. You're safe with me."

"You deserve better," Grey said sorrowfully. "I am so messed up. I'll only hurt you." His voice broke as Emma held him tight. "My nightmares are starting to come back, and I don't know why. They remind me of the dark places in my soul. I hate myself for what I did in the war, what I did to Joe and Isaac, how I ruined my marriage. The only time I don't have them is when I'm with you." Emma stroked his hair as she listened. Her heart was breaking for his suffering. "I love you, Emma… so much. And I hurt the ones I love," he said desolately. "I had to run, so I won't hurt you."

Emma hugged him as tight as she could, kissing the top of his head. "It'll be alright, Grey. I love you too. We can work through this together."

She lifted his head from her chest, her hands cupping his jaw, slowly kissing his forehead, his eyes, the tears as they coursed down his face. "You're a good man," she said fiercely. "And I'm the strong woman who loves this good man. I see your true colors."

Grey's eyes met hers. He saw the love and strength radiating from her. His heart was soothed. Maybe we can do this he thought as he laid his head back down on her.

Emma saw so much love and despair in his face. She knew he was afraid, but maybe his love for her could help him overcome his fears. We can do this, she thought as she rubbed his shoulders.

"Do you have an appointment with Celeste this week?" she questioned kindly.

"I do. Since the nightmares have returned, she sees me at least once a week. She tells me it's because I'm beginning to open up and that the nightmares are a sign that I'm making progress. That my brain is trying to work through all the trauma. But it doesn't feel like progress. It feels like hell."

"Sometimes we have to wade through the crap to get to the good part. I can walk this journey with you." Emma reached up and kissed him. "As long as you're trying, I can deal with whatever you throw at me."

Grey rested his forehead on hers. "Not sure what I did to deserve you, but I thank God I have you."

Emma grabbed his hand. "Okay old man, how about watching *Wheel of Fortune* and *Jeopardy* with this old lady. Haven't seen them all week. It's the Tournament of Champions and I want to root for Amy."

"Oh man, we are old. That sounds perfect." He ran his hand over his head. The panic was over for now. He relaxed. Emma made him feel safe. *Who knows what the next few weeks will bring.* He reached for the remote as they settled back into the sofa cushions. Emma nestled next to Grey, and he draped his arm over her shoulder. "I love game shows," he said excitedly.

Who is this man? Games shows? Romance novels and sappy movies? How did I get so lucky? Emma shivered and reached up for the throw and covered them both. "Wonder which one of us will fall asleep first? I'm betting it's you," she teased.

Grey smirked at her. "Maybe. But if it's you, I won't be able to hear the show over your snoring."

Emma punched him in the arm. "Hmmff. I don't snore" she huffed.

That night as they climbed into bed she kissed him lightly on the forehead. "I love you Grey" she whispered.

"I love you too," he mumbled back. Grey slept peacefully next to Emma, his arm hugging her close all night.

*****

"Wake up beautiful." Grey pressed himself into Emma. "We've only got one more day before we go public. Let's enjoy it!"

182

Emma pulled the covers over her head. "Go away," she grunted. "I need my beauty sleep."

"You're beautiful enough." He ripped the covers off her. As she screeched, he began kissing her face, snuggling in to keep her warm.

"Mmm…" she turned towards Grey, pressing her hips into his.

"Nope! We're getting up and doing something fun," he whispered into her ear as he pressed his growing erection against her.

Emma said in a sultry voice, "Isn't this fun?"

"Emma Griffin, yoga teacher extraordinaire, you are a sex maniac! We've had sex all weekend. We need to give my manhood a break. I'm not the stud I used to be. Let's go on a hike. It's a beautiful day."

"You sure look studly to me." Raking her eyes down his naked body. Her hand reached down to touch him. He gasped as her hand closed around him.

Catching his breath "You are a temptress. But no!" His hand slid down her body, weaving around to her backside and giving her bottom a gentle swat. She moaned, a little startled. *That felt good.*

"Hey! What was that for?" she purred.

"Huh. You like that, bad girl?"

Emma gulped and nodded her head. *Well now, isn't she surprising.* Grey filed that away for future exploration. "As much as I would love to spank you and do naughty things to you, let's get going."

Emma pouted but moved away from Grey. "Where are we going hiking? Its cold out."

"Let's drive up to Asheville. We can do a short hike and have lunch. Then come back home and…" Grey grinned a wide grin, "…if you're a good girl, I'll spank you."

Reluctantly, she got out of bed. As she walked by Grey, she rubbed her naked body up against him. "Sure I can't change your mind?"

Grey grabbed her and gave her a passionate kiss that left her breathless. "Nope!" he said cheerfully. "Dress warmly. It'll be cold in the mountains." As she walked away, Grey smacked her bottom again. "Nice view."

*****

Asheville was beautiful. The weather was cold and clear, a perfect fall day. They hiked a beginner trail at Mt. Pisgah near the Blue Ridge Parkway and then headed into the city to have a late lunch. "I love Asheville!" Emma gushed as they strolled through downtown. "It's so eclectic and yoga-like." She grinned as they walked by a couple of yoga studios.

"You mean it's a hippie city? I feel like I'm back in the '70's. Patchouli scents and unwashed hair." He looked disgusted.

"Asheville has the best food, grumpy boy." They stopped and looked at a few menus outside the small restaurants, finally settling on one that had a variety of options and outdoor seating. Grey ordered a barbeque sandwich, Emma a veggie burger, and they split an order of sweet potato fries.

"I hate to admit it, but that hike was fun. All my working out has paid off."

Grey agreed. "You did really well. The trail was a little harder than I thought. And your idea of doing a walking meditation was cool." Emma sipped her tea and Grey sipped his water as they people watched and enjoyed the mountain vistas. "I wish I could always feel this content," he sighed.

"You know, there's a saying: 'Feelings are like waves; we can't stop them from coming, but we can choose which ones to surf.'" She

184

smiled gently at him. He squeezed her hand, thinking about what she had said. It made sense. If only he could.

*****

When they got home that evening, both of them were beat. They grabbed a pizza on the way home and ate it in bed.

Emma's phone buzzed:

Lisa: I've got my text all lined up and ready to hit send tomorrow morning. Be prepared.

Lisa: How was the rest of your weekend?

Emma: Interesting. We're in bed.

Lisa: Mom! What are you doing answering my text. Go enjoy your boyfriend.

Emma: It's not what you're thinking! We went hiking today and are tired.

Lisa: Is that what the old folks call it nowadays . 😃

Emma: Good night miss troublemaker.

Lisa: Good night. Love you. 🖤

"Those kids are going to drive me crazy," she told Grey. "I'd better be ready for the big reveal tomorrow."

"It'll be fine. They'll just tease you mercilessly." Grey looked at Emma, "Sorry, I'm too tired to spank you."

She laughed. "Not really in the mood anymore anyway." Snuggling together, they quickly fell asleep.

Chapter 12

Whenever I See Your Smiling Face – James Taylor

Lisa: I know a secret about mom.

Marie: Ooooo I love secrets. Spill!

Aaron: Lisa! You're breaking your promise.

James: Tell me! I'm a lawyer so you know I can keep it a secret.

Steve: No me! I wanna know!

Lisa: Awww. Aaron's right. I can't share until tomorrow. But it's killing me.

Marie: That's not fair! Let me guess. If we guess, can you tell us? Just a thumbs up emoji.

Lisa: I promised I wouldn't tell.

James: Who'd you promise?

Steve: Good one Mr Attorney

Ashley: Let James ask the questions. He's good at interrogations. Believe me I know.

Steve: Yeah and he's sneaky about it. Remember the time he tricked me into admitting I had snuck in past my curfew.

James: You deserved that! Mom was so mad that we wouldn't tell her who broke the bedroom window lock. She was gonna punish all of us.

Emily: You devil! You told me you never got into trouble.

Marie: He's got you fooled. He was the ringleader of bad behavior.

Steve: Was not!

James: Soooo… who did you promise?

Marie: Tricky James. . 🙃 Catch her off guard.

Aaron: Lisa. Don't answer that!

Marie: I got a guess. Mom went out with Grey.

Lisa: Can't say.

Lisa: But….. it's bigger than that!

Aaron: Lisa!!

Steve: Who's Grey?

Emily: You remember he went to the park with the kids a few weeks ago. Him and his son. Ellie and Olivia loved him.

Lisa: So did Graydon, Ayden, and Jaden. Thought he was cool.

James: This is the first I've heard about any guy with mom.

Marie: Oh yeah. He's a hottie. I told mom to go for it.

James: What??!!! Who is he?

Marie: He owns The Core Connection gym downtown.

James: How'd she meet him?

Marie: At the gym. Where have you been? She's been going to the gym for weeks now. She's got osteoporosis and needs to build up her bone strength.

James: What? Why don't I know this?

Steve: Because you're too busy working and partying with friends.

Lisa: Anyways. Me me me… Back to my secret.

Aaron: Lisa! Stop teasing everyone. You promised your mother you wouldn't say.

James: Ah ha! So *mom* told you a secret that she hasn't told us.

Lisa: Aaron!

Aaron: Whoops!

Marie: Why you? I'm hurt.

Lisa: It wasn't like she told me. I stumbled upon it. And she made me promise not to tell you guys until tomorrow.

Marie: Why?

Lisa: Because she said you guys would blow up her phone.

Marie: Spill

Emily: Spill

Steve: Spill

Ashley: I'm so curious. Tell us!

Rob: I've tried to stay out of this thread. But now I need to know too.

James: As official attorney for this group, it's imperative you tell us the truth.

Lisa: Only if you promise not to bug her until tomorrow.

Marie: Scouts honor.

Steve: Yup

Rob: you know I'm trustworthy.

Aaron: I already know.

Ashley: I'm in. Lips are sealed.

Emily: I promise.

James: Of course

Lisa: Mom's been sleeping with this guy.

Marie: How do you know?

Lisa: I walked in on them Saturday. She was supposed to babysit the boys. I guess she forgot. She didn't answer the doorbell. So I walked in and she came out of the bedroom all hot and messy. And she kept looking towards the bedroom and all of a sudden Grey came out of there in his underwear.

Steve: OMG.

James: TMI

Ashley: Go Emma!

Emily: It's about damn time.

Rob: Good for her. She's been alone for so long.

Marie: How'd he look? Tightie whities or boxer briefs.

Lisa: Navy boxer briefs. He filled them out quite nicely. Lucky mom.

Steve: Stop!

James: TMI

Marie: I knew it!

Rob: OMG. You guys are awful. Give the guy a break. He was probably embarrassed.

Lisa: Oh he was embare-assed alright. The boys saw him and were chanting, 'Grey is in his underwear.' He'll never live that down.

Steve: Enough! He seemed like a nice guy when I met him. Hope he doesn't hurt mom.

Lisa: Umm I don't think she was hurting. She seemed pretty satisfied.

James: TMI. Please stop! That's my mom.

Ashley: Grow up James. She's entitled to a life.

James: But she's in her 60s. Do old people have sex?

Marie: OMG! How old are you?

Lisa: People can have sex their whole life. I mean they might need Viagra or hormones but still.

Steve: Please stop. I'm glad mom has a boyfriend. BUT I do NOT want to hear about her having sex.

James: Well don't worry about me texting mom. I can't even think about it.

Steve: I'm with you.

Emily: It might be nice if you tell her you're happy she's got a boyfriend. Support her. After all she's done for you guys.

Marie: No worries I'll be texting her right away!

Steve: James maybe you and I should go check out Core Connection. Tell him to be nice to mom. Go all alpha male on him.

Marie: I already did. I thought something might be going on when we were at the park. So I told him not to hurt mom.

Steve: What did he say?

Marie: He said he wouldn't. I can be pretty scary sometimes.

Lisa: Poor Grey.

Steve: He must like mom if he stuck around after Marie threatening him.

Marie: I think he does. He seems like a good guy.

Lisa: Fingers crossed this goes well. Mom deserves love.

Lisa: Not a word until tomorrow!

*****

Emma's phone buzzed non-stop the next morning. OMG, she thought, her kids were relentless. She finally put her phone in airplane mode so she could get through the morning. They had actually been pretty encouraging, everyone except for James. She hadn't heard from him, but that was par for the course. He didn't answer phones or texts on a regular basis, at least when they were from his mother.

Marie had been relentlessly pressing her for details, some of which Emma felt fine sharing, some were none of her business. Steve told her he was happy for her but would beat Grey's butt if he hurt her. *Good to know.* Lisa was pleased for her, but still a little wary of how fast it happened.

After class, Emma headed to Meadow Wood to have lunch with her mom. When she arrived, she was surprised to see Grey waiting for her in the lobby.

"Hi sexy. Thought I'd visit your mom with you today. Tell her about us."

Emma looked surprised and pleased. "That's so nice of you." She stood on tiptoes to give him a quick kiss.

"And I stopped at Café Amore and got you both a dessert."

"You didn't?! Suck up!"

"Yup. Gotta keep my girls happy."

"Keep it up and Mom might even remember you," she teased as they walked to her room.

"Hi Mom! It's Emma."

"You're not Emma." She pointed to Grey. Squinting, she scrutinized him suspiciously.

"Nope. I'm Grey, Mrs. Perilli. Emma's boyfriend. And I come bringing gifts." He held out the bag with the pastries.

"Trying to bribe me, young man?"

"Yup!"

"I like this one, Emma. He's got his priorities straight." She grinned at him.

"Sure, Mom! I bring you a homemade lunch, but you prefer the dessert from the handsome man." They both laughed.

"He's not the only one with their priorities straight."

"How about you eat some of the minestrone soup I made while I cut up this lovely apple tart that Grey brought for you?"

As Linda cautiously slurped her soup, she quizzed Grey. "What do you do besides flirt with old women?"

"I own a fitness place. We have spin classes and boot camps and all kinds of exercise classes."

"Huh. Do you make any money?"

"I do alright. Do you like to exercise?"

"Nah…not anymore. I'm too tired. Muscles and the brain don't work the way they used to." She snorted in disgust. "Old age is not for sissies."

"Mom goes to Isaac's class. Apparently, he's very popular with the ladies," Emma added. "Mom, Grey's son teaches your exercise class. The one where you get your heart rate up."

"Exercise class? I don't go to any exercise classes." Linda looked confused.

"Sure, you do. On Tuesdays. It's got the music you like to dance to."

"Pfff. I don't dance. I got two left feet."

Grey chuckled, "So does your daughter."

"I do not!" Emma huffed.

"How's your soup, Mrs. Perilli? Emma made it herself."

"Oh, it's alright. I don't taste things the way I used to." Even so, she had made a big dent on the soup. Emma was happy. It was nourishing, more so than the pastry she was anxious to consume.

"Where's my dessert? What's your name again?"

"Grey. How about one more spoonful of that soup? You know Emma doesn't cook much, so enjoy it while you can." Emma smiled at Grey. He was so patient with her. She loved seeing that side of him.

Linda sniffed, "Ain't that the truth. She never was much of cook. Now Lizzy! She's a natural." She took a few more spoonfuls. "Done! Where's my apple tart?"

"Here you go, Mom. Enjoy."

"Ahhh… now that was tasty." Linda smacked her lips and smiled at Grey. "Thank you. I enjoyed that."

"Time for your nap, Mom."

Grey moved the table away and helped Linda get into bed. Emma tucked her in and waited until she closed her eyes and began to doze. She kissed her forehead. "Sleep tight, Mom," she whispered.

Emma and Grey walked back down the hall. She elbowed Grey. "Look who's here flirting with the staff."

Isaac was at the nurse's station talking to Anna. She was giggling away at whatever he was saying. Grey shook his head. "That boy has an eye for the women. Does he even have a class here this afternoon?"

As he walked by the nurse's desk, he said sternly, "Isaac. Who's watching the gym?"

Isaac jumped and came to attention. "Hi, Dad. What are you doing here?"

"I might ask you the same question? I thought your classes were in the morning."

"They were. Ummm… I just stayed behind to ask Anna about one of the patients. Trying to make sure I don't overdo some of the cardio."

"Again, I ask. Who's watching the gym? And don't you have clients this afternoon?"

Isaac looked guiltily at his watch. "Oh crap! Mr. Johnson's going to be there shortly. Better run. Thanks, Anna, for the info." He winked at her as he turned to his dad. "Geez, Dad. I'm not an idiot. Kayla's at the gym. She said she would hold the fort until I got back. I'm heading out now."

Emma looked at Grey. "You were kind of hard on him. He's an adult and I think he manages his time well."

"He's got to learn to be a little more responsible. We agreed that, unless it's an emergency, either he or I would be at the gym whenever it's open."

"Seems like he had it covered. Kayla is very responsible."

"I guess. I just worry. I want him to be able to take over the business someday and spending unpaid time flirting with the nurses shouldn't be a priority."

Emma rolled her eyes. "He's right. You are Mr. Grumpy Pants."

Grey harrumphed.

"But one with a sweet side." She kissed his cheek lightly. "Thanks for being so good with my mom."

"Will I see you after Boot Camp tonight?"

"Yes, but I have to go right home afterwards. My house will be a disaster after I babysit this afternoon. And I have to shower."

Grey looked disappointed. "I can help you clean. Tell you what, I'll bring you supper and then we'll clean up."

Emma hesitated. She gave him the look. "No funny stuff. I need to clean and shower and get ready for classes tomorrow."

"Deal. I can help you shower though." He grinned.

"Do you not remember what happened last time we tried that?!"

"Oh yeah. No showering together. Remind me sometime to replace your shower fixture. Okay I promise we'll eat, we'll clean, you shower, and work on your yoga. I'll watch TV and then we can spend the night together. No funny stuff. Deal?"

"Sounds good. What are you going to make? Something good. I'll need carbs after that workout. Maybe mac 'n cheese?" she looked hopefully at him. "And don't forget dessert."

Grey rolled his eyes. "Yes, ma'am."

*****

Grey kept his promise to bring mac 'n cheese and, to Emma's delight, it was delicious. She thanked him profusely after dinner.

"My pleasure madame. It's nice having someone to cook for." They were sitting on Emma's couch comfortably, Emma working on her class plans and Grey reading. She got up every once in a while, to practice her yoga sequences. Grey always looked up to admire the view. She was graceful and strong, and he really enjoyed her down dogs. Her phone buzzed. She glanced up and saw it was a group text from the kids. Oh boy, thought Emma, what now?

Lisa: What are we all doing for Thanksgiving? Aaron needs to know so we can work out the holidays with his parents.

Marie: I'm eating as much food as I can. This baby has turned me into an eating machine.

Emma: Not much longer honey.

Lisa: Pretty soon your life will turn to no sleep hell, and you'll be eating whatever crumb you can find because you're too tired to cook.

Emma: Lisa!!

Emma: Thanksgiving plans?

Steve: I think it's our turn to be at mom's.

Emma: Yeah. I was planning on having you all but it's ok if you need to be at the in-laws.

James: We'll be there for part of the day and then we need to go to Ashley's later.

194

Marie: How's the love life going? Inviting Grey for dinner?

Emma: I was thinking of it. How do you all feel about it?

Lisa: That's fine. As long as he keeps his pants on . 😆 The boys still sing about Grey in his underwear.

James: OMG!

Emma: If I invite him you guys better act like grownups!

Lisa: I'm in. Let me know what I should bring.

Marie: Me too. I'll bring a dessert. Something creamy like a trifle and a pumpkin pie.

Steve: Us too. I'll check with Emily, see what she wants to make. She's all into roasted vegetables right now.

James: Let me know what I should buy. Maybe rolls and some wine?

Emma: So we've got a plan for turkey day! Thanks guys.

"Are the kids still blowing up your phone? Grey asked, a little annoyed. Her phone had been buzzing non-stop for the last half hour. He liked Emma's family, but they relied on Emma an awful lot.

"Yeah, but it's not about us. It's about Thanksgiving."

 "I guess that's coming up soon. What do you guys usually do?"

"Usually, we have a big family meal. The kids come-- well, those who don't go to their in-laws. My sister and her family. I try to make it casual because people come and go; and with the grandkids…well, you know. It can get crazy."

Grey nodded. Sounded like a lot of work and noise.

"What do you do?'

"Varies. Isaac and Joe generally go to Alisha's for the holidays. Sometimes I go with them. Sometimes I stay home."

 "Why don't you come here for dinner? I'd love everyone to meet you."

 "Not sure that's a good idea. I mean your kids are fine. I'm just not that good in large, loud groups. My anxiety tends to flare up."

"Oh." Emma looked disappointed. "Why don't you think about it. You can let me know later. But I'd love to have you. Holidays mean a lot to me."

"Alright," he said grudgingly. "I'll think about it. Let me see what the boys are doing. But Emma, situations like that are not my strong point. Will you hate me if I don't come?"

"No, of course I won't hate you. I'd be disappointed and perhaps a little sad, but I'd understand."

Grey put his arm around her. "Thank you for wanting to include me."

Emma felt a little unsettled. She loved the holidays and wanted to share them with Grey. She'd had visions of a Hallmark holiday with everyone laughing and eating and enjoying-- and finally having a partner to help share the joy. She felt a lump in her throat. She knew in her head that holidays could be triggers for people. Nonetheless, she yearned in her heart for everything to be perfect. She wanted Grey beside her. She sighed. At least he hadn't said no outright.

Grey knew he had upset Emma. He didn't know what to do about it. He hated holidays. They only brought bad memories. And loud crowds still freaked him out. Celeste had suggested avoiding situations that would trigger his anxiety until he had a better handle on them. He was still uncertain about what had triggered his panic attack a few days previously. It had surfaced when he was feeling content and safe with Emma. Celeste thought it was precisely because he felt safe that his mind allowed unsafe thoughts to bubble to the surface. Possibly, but he couldn't risk having a panic attack in front of Emma's family. What would they think of him? Marie had already warned him not to hurt her. He'd have to find an excuse. He texted Isaac and Joe to see what was going on for Thanksgiving.

Grey: What are the Thanksgiving plans?

Joe: Funny. We're just discussing that. Amanda's parents are coming to town so thought we'd host Thanksgiving this year.

Isaac: Am I invited?

Joe: Of course, douche bag. But don't bring your flavor of the month girlfriend. Her parents are very conservative.

Isaac: Hey, don't insult my girlfriends. I can't help it if I have so many.

Grey: What's your mother doing?

Joe: She and Bill are going on a cruise. I invited her to our house, but she chose the cruise . ☺

Joe: Are you going to come? Or do you have plans with Emma?

Grey: I'll be there. Emma invited me but she has a big chaotic family. Not sure I can handle it.

Isaac: You better get used to it. You guys seem pretty serious, and her kids aren't going to go away. Besides I like them. They're fun.

Grey: And loud. You know I can't handle crowds.

Isaac: Maybe you need to think this through, grumpy pants. Emma loves her family. If she has to make a choice, you know who'd win.

Joe: We're glad to have you. Just be nice when you tell her. Don't hurt her feelings. Tell her the truth. We like Emma.

Grey turned to Emma again. "It looks like I'll be going to Joe's house for Thanksgiving. Amanda's parents will be in town, and she wants to host dinner."

Emma stuck her lower lip out. "I guess that's alright." Her eyes lighting up, she said, "Maybe I should invite them here. We can have a really big party!"

Grey's heart sunk. Thinking quickly, he squashed that idea "No, they want to spend time with the boys. They don't get to see their grandkids very often."

"I get that." She was disappointed, but she understood. That was his family, his loyalty was there. Just like hers. "Can you come by for dessert afterwards?"

"Sure, I'll try my best." But he knew he wouldn't come by. It was too stressful.

Emma sensed something was off with Grey, but she didn't know what. She shrugged the feeling off. *Probably just tired.*

Changing the subject, Grey mentioned to Emma that he had suggested to Casey she become an instructor. "I remembered you said she might be insecure. In trying to encourage her, I realized she is very athletic and might make a good instructor. I mean, she likes being the center of attention. She seemed excited to have a new direction."

"Good for you, Grey!" She hugged him. "That's wonderful! What a great idea! What kind of certification?"

"Zumba and Cardio Fusion. Seems like her style. Which reminds me, I need to follow up with Isaac to make sure he hooked her up with some training workshops. The gym needs some new classes anyway."

"You're a good guy, even if you're not coming for Thanksgiving." She kissed him on the cheek. "A grumpy sweetie."

"Are you ready for bed? I'm tired." Grey yawned. "Think I'll turn in early. We've got several new clients tomorrow."

She looked up from her paperwork. "You feeling okay? You seem a little off. Usually it's me who's hits the sack first."

Grey avoided looking at her. "Nah. I'm good. Just a little tired. I'm old remember?"

"Okay, I'll be in soon. Just need to finish my lesson plans. Keep a spot warm for me."

"Will do. Good night."

Huh, that was weird. He's been a little off all night. Hope he's not getting sick. Emma went back to her planning.

Grey couldn't get to sleep even though he was tired. He didn't like lying. Well, he wasn't actually lying; but he was not telling Emma the whole truth. *Is that lying? It's a slippery slope.* Everything seemed so great between them. Perfect. In fact, too perfect. He didn't deserve such happiness. His feelings darkened and swirled around him as he worried. *How can she love me? She is so good. I'm so damaged. I'm no good for her. She wants one big happy family, and I can't give that to her.* Over and over, the thoughts flew through his brain.

Emma slipped into bed a little later. Grey was lying on his side. "You still awake?" she whispered.

Grey nodded. "I'm tired but I can't sleep," he sighed.

"Let me help." She wrapped her arms around him, pressing her body tightly to his. She could feel him relax as she gently kissed his back and shoulders and lightly massaged his lower back and arms. She let her hands slip lower.

"I thought you said no funny stuff tonight." His voice was hoarse.

"A girl can change her mind, can't she? Let me help you relax." Her hand gently stroked him.

He rolled over onto his back. She climbed on top and kissed him lightly on his face and neck and shoulders. She slowly guided him into her.

"Oh, Emma." He moaned. He took her face and kissed her so tenderly it brought tears to her eyes. "I don't deserve you." They moved together in a gentle dance until both were satisfied. Resting on his chest, cradling his body, his arms holding her close, she stayed quiet until she heard his breath slow down and he dropped off into sleep. *My poor Grey.* She knew something was troubling him. All she could do was wait. Maybe he would open up to her before it was too late. She rolled off to one side. Grey turned to spoon her, clinging to her in his sleep.

Later that night Grey woke up crying. Emma startled out of her sleep and hugged him to her. "It's alright, baby. It's alright. I'm here. You're not alone" she crooned until he went back to sleep. When she woke up the next morning, he was already gone.

*****

Emma didn't hear from him all day. She texted him and even tried calling, but it went straight to voicemail. It was unusual, but she knew he had some new clients, so she shrugged it off. Later in the afternoon, she got a text from Marie.

Marie: Mommy. What does labor feel like?

Emma: Are you asking because you're curious or because you have some contractions.

Marie: Contractions. They hurt. A lot!

Emma: Have you checked with Lisa?

Marie: She's been with patients all morning. I can't get through.

Emma: It's a little early for labor but anything's possible. Call your midwife.

Marie: I did. Waiting for a call back.

Emma: Ok. Tell me about how far apart are these contractions? Are they regular? And are you sure they're not just Braxton Hicks?

Marie: Seven minutes. And no

Emma: Hmmm. You call that doctor's office right back and talk to the nurse. I'm sure they'll have you come in to check. Where's Rob?

Marie: On a business trip. Won't be back until tonight.

Emma: Ok. Hang tight and I'll be right over.

Marie: I'm scared. Can I stay on the phone with you?

Emma: Of course. I'm in the car. Be there in ten minutes. Actually, call the doctor's office back and tell them the contractions seem to be seven minutes apart. Then call Rob and tell him what's happening.

Marie: Yes mom. Hurry!

Emma hung up and immediately called Lisa's office. She spoke to the receptionist and asked her to get Lisa right away. The girl hemmed and hawed until Emma put on her best strict mom voice. Lisa came to the phone after a few minutes.

"Mom? Is everything all right?"

"Yes, but Marie called me. She thinks she's in labor. Contractions are seven minutes apart. And Rob's out of town. I'm headed there now, but she's scared."

"It's a little early but you never know. Babies can't read a calendar. Let me see if I can cancel my appointments. Tell her not to worry. I'll be there as soon as I can."

Emma knocked on Marie's door. Marie rushed to open it. "Mom, it hurts," she sobbed. "I'm scared."

Emma hugged her and assured her it would be okay. Just then, Marie's cell phone rang. It was the midwife's office suggesting she go to the hospital.

"Let's go, baby girl. Looks like you might be having a baby."

Arms crossed, feet firmly planted, eyes scared, Marie froze. "Nope. I'm not going. I'm not ready."

"You may not be ready, but this baby might be. Let's go, young lady," Emma said in her mom voice. Marie looked at her, Knowing she had no choice, she shoved down her fear, gathered her wits, and took off behind her.

"Mom I'm so scared and nervous. What if I'm not meant to be a mom? I'm not nurturing like you. And I'm afraid of the pain." She was sobbing.

Emma reached out and took her hand. "Honey no one's ever prepared to be a parent. There's no wrong or right way. You just do you. You're amazing and fun and if you can sit for hours on end listening to your patients, you know you have the patience to raise a baby. Besides you have calm cool and collected Rob. You're not alone."

"I know." She grimaced as another contraction hit. "Rob is a good guy. I just wish he was here."

The hospital immediately took her upstairs to Labor and Delivery for a labor check. Emma paced in the waiting area. She texted Rob to let him know what was going on. He replied he was on the way and should be there in a few hours. Lisa came running in a few minutes later. "I'm so excited for her! She's waited so long."

"I know. But isn't it too early? What if something's wrong?" Emma was anxious. Birth was normal, but there were always risks. "I just hope Rob gets here before the baby."

"Me too! If he doesn't, one of us will have to go in with her." They looked at each other in horror. Marie tended to be dramatic and very vocal.

"It should be you. I'm not fond of blood."

"Sure, Mom, send me into the lion's den! Coward. Let's go together. You can calm her and when it gets too gory for you, I'll take over." Lisa reasoned that two heads were better than one.

As Emma had suspected, Marie was in labor. The midwife came and said the labor pains were now five minutes apart.

"Where's Rob? Isn't he her birthing coach?" she asked, looking around the lobby.

"He's on an airplane headed here. But he won't be here until tonight. Mom and I agreed to be interim coaches. We thought we'd take turns."

"She'll need a lot of extra support if the dad isn't here. So maybe better if both of you can come in. Either of you squeamish?"

"I'm a PA. I should be fine. Mom, not so sure about."

"I'll be okay. I had four kids, so I know the drill. Although if you see me crossing my legs, it will be in sympathy."

The midwife laughed. "She's in good hands then."

When they walked into the birthing room Marie was in the middle of a contraction. Emma's heart lurched as Marie screamed. Emma rushed over, taking her hand.

"Focus on your breath honey. Out, out, out." Marie looked at her with wild eyes, but she did it. When the contraction was over, Lisa put a cool compress on her head and gave her a few ice chips. Marie took them gratefully.

"So much for my birth plan. I live in awe of you guys having more than one baby. I will never…." Her face scrunched. "Oh no, another one's coming," she moaned. "Where is that bastard of a husband. He will never touch me again!"

Marie was a trooper for the next two hours, but she was starting to lose it, alternating between crying and anger. "Moommm, I'm dying," she cried. "I can't do this. I'm going to chop off Rob's penis. He will never touch me again."

Emma took a short break to get a cup of tea. Sinking into a chair in the cafeteria, she texted Grey to let him know she wouldn't be around tonight.

Emma: Gonna be a grandma again. 😍 Marie's in labor. Rob's out of town. Lisa and I are being her coaches.

She waited for a reply. But none came. *Huh... guess he's busy with clients.* But still, she had an uneasy feeling. Something wasn't right. It wasn't like Grey not to reply even when he was busy. He was always checking his phone.

Eventually, he answered her.

Grey: Nice.

Emma looked at her phone in disbelief. That was it? Nice? Not even congratulations or keep me posted? She was beginning to get angry. What was up with him? She looked at the time. *Better hurry back. Lisa might need a break.* On the way back to the room, she got a text from Rob.

Rob: I'll be there in 30 minutes. Plane landed. Going to speed to the hospital. Tell Marie I love her and she's brave and strong and I love her.
Emma: Will do! Hurry. Oh, and when you get here, keep your nether region protected.
Rob: ????

Emma raced back up the stairs to tell Marie the good news. Lisa was holding her hand and chatting with her. She was resting between contractions while the midwife checked her dilation. Emma stood next to her and gently stroked her head.

"Rob will be here in thirty minutes."

The midwife glanced up, finished with her exam. "Good thing! Papa might make it for the birth. Marie, hang in there. You're nine centimeters. Moving along quickly. The baby should be here in a while."

Marie moaned, "A while? She needs to come now. I can't do this."

The midwife looked at Emma and Lisa and smiled. "Have the nurse get me if she starts having the urge to push."

Lisa and Emma exchanged glances. Getting close to go time. They both knew the hard part was coming.

"Marie, let's get you in the shower. That might help." Lisa got her up. All modesty gone, Marie tore off her gown and stepped in the shower.

Exactly thirty minutes later, Rob rushed into the room. "Oh my god, Marie. I'm so sorry I wasn't here."

Marie burst into tears. "Rob, it hurts! Really hurts!"

"I know, baby, I know." He gathered her up in his arms.

"Do you?" she shouted. "I'm standing here naked with my insides being pulled out. You have no clue."

Emma and Lisa quickly backed out of the room. "We'll let you take it from here. Unless you need reinforcements, we'll be in the waiting area."

Once outside, Lisa laughed. "Whoa, that was intense. Poor Rob. He will never live this down. Thank goodness he's here now."

"I don't remember any of my labors," Emma mused. "Just that it hurt. Not sure why I did it four times."

Lisa agreed. "It's nature's way of ensuring the survival of the species. We don't remember the pain, only the joy of holding that baby."

"Why don't we go home and change. I'm wet and sweaty." She glanced down at her clothes. "Childbirth is messy."

"You go first and, when you come back, I'll leave and check on the boys and Aaron." Lisa said. "It'll be a while before the baby is born."

"Sounds good to me. I'll be quick. I'm afraid to leave Rob too long. Marie might kick him out. You know how transition is."

Lisa nodded knowingly. "Yeah, I almost murdered Aaron when Graydon was born. He suggested I wasn't pushing hard enough."

Emma laughed. "Rookie mistake. Okay, I'm off. Oh, crap, I forgot to text James and Steve!"

"No worries. I texted Ashley and Emily earlier. I figure they'll fill in the boys."

Chapter 13

You're My Soul and My Heart's Inspiration - Righteous Brothers

Emma checked her phone for any messages from Grey. Not a one. *What is going on?* Her shoulders slumped as she walked back into the hospital. She was afraid and confused. Everything had seemed fine between them, she thought. Except, she remembered his face when they talked about Thanksgiving. And his panic attack out of nowhere the other day. Something was up.

Grey kept reaching for his phone, lifting his hand to text Emma, then stopping. He wanted to text her to find out if Marie had her baby. He wanted to hear her soft voice all excited about having another grandchild. He wanted to see her smile when she held the newest addition to her family. He dropped his head between his hands. *Oh Emma,* he thought with despair. He knew what he had to do. He loved her too much to drag her through the emotional firestorm going on in his head.

He wasn't worthy of Emma. She shouldn't have to hold him in the middle of the night while he cried. She shouldn't have to talk him down from a panic attack. He couldn't put her through what she'd already been through with Brian. *She doesn't deserve to inherit my hell. I can't use her as my emotional support person anymore. She needs a fully functional human being, one who isn't tortured by the past or afraid of the future. Someone who can love her wholeheartedly with no reservations. Someone who is whole rather than broken. I need to learn to deal with my flaws on my own before I can come to Emma with an open heart.* It would hurt her, but better now than later. Grey shook, his chest tight with sadness, as he resolved to set Emma free. It would be the best and the worst thing he'd ever done.

He picked his phone back up and texted Emma.

Grey: Can we talk?
Emma: So, you're still alive?
Grey: How's Marie?
Emma: About to have a baby any minute. I've been at the hospital since lunch time.
Grey: I need to talk to you. Can we get together tomorrow?
Emma: Sure. When?
Grey: Text me when you have a moment. And I'll come over.
Emma: Ok. Is everything alright?
Grey: Let's talk tomorrow.

Rob came running out just then. "We're having a baby! I mean we had a baby! She's beautiful and so is Marie. Come and see."

Emma: Gotta go Marie just had the baby. I'll text you tomorrow.

Emma went home that night exhausted and exhilarated. The baby, Ameila, was beautiful. 6lbs 8 oz. She was little, but feisty like her mother. *Good luck Rob*, she thought. *Surrounded by strong, opinionated woman*. Good thing he was so laid back.

As she scrounged around for some food, she wondered what was up with Grey. His text was rather terse. And he hadn't asked to come over tonight. She already missed his warm body, his handsome face, his strong arms cradling her at night. *Hope everything's ok. Don't be ridiculous*, she told herself. *Don't be so needy. It's only one night and they both had had a busy day.* He just needed sleep and so did she. She yawned. Not every day in a relationship was easy. But she had a niggling thought that something wasn't alright, and it was more than a busy day that was keeping him away. She climbed into her bed and texted Grey good night. He never replied.

*****

Emma visited her new granddaughter at the hospital first thing after lunch. Marie was besotted with her tiny baby. "I'm so glad you came early," she cooed sweetly to her. "Isn't she just the sweetest thing?"

"She is! She looks a lot like you did when you were born. Except for the hair color." Amelia had a full head of black hair. "You were bald as a bowling ball."

Amelia squirmed, opening her eyes and staring at Emma. "Hi there, sweetness," Emma cooed. "You're so lucky to have a wonderful mom and dad who love you so much."

Marie reached out for Emma's hand. "Thank you so much for being there yesterday. You guys gave me the courage to get through it."

"That's a family's job, to support one another."

"Speaking of family….How's Grey? I thought he might come with you to see my Amelia."

Emma hesitated before speaking. "I'm not sure. He's been acting weird lately. And yesterday, he didn't answer my texts until nighttime. He said he wanted to talk."

Marie looked sideways at Emma. *Hmm. That's never good.* "Did you two have a fight?"

"No. But he seems withdrawn lately. And he had an anxiety attack the other night. He's been having nightmares."

Marie looked concerned. "I know he goes to counseling. Has he still been going?"

"He says he has appointments with Celeste." She shrugged. "But who knows."

I will kick his ass if he up and runs! Marie angrily thought. *I warned him not to hurt my mother.* "Mom, maybe you should think twice before getting any more serious with him." She paused. "He's got issues and might not be ready for a relationship. I know you don't want to hear that, but I don't want your heart broken."

Too late for that, Emma thought sadly. "I'll see what he says. We're supposed to talk later." Marie's words scared her. She didn't want to lose Grey. She wanted to help him. Isn't that what friends do? Support each other through the good and the bad? Didn't he trust her?

"I love him. He loves me. We'll get through the muck."

Well sometimes love isn't enough, Marie thought sadly.

Emma texted Grey on her way out of the hospital.

Emma: I'm headed home now.
Grey: Be over shortly.
Emma: 👍 Front door will be open. Come on in.

She puttered around the kitchen anxiously. *Wonder what he wants to talk about?* Lost in thought, she was startled when Grey put his arms around her, kissing her gently on her head.

"Well, hello stranger. Didn't hear you come in."

"Hi. How's Marie and her new baby? Amelia?" Grey held her tight knowing this would be the last time.

"She's doing well, and the baby is gorgeous. Just like her mama."

"And her grandma." He kissed her but it had a touch of wistfulness to it.

"Hey, what's up?" She reached up and caressed his face.

The concern in her face was breaking his heart, but only confirmed he was doing the right thing. He steeled his nerves.

"I can't do this anymore. I think we need to stop seeing each other."

Emma shocked, "What! What do you mean?" Tears filling her eyes, she stared at Grey.

"Break up. Not be together." His eyes avoided hers.

"But why? I love you, Grey! You love me."

"Because I love you," he said tersely.

"That does not make any sense. You're breaking up with me because you love me?" She stepped away from his embrace.

"Emma," he said helplessly, "I'm not ready for a full loving relationship yet. You've seen me the last few days. Panic attacks, can't sleep, nightmares. I'm not whole. The fact that you love me scares the crap out of me. I always seem to hurt those who love me. Look what I did to Alisha. I wrecked my marriage. I abandoned the boys. I spend all my time at work or worrying about work. I'm not a good person." He took a breath.

"Grey, this is crazy," she said calmly. "Those things don't scare me. I calmed you through your anxiety. I held you in your nightmares. It's okay. You don't have to struggle through this alone anymore. I'm here to help you. Look how far you've come. You and Alisha are friends. You and the boys have a great relationship. As for work, you're getting near retirement. Isaac can take over. We can finish this journey together."

"Emma," he said gruffly, "I don't want your help. I need to be able to do this on my own. To stand on my own two feet." He backed away from her. "I'll only hurt you more if I can't." He reached out for her. She stood still. Hands by her side.

Her heart shattered into a thousand pieces. She heard what he was saying but didn't understand anything except *I don't want your help*.

"Grey…"

"I've got to go, Emma." His voice cracked. "I love you and always will. I hope you can forgive me." He pivoted away from her, back straight, shoulders back, like a soldier marching off to war. Only this war was being fought against himself. He wiped the tears from the corners of his eyes as he walked out the door and into his truck.

Emma stood there in shock for a few minutes. Watching Grey's truck pull away, she cried. *What the hell just happened?* He didn't give her a chance to fight for them. He just walked away. *Why does he get to decide what's best for us? Us! Not just him!* Angry, she strode into the kitchen, put the water on for tea, and pulled out a bag of cookies from the freezer. Frozen for a special occasion. *Well, this was an occasion: my life being blown apart.* She put her tea bag in her favorite cup and let it steep as she sat at the kitchen table eating frozen cookies.

Emma picked up the phone to call Lizzy. But voicemail picked up. "Grey dumped me. Call me when you can." Emma hung up. She needed to talk to someone, to make sense of what had just happened. She needed a shoulder to cry on. Maybe Lisa was free, she thought desperately.

Emma: Can you come over?

Lisa: I'm at work right now. What's up?

Emma: Grey walked out on me.

Lisa: What? What happened?

Emma: I'm not really sure. He'd been acting a little strange the last few days but with everything going on I didn't pay that much attention.

Lisa: Oh mom. I'm so sorry. Are you ok?

Emma: No. Not really. I tried calling Lizzy but she didn't answer.

Emma: I'm just so shocked.

Lisa: I'll come right over after work. Can you survive an hour? I can text and see if Emily or Ashley are available, so you won't be alone.
Emma: It's alright. I'll be alright.
Lisa: Just hang on mom.

Oh mom. I'm so sorry. I was afraid this would happen. Lisa texted her siblings and spouses to see if anyone was free. One of them had to be available.

Lisa: Grey dumped mom. She's a mess, can anyone get over there right away? I can't leave work for another hour. I don't want her alone.
Steve: That bastard! I'll beat him up.
Emily: Steve and I are off today. Kids are with the babysitter. We'll be right over.
James: I can be there in half an hour. Steve and I can go round him up and make him sorry.
Lisa: Just go over and be supportive. 😐 Act like grownups. I'll get there a quickly as I can.

Emma heard knocking at the door. She rushed to open it, hoping beyond hope that it was Grey. Her shoulders sagged as she saw it was Emily and Steve. "Why are you guys here?"

"We heard the news. Are you okay?" Emily put her arms around her, hugging her closely. Emma started crying.

"No," she sobbed. "I don't know what happened. He just said he didn't want my help anymore."

Steve chimed in, "It'll be alright, Mom. Did you guys have a fight?"

She wiped her eyes, sniffing, her chest heaving. "No. Not really. He said he was having some struggles and didn't want to hurt me. That he needed to figure out what was wrong with him on his own."

Steve and Emily exchanged glances. "What kind of struggles?" Steve asked quietly.

"Well, he's had some anxiety attacks lately. But I've been able to help him through them." She sniffed.

"Anxiety attacks like dad used to have?" Steve's voice was grim.

Emma nodded. "He has some PTSD." She looked up to Steve's unsmiling face. He was remembering all they went through as kids. His dad crying in his bedroom. His mother in tears or grim faced. The hospitalizations. He, of all the kids, witnessed his dad's pain and his mom's struggle. Emily reached out and gave Steve's hand a squeeze. She knew he had suffered as a boy.

"Mom. Why would you put yourself through that again?"

"Grey is different than your dad. Different issues. He's trying hard to heal himself. He's a good guy." Her voice trailed off. "At least, I thought he was. I thought we could do it together." The tears started rolling down her cheeks again.

"But why, Mom? I don't understand." Steve's voice was angry and confused.

"Okay, Steve that's enough." Emily hugged Emma again. "Let's get you a cup of tea." Turning to Steve, "Can you handle that please?"

Steve's hands were clenched. He was angry. Grey had seemed like a nice guy. Had he been honest with Emma from the beginning? He hoped so. He loved his mom and respected her strength; but why would she get involved with someone like that? It was a guarantee of hurt and disappointment. He started the electric kettle and then stuck his head back into the living room. "Chamomile okay?"

Emma looked up. "With honey, please." She said between sobs.

Just then, James came bursting in the front door. "Hi, Maw. Heard you needed the calvary." He grabbed his mom and gave her a bear hug. "Steve and I are going to give Grey a piece of our minds.

He thinks he can break up with my mom and not pay for it, he's got another thing coming. I know people who can make his life miserable."

Emily rolled her eyes. "Let's act like grownups. This isn't the wild west."

"I appreciate the offer, son, but no thanks." She gave them a weak smile. "Nice to know you guys want to protect me but I'm a big girl. I will survive." *I'll survive, but my heart might not.*

They sat around the living room, chatting quietly. Emily asked about how Grey and Emma met. Emma seemed eager to talk about it, reliving the beach trip, making everyone laugh about her fixation on donuts. She told them about his past and how he had moved forward.

As Emma spoke, Steve unwound a little. He could tell that he ought to give Grey credit for acknowledging his anxiety and working on it. He had met Isaac, and he and his dad seemed to be on good terms. Clearly, he still had problems; but maybe they were not as bad as he first thought. He had to give him credit for seeing that he had more to work on and for trying to protect Emma from more pain. But he still wanted to talk to him, with James.

Lisa arrived, bringing a pizza and some salad. "Hi, Mom." She hugged her tightly. "Let's eat. Food helps you think more clearly. Unless you're Marie," she joked. "Nothing can help her now,"

"How is my newest grandchild doing? Can Marie come home tomorrow?" Emma's phone buzzed just then. It was a picture of Marie, Rob, and little Amelia, with the caption *We love you, Mom. Hang in there.*

Emma's glanced around at her family. She knew she'd be okay with their support, she just wished things were different. She went to bed after everyone left but didn't sleep much. She texted Grey and asked if they could talk some more. She was confused and angry and hurt. But she got no reply. *Damn him and his stubbornness.* She went over and over what he said, always coming back to, "I don't want your help." That hurt the most. She wrapped her arms around herself as rolled to her side to sleep. I need to do this on my own, he had said. Deep down, she knew that made sense. Change and healing can only come from within. He needed to let go of the thoughts and behaviors that kept him 'safe' but were actually destructive. But why couldn't they walk that road together? Her heart ached. She cried herself to sleep.

Grey saw her text. His fingers itched to answer her, though he knew talking with her wouldn't change his answer. He put his phone away so he wouldn't be tempted. He had to do this himself. Calling Celeste was first on his to-do list for tomorrow. He needed to see if she'd have time for an emergency appointment. He was determined to fix himself. He no longer wanted to run in fear of his emotions. Healing was the only way to get his life back.

Chapter 14

Hello Again by Neil Diamond

The next few weeks for Emma were a blur. She stayed busy, but she felt numb. She wasn't sure what to do about Core Connection. *Probably best not to go there anymore.* Too bad, she thought. She loved her classes, but she didn't think she could stand to see Grey yet. Good thing he wasn't in her yoga class anymore. *Wonder if he'll stop coming to Half Moon Yoga.* For his sake, she hoped not. For her sake, she hoped so.

The new baby was adorable, and Emma loved cuddling her while Marie rested. Marie was grateful for her mom's help and Emma was grateful for the distraction.

"I'm so in love with this little sweet face. I could eat her up!" Emma gushed as she held Amelia tight.

Marie laughed. "She is rather adorable, if I do say so myself. But I tell you, she'll probably be the last." She sighed dramatically as she started folding the pile of laundry in front of her. "It hurt. The human body is not meant to expand like that! And my bottom is still not back to normal! I told Rob to forget sex forever!"

Emma laughed heartily. Marie was always so dramatic. "I hear you. I felt that way too, after each one of you."

"Seriously, Mom, I think for us, one is enough. I love being a mom, but it's so all consuming. The feedings, the crying... the laundry!!!" She flopped back down on the couch. "And I miss my job. I feel like my brain has turned to mush these few weeks."

Emma nodded. She was empathetic. Her brain, too, had turned to mush the last few weeks. All she could think about was Grey and what went wrong and how she could fix it. She was so angry he had unilaterally decided the course of their relationship. *Disrespectful! That's what it was!* Didn't he trust her?

*****

Slowly, her life resumed its usual flow. She babysat and lunched with her mother and sister. But the nights were lonely. She taught her classes but made a point of not being around when Grey's meditation class was scheduled. Gwen said Grey seemed more intense about the class lately and asked her why she didn't pop in like she usually did. Emma just smiled and told her she was busy.

Isaac stopped her when she was at Meadow Wood and said he missed her in boot camp. "I'm sorry about what happened. Dad's an ass sometimes, but I think he thinks he did what was best. He's going through a rough patch. He is going to therapy, though. Don't give up on him yet."

"I'm not the one who gave up," she said sadly. "Glad to hear he's getting help." She teared up and Isaac hugged her. "I miss boot camp too. Just not sure if I can come back to Core Connection."

"Please come back. Don't give us up just because my dad's messed up. You love working out. I'll make sure dad is not around when you want to come work out. Just call me. He's cut back his hours a bit. Besides, we've got Casey on staff now and she teaches a killer dance class. You'd get your weight bearing and some fun at the same time… and avoid Mr. Grumpy."

Huh, cut back his hours. That's a step in the right direction, she thought. *Although, what do I care? Isaac's right. I shouldn't have to give up what I like because of him. He still goes to yoga. Let him deal with my presence. Casey's class sounds like fun. Maybe I'll start there.*

"Okay, you've got a deal. Sign me up for Casey's class," she said firmly. It was time to move forward with or without Grey. She felt her armor slide into place. She was strong with or without Grey. Wistfully, she thought, *though I wish it was with him.*

*****

Grey's life fell into a routine. He worked. He ate. He ran five miles or more a day. He thought about his past. He thought about his future. And he thought about Emma. Emma was the first thing he thought about when he opened his eyes in the morning, and the last thing he thought about as he fell into bed at night. He pictured her smile that lit up her face. He heard her laugh. He saw her face as they made love. And he saw the hurt in her face when he broke up with her. He would do anything to erase that look.

Therapy helped. Celeste suggested he have sessions two to three times a week. They explored, in depth, what set off his anxiety, what triggered his fear of not being worthy, and what events caused his panic attacks. After a week, they set up specific goals and actions for Grey. Celeste had never seen him so determined and honest. *This is good,* she thought. *He's really trying.*

They discussed his relationship with Alisha. Grey had never followed through in making amends to her. He was afraid of what she might say to him. Celeste suggested he do it anyway. "You can't change without some struggle," she told him. "And struggle involves pain. But is that pain any worse than the pain that you have now?" she asked.

He shook his head no. "I just ruined the best relationship I ever had." His voice was sad.

She thought Alisha's forgiveness would help him see that he was worthy of love. "Let's make that goal number one. It's up to you when you do it. But the sooner the better," Celeste said encouragingly. "You can do it and we can check that off our goals list."

Although skeptical that it would make a difference, he agreed to give it a try. He needed to get better. So, he called Alisha the next day and made a coffee date for later in the week.

*****

Alisha gave Grey a big hug and a smile. "How are you doing?" She was a tall, slender, very attractive brunette. "Haven't seen you in a while." She looked questioningly at him. "What's up?"

Grey hemmed and hawed, but finally looking at her and said, "I owe you an apology for the way I treated you when we were married."

Alisha looked surprised and searched Grey's face. "You're not sick or anything are you?"

"No, nothing like that." He sighed as he continued, "I'm trying to fix my life, and one of the ways is to make amends for things you've done wrong. One of my biggest regrets is our divorce. I mistreated you. You tried to help me, and I shut down."

Alisha took his hand. "It's all water under the bridge. I've moved on. Bill is a nice guy, and he was a good stepdad. You've moved on too," she said with a sly smile. "From what I hear. Got a girlfriend."

Grey shook his head. "Had a girlfriend. I did to her what I did to you, panicked and shut down."

"Oh Grey. I'm so sorry. You deserve to be loved."

Grey looked at her despondently, "Do I? I ruin everything I love. She loved me but I couldn't handle the feelings. Just like I did with you. I am not worthy of love."

"Grey," she said fiercely. "You were a victim of that war. I tried to help you because I loved you. But I was a kid and didn't know what to do when you closed up. And the service was in denial about trauma victims and PTSD. We had two kids. They needed their dad, but you were hurting so much you couldn't be present for them. I needed to protect them. I couldn't be a mom to them and a counselor to you. I was too young and stupid. It wasn't because you weren't worthy. I loved you with all my heart."

His head bowed as she talked.

"I'm sorry I did that to you and to the boys. If I had to do it over again…" he paused. "I guess we don't get do-overs, do we? We just move forward."

"Exactly. You did make our life hard. But you know what? We're okay. You and I are fine. You're a great co-parent and the boys love you. You have come along way."

"So, you loved me? And you forgive me?"

Alisha nodded. "Yup, still do love you, but not in the same way. You're a great guy. Share that goodness. Don't hide it. Go talk to your girlfriend the way you're talking to me. Bet she loves you and bet she'll forgive you."

"Thanks, Alisha."

"You're welcome. Hope it helps. Now where's the coffee you promised me? We need to talk about Isaac. Will that boy ever settle down?"

Grey laughed. "He's doing a great job at Core Connection. I'm thinking of turning the business over to him. He's got a way with people. And he's got great marketing skills. Not so sure about his financial acumen though."

"Wow! That's great to hear. He's finally maturing. Maybe Joe could handle the finances and let Isaac do the rest?"

"Hmmm. Hadn't thought about Joe joining us. Do you think he'd be interested? May be just a few hours a month."

"I'm sure he would. With two kids, they could use the extra money."

They chatted for a long while, enjoying each other's company. He asked about her cruise and her job. And Bill. She asked about business and about Emma. Finally, she looked at her phone. "Gotta get back to work. It's been wonderful catching up with you."

"You too. Thank you again."

"Grey, you are worthy of love and respect. I'm glad you're back at therapy. Work hard. And give love another chance. Emma sounds wonderful."

He kissed her on the cheek and hugged her goodbye before sitting back down at the table to finish his coffee. Celeste had been right. Talking to Alisha had been stressful, but eye opening and necessary. He had faced his fear and was okay. He felt like a weight was lifted off his chest. She didn't hate him. She even still loved him. That was so valuable to hear.

When he was done, he headed back to the gym. He was teaching spin class tonight and had some paperwork he needed to finish.

On his way through the front door, lost in thought, he nearly ran smack into Emma. She froze when she saw Grey. He stopped and looked at her. "Hi Emma," he said softly, shocked.

"Hi Grey." She stared at him. He looked different. More at peace. *That was good. Guess I wasn't so good for him after all.*

"Haven't seen you around here lately. I'm sorry if I drove you away." He stumbled for words. "I mean…I'm glad to see you."

Emma looked away. "You too. Hope you're doing okay." She mumbled as she walked away as quickly as she could.

Grey stared after her. *You idiot. Leave her alone. It's obvious she hates you.*

Emma rushed into studio two where the dance class was, tears in her eyes. Casey greeted her cheerily. "Hi Emma. So excited to see…" she paused. "What's wrong, honey?"

Emma burst into tears. "Grey." She sobbed. Casey gathered her into her arms.

"There, there. What did he do?"

"He said hi." She blubbered. "We broke up and all he can say is hi, like nothing happened."

Casey stuck her head out the door and glared at Grey. "Men are idiots," she said loudly-- loud enough that Grey could hear.

Emma nodded in agreement. She wiped her eyes. "So, so sorry. I didn't mean to make a spectacle of myself. Just wasn't expecting to see him. Isaac promised he would warn me if Grey was here." The other students were beginning to stare at her. She gathered her wits about her. "Thanks, Casey. Maybe I should leave. I'm a mess."

"No, honey. Don't let him win. No man should make you feel this bad. You came here for a reason. Your body and mind need the stress relief. Let's dance."

The other students gathered around Emma. "It's okay. We've all been there," one younger woman said in sympathy.

Casey clapped her hands, "Yeah, ladies, let's go." As Beyonce's 'Single Ladies' song boomed out of the speaker, Emma smiled. It was nice to have support, she thought as she moved her body to the music, letting the sadness and anger melt away.

Emma walked out after class sweaty and happier. Ignoring Grey, she waved goodbye to Isaac and Kayla. "See you tomorrow."

Casey waited until Emma left, then went up to Grey, furious. "Leave her alone. You obviously screwed her over. Let the woman have her dignity."

Backing away from Casey's fury, Grey stammered an apology "I just wanted to say hi. I miss her."

"Well, you should've thought about that before you broke her heart! Leave the girl alone!" she hissed. "Emma is a nice person. Be kind to her. Let her heal. Stay out of her face." Pivoting on her heels, Casey stalked away.

Grey, Isaac, and Kayla all stared after her. "Way to go Casey, guess she's not afraid of you." Isaac said with a smirk. Kayla nodded her head in agreement. "She's my new hero," she said in wonderment.

"Dad, you've got to be more careful. Emma is very popular here. Give her space."

Grey hung his head. He was embarrassed and dejected. "Yup. I will."

*****

The weeks flew by. Christmas was closing in. Emma normally brought the Christmas decorations out right after Thanksgiving. *Holidays used to be fun,* she thought sadly. But this year she didn't have it in her to do much. She hung a wreath with a sparkly gold bow on the front door and put gold and red bows on the front lanterns, but she skipped the lights over the railings and the bushes in front of the house. It looked very lackluster, just the way she felt. Dull, lifeless, empty. The delight she normally felt for the season was absent.

She went with Steve and Emily and the girls to get a fresh tree. The girls' excitement at picking just the right tree was fun to watch but it didn't rub off on Emma. She looked listlessly at the trees on the lot. Eventually, she found one that fit the bill-- tall and green--and took it home. It didn't spark any joy in her heart, though. She had imagined Grey helping her decorate the tree, sharing laughter and memories of Christmases past. Their first Christmas together. Creating their own new memories and traditions.

Instead, she hung the ornaments by herself, tears occasionally running down her face. *I miss his smiles. His grumpiness. His hugs.* When she was done, she stood back and admired her work. It was lovely, but no smile broke on her face. *I wish Grey could see this. He would love it.* She turned on the tree lights and sat on the couch, staring at the tree. The ache for Grey was almost unbearable. Taking her phone out of her pocket, she took a picture of the tree. She hesitated, then before she could change her mind, she hit send.

Emma : It would be better if you were here with me

She saw the little dots start and then stop, start and stop. Her heart raced.

Grey: It would be better.... I'm sorry.... The tree is beautiful, just like you...

Emma: I miss you.

Grey: I miss you too... but my decision was for the best. Maybe someday I'll be healed. But not yet.

Emma: What about me? Where was my input in that decision?

Grey: I'm sorry.

Emma: I'm angry and hurt. But you need to know I'm here for you whenever you need.

Grey: I know….If I could fix it I would. But I can't.

Emma: … … ….

Emma: I won't bother you anymore.

Grey stared at his phone, his heart shattering into a million pieces. He knew what he was doing to her. He knew he was cruel to her and yet she still wanted to be there for him. *Why can't I accept her help?*

He yearned to be beside her as she decorated that Christmas tree, to put his arms around her as they admired their handiwork. But his demons hadn't been conquered yet. He wouldn't, couldn't, come to her until he was healed. It might already be too late for them. He hoped not, but her last text was scary. Maybe he had pushed her away permanently.

Grey wandered into the bedroom and lay down on his bed. He felt heavy and sad. Looking at his pile of seashells, he picked up the sand dollar they had found at the beach. He gently rubbed the surface, feeling the small indents and rough surface. He smiled as he remembered their beach trip. Closing his eyes, he recalled the peacefulness of the cove. The way he felt in touch with his inner calm that day. The strength of Emma's belief in him. He rolled over onto his belly as the tears rolled down his face. He would conquer this. He would get Emma back no matter how long it took. *Believe in me, in us, Emma, just a while longer,* he prayed.

*****

Emma was downhearted at New Year's. She had survived Christmas. Her family celebration had buoyed her spirits. Her children had gathered around and supported Emma in her grief. Marie had pulled her into a big hug and told her Grey was a regular at counseling. She knew her mom was still in love with Grey. And, if truth be told, she believed Grey was trying to be whole. She hoped they might eventually work it out. Emma and Grey had a special connection. She had never seen her mom so happy, so alive, as those months they were together.

Steve and James had kept their word and had spoken to Grey. They had corralled him at Core Connection one night as he was leaving. Both of them, united, arms crossed, standing tall, had let him know they were protecting their mother.

"You hurt her." Steve spoke angrily, advancing towards Grey. James put out his arm to stop him. Steve pushed it off, "No! I want to hear what he has to say." He stood right in Grey's face. "She went through hell with our dad. She didn't deserve a second trip there."

Grey paused for a moment before he spoke. "Son, I love your mother. I never meant to hurt her. It all happened so fast …and I realized I wasn't prepared to be a good partner yet. I would only hurt her more by staying." He looked them in the eye and told them he was trying to be a better person for Emma. "I'm working on my issues. PTSD just doesn't disappear. But I'm learning to manage it. War damages you in so many ways. Your dad suffered because he didn't have the help he needed."

Steve looked away. His eyes tearing. "I know that now. But as a kid all you see is the person in front of you. He was troubled and sad and violent. And my mom suffered because of it. She shouldn't have to deal with it again."

Grey reached out, placing his hand on Steve's shoulder. "You did the best you could son. PTSD is overwhelming. The anxiety and the fear take over all your being. He really couldn't stop it. He wasn't rational. It wasn't that he didn't love you. It was because he didn't love himself. He couldn't overcome the demons inside. They are powerful," he sighed. "Believe me, I know. That's why I backed away. I still have nightmares… might have them all my life. I respect your mom too much to put her through it again." He paused, dropping his arm from Steve's shoulder. "You know your mother felt bad about relying on you so much. She knew you suffered. You all did," he looked at James. "But so did she. She did the best she could. And she was proud of you, the way you stepped up."

Steve looked at them both. "Thanks." That simple acknowledgement eased some of the burden of the past. "I appreciate it."

An awkward silence followed.

"But look man," James said firmly to Grey, "leave my mother alone if you're not serious about the whole rehabilitating thing. She's a good person who deserves someone to be a partner with, not a nursemaid for. We'll be watching." He liked Grey's forthrightness and compassion. As a lawyer, he had learned to be a good judge of people. Grey passed the test of sincerity. Maybe there was hope for both of them after all.

Grey offered a hand to James and then Steve. "You have my word."

They turned to leave and Isaac stepped out of the shadows. He had seen the boys approach Grey and had been concerned. He listened to the whole conversation and was impressed by the discussion.

"Oh, by the way, we have a special this month for new members. Love to see you join."

Steve and James laughed. "Maybe we will." Steve said, "We do like to see local businesses succeed."

"See you next week. Just ask for me and I'll hook you up."

Grey stood back shaking his head, hiding a smile. Isaac would do well as the manager of Core Connection.

As Steve and James walked away James dipped his chin. "Yeah, I was much younger than you, so I didn't really know about all that, about what you went through. I knew it wasn't normal but... I'm sorry, dude."

"It's okay. As the oldest I had to pick up the slack and protect you guys."

"You did a great job and I'm sorry." He gave him a quick hug. "It must've been hard."

"It was," Steve acknowledged. "But we all survived. I just hope Grey can help himself. He's a decent guy."

"Yeah, and mom loves him, at least Ashley says she does. She says true love never dies."

"So, when are you and Ashley going to settle down?" Steve asked with a sly grin.

James gave him a gentle punch and smiled. "Maybe someday."

Chapter 15

Time is a Healer by Eva Cassidy

Another year, Emma sighed. *Guess it's time to move forward*. Lizzy invited her over to her house for a small New Year's Eve party. She left early though; she didn't have anything to celebrate. At midnight, she pulled up a picture of herself and Grey at the beach. They looked so happy. Damn it! They were happy. Why did Grey have to blow it all up?

"Damn you, Grey! Why don't you realize what you gave up?" she shouted into space. She texted the picture to Grey. No words. She waited. The response was quick.

Grey: You're so beautiful.
Emma: We look so happy. Guess appearances can be deceiving.
Grey: We were happy.
Emma: And now?
Grey: Happy New Year Emma. Are you at home?
Emma: Yes. Alone. You?
Grey: Same. Lonely. Are you in bed?
Emma: No. Are you?
Grey: No. I don't sleep the same without you beside me.
Emma: ... ... Your choice.
Grey: I know.
Emma: ... .
Grey: What?
Emma: Want to come over?
Grey :.... ... More than anything. Do you want me to come over?
Emma: More than anything.

Grey hemmed and hawed. He desperately needed her touch. But would this just be a booty call? His feelings for Emma were too deep to play with her.

Grey: Do you think that's a good idea?

Emma mulled the idea. Sex with Grey would be a great start to the new year. A booty call?   But she couldn't make love and then have him desert her again.

Emma: Probably not…. Happy New Year Grey. Goodbye.

She put her phone on the charger and crawled into bed, wide awake and lonely. *Why does he get to make all the choices?* She grabbed her phone again. *Should she? What can it hurt?* She missed sex with Grey. Before she met him, she was an innocent about lovemaking. Brian and she had married young. She had had no sexual experience and Brian very little. When the kids came and his depression grew, their love life evaporated. But now she felt like a new woman. Older maybe, but more open to trying new things. Sex with Grey was fun and adventuresome. He made her feel confident. She didn't feel embarrassed by her older woman body. He wasn't shy about letting her know what he wanted, and neither was she. He worshipped her body. Tonight, Emma needed to be worshipped.

She thought about how shy she had been in front of Grey the first time they made love. That certainly had changed. She accepted her body for what it was-beautiful in its own way. She's even taken a few selfies, not that she'd show anyone other than herself. But when she was feeling down they reminded her of how far she'd come

She was doing all she could do to keep healthy. Now it was time to enjoy the fruits of her labor.

Her finger hovering over the phone… *Just do it…* she FaceTimed Grey.

Grey still had the phone in his hand when it rang. Surprised, he saw it was Emma, and answered right away.

"Is everything okay?"

"Yes." She hesitated. "Hi." She was a little unsure how to do this. She drank in his face. He looked tired, but less tense. "I see you still don't wear a shirt to bed." She gulped. He was so sexy. His chest muscles looked more defined. He must be working out harder. She ached to be in those arms.

"Nope." He smiled at her. "I see you still do."

Emma replied, "Yup. But I can fix that." She whipped off her tee shirt before she lost her courage.

Grey gulped and stuttered, totally shocked. "Oh… my." His eyes raked down her newly toned physique. She must be working out really hard. "You look good."

Emma was emboldened now. *Might as well go all in.* "Take off your pants." Her voice sexy and firm.

Grey did as she asked.

Emma's voice was husky. "Nice. I've missed that view."

"Can you do the same for me?" he asked sweetly.

"Since you asked so nicely… yes, I can. Hold on." Fumbling with the phone a bit, she took off her bottoms.

"Oh, Emma." His breath was heavy. "I want to touch you so badly."

Emma slid her hand down her body, gently caressing herself. "Like this?"

"Yes," Grey answered. His voice deep and eager. His penis twitched.

"Well, I need to touch you just as much. Show me how I would."

Grey's hand surrounded his manhood. He groaned with pleasure as he kept his eyes on Emma, watching her hand moving slowly, her hips responding to her touch.

"Touch your beautiful breasts," he growled.

She caressed her breast, rolling her nipple between her fingers. Her back arched in enjoyment and need. "Oh, Grey," she moaned. She watched as Grey's hand slid slowly up and down, pleasuring himself.

He stopped and looked at her. "Emma, put your phone down beside you and lay on your side so I can see your face and hear you. I want you to focus on just you." She did as he asked. "Damn you, Emma! You are my magical enchanting witch! I miss your beautiful sexy body. I miss your sexy voice."

Keeping her eyes intently on Grey's, she took her time, reveling in the feeling of teasing him, watching him as his eyes widened, enjoying the power she had. She brought herself close to the edge and then retreated, just as Grey had taught her to do.

He groaned, "Come for me. Please?"

She looked at him with need. "Yes! Oh god, yes!" She sank back down and beamed. Satisfied. *That was easier than I thought.*

"Your turn," she said huskily. "I want to see you come."

His gaze, full of need and desire, held her eyes. He wished he was holding her. He whispered her name over and over until he came. Breathing together, they stared at one another. Emma's face reflected her love and sadness, Grey's his love and regret. No words could capture their feelings.

"Happy New Year, Grey. Hope you sleep well tonight." She smiled, then sighed with satisfaction and sorrow, and ended the call.

Grey whispered, "Happy New Year Emma. I love you." He fell asleep, his arms wrapped around a pillow.

*****

January and February both flew by and dragged. Emma kept busy. New Year's Eve became a distant memory. She wasn't sure why she had done it, but she was glad she had. She was convinced he still loved her. She had read it in his face. And, god knows, she still loved him in spite of what he had done. Maybe that little reminder of their connection would help him.

Emma nodded to Grey when she saw him at the yoga studio. At the gym, she avoided him as much as possible. He seemed to stay out of her way which made her feel… well, she wasn't sure what it made her feel. She still yearned for him, but thinking about him made her miserable. He had rejected her and that hurt. She didn't know if she could ever forgive him, but she did know she still loved him.

In March, she decided to change up her hair. Her hairdresser, Crystal, had been encouraging her to try a keratin treatment and a more up-to-date hairstyle. *Why not*, she thought. It was expensive but would help tame her course wiry hair-- no more frizzies! *What have I got to lose? New year, new Emma*, she thought.

After several hours in the chair, Crystal exclaimed, "OMG! You look fabulous!" Crystal swung the chair to face the mirror. Emma was shocked as she admired her soft, fluid hair flowing around her face. *Wow!* She thought she looked years younger and more polished. Her hands kept reaching up to touch the softness and the straightness. Although she sort of missed the curls, she loved the new look.

"Men will be chasing after you like crazy!" Crystal wiggled her eyebrows. "You look hot!"

"Too bad the one I want doesn't care," she smirked, her hands still running through her hair. "But it looks great! Thank you so much." She stopped on the way out and admired herself in a window. *I do look good*, she thought with satisfaction. *Who needs a man to make you feel beautiful!?*

After her haircut Emma went to the Athleta store. She needed some new workout clothes, and she was excited to see if all her hard work had paid off. She grabbed the outfits she had tried on three months before, just for a laugh. As she slid the tight leggings on, she was excited to see there were pockets. She smoothed her belly down and pulled the pants up. They fit- still a little muffin top but… She grinned and pulled her phone out for a selfie. *Hey not bad for an old lady*! She covered her breasts and turned sideways, angling the phone until she found just the right view. She focused on her newly toned arms and abds. Twenty pictures later she had a keeper. She grinned as she sent it to Grey, revenge selfie, she thought with satisfaction.

Emma: Thanks!
Grey: My pleasure.

*****

When she visited her mom later in the week, Linda kept mentioning 'that pastry guy' and asking Emma when her boyfriend was going to come again. Apparently, Grey had made a strong impression on her, considering he had only met her twice. Emma just laughed it off. Grey had been charming, and dementia was an unpredictable disease. You never knew what Linda would remember.

On the way out, she had asked Anna about it. Anna looked weirdly at Emma and said, "You know he comes and visits her once a week, don't you?"

Emma, shocked, just nodded her head. "Guess I forgot! Hope I'm not getting senile."

Anna laughed and shook her head. "We all forget things."

As she left, Isaac was walking in. "Hi Isaac! How's it going? Headed to class?"

He smiled a big smile at Emma. "Actually no. Just dropping something off. See you at boot camp tonight?"

She smiled, "Yup! Don't be too hard. I'm tired."

He looked at her closely. "Somethings different. New 'do?" Emma nodded. "Wow! You look beautiful! Not that you didn't before… just different beautiful. Dad will be surprised. Umm. Not that it matters what he thinks."

Emma noticed he made a beeline for Anna, whose face lit up. *Hmmm… wonder if there's something going on there? They do seem to be attracted to each other. Well, he deserves someone special. Those Erikson men are charming,* she thought ruefully. *They get deep into your soul.* Case in point, she couldn't believe that Grey was visiting her mom. *He's a sweetheart deep down. Wish he could see that.*

*****

In April, Caitlyn, Melinda, and Emma headed to Asheville for a yoga retreat. They'd been looking forward to some girl time, as well as to fine tuning their teaching skills.

"I really need this," Caitlyn sighed as they pulled into the retreat parking lot.

"Me too!" Emma and Melinda chimed in. They unpacked the car and settled into their rooms.

"Ladies, I'm going to check out the meditation garden. Be back in a while." Emma grabbed her jacket and headed out the door. As she stepped into the elevator, she heard someone running down the hallway.

A deep voice yelled out down the hall, "Hold the door please!"

Emma reached out and grabbed the door, peering around to see who was coming. She saw a tall, slender, older man hurrying towards her. *My, he's good looking.*

Breathless he stepped into the elevator. "Thanks!"

"No problem," Emma said politely as she edged to the back of the elevator.

He glanced at Emma with interest. "You here for the retreat?" His voice was deep and soothing.

She nodded her head. "Yeah, just going to check out the meditation garden."

"Me too." As the door opened, he stepped back. "After you."

"Thanks. Wonder which way to the garden?"

"No clue. I'll ask at the front desk. Do you want to wait here, and we can go together?"

Emma hesitated. Was he just being polite? Or was he hitting on her? He was very handsome with silvery brown hair and beautiful eyes. She noticed lately guys had been noticing her. Flattering as it was, she didn't know how she felt about that. For years she'd been invisible. Until Grey. And he saw her completely. She sighed. *Or he used too, anyway.* Maybe it was time to let go and move on.

She shrugged. "Sure." He looked pleased as he headed off in search of the concierge.

As he returned, he boomed, "Okay, got directions! I needed to know anyway because I'm leading a morning meditation in the garden tomorrow. I'm Samuel, by the way." He offered his hand. She took it with a smile.

"Emma. Are you Samuel....as in Samuel Edwards? Leading the trauma based workshops tomorrow?"

"Pleased to meet you, Emma." He paused. "And, yes," he smiled, "that's me. The garden is this way. So, are you a yoga teacher or a student?"

"Both," Emma replied. "There's so much to learn."

"Agreed. It's a lifelong pursuit."

After a few minutes of quiet walking, he pointed to the left. "I believe the labyrinth is this way."

At the entrance of the garden area, Emma stopped and took it all in. The early spring flowers, crocuses, and daffodils were blossoming. They were all planted in a carefully arranged circular pattern. It took her breath away. "It's so beautiful!"

Samuel nodded. "Indeed. Spring is a wonderful time for a morning meditation. Are you signed up for it?"

She nodded. "Although, I'm not a morning person. But you have such a good reputation, I will force myself to get up early."

He laughed. "Can I tell you a secret? Neither am I. But I've found if I don't meditate early, the day gets away from me. Shall we walk the labyrinth?" He gazed into her eyes with a quiet intensity.

The warmth of his gaze was calming. He had an aura of peacefulness. *Guess that's why he's a meditation expert.* She relaxed and let go of her anxiety. "Yes."

He led the way, placing one foot firmly but softly in front of the other. Eyes cast down; Emma followed his lead. No words. Just listening to their footfalls, the birds, and the wind as they walked slowly around the circles.

Afterwards, they walked back to their rooms and talked. "That was simply amazing!" Emma murmured.

Samuel agreed. "Walking meditation is powerful. We use our bodies as conduits for our thoughts. We can let go of our anxieties, our fears for the future."

"I know someone who needs to hear that message. But how do I get him to listen?" She looked earnestly at him.

"Someone you love?"

Emma nodded shyly.

He looked disappointed. "You can't make him listen," he said kindly. "He has to be open to the message, to want a solution.   All you can do is share the information with no attachment to the outcome. Sometimes it takes a long time for that to happen. Be patient. He's lucky he has you to guide him. You are a beautiful woman, and I can see you have a compassionate heart."

"If only he would hear me."

Samuel gazed at her for a moment, "I have a feeling he will."

As they rode back up the elevator, Emma turned to Samuel "I see why you have such a great reputation. Thank you for your words of advice. See you in the morning." They stepped off the elevator together. He headed in one direction, she the other. Emma stopped and turned back. "Oh, by the way Samuel, if you ever want to come teach at our studio, we'd love to have you."

Samuel smiled.   "I'll take that under consideration. Lovely meeting you, Miss Emma. I wish you luck."

*****

The holidays had been hard on Grey. He spent Christmas with Alisha, the boys, and the grandkids. He had spent New Year's at home watching tv until Emma had called. He couldn't get the image of Emma on New Year's Eve out of his head. *What was that? Did she just need some relief? Or was she showing him what he was missing?* If that was the case, he was aware of what he no longer had. Although, that little reminder motivated him to work harder with Celeste.

He stuck to achieving the goals he set in therapy, practicing techniques to handle his emotions. He missed Emma so much. Still, visiting Emma's mother once a week and bringing her pastries helped him to still feel closer to Emma. Linda still didn't remember his name, which was probably good. She did remember the pastries though. She greeted him with, "Oh here's my favorite guy. Do you have a pastry for me today?"

She had a smart mouth, just like Emma, and made him laugh. Somedays, they chatted about Emma's childhood, somedays about his gym. And somedays, she thought he was her late husband. Grey went along with it. As he left, she always gave him a quick hug and said, "Goodbye, pastry guy. See you next week!"

He knew Emma might be mad at him for insinuating himself into her life, but it was one small way he could keep in touch with her. Still, he thought it best to keep it a secret. Isaac ran into him one time when he was visiting Linda, and Grey told him he was seeing an old client. He didn't know it, but Anna had whispered to Isaac in confidence what Grey was really up to. *Interesting*, Isaac thought. *That's a side of Dad I've never seen. Wonder if Emma knows? Probably not. Wonder if I should mention it in passing. Nah, Dad's just being thoughtful. I'll keep his secret.* Grey had mellowed over the last few months. He was less likely to fly off the handle, more likely to be compassionate, and more respectful of Isaac's ideas. It was a new Dad. Isaac liked it. He hoped it would stay that way.

*****

In March, Grey decided to make fishing a regular activity. It soothed and calmed him. He found a lake nearby and made a point of inviting Isaac or Joe or both to go fishing with him. One week, Joe brought Noah and Elijah with him, and Grey showed them some basics. "You know, I learned all my fishing tricks from my dad, your great-grandpa. He took me fishing whenever he could. Of course, that was before TV and computers and iPhones." It made him happy to talk about his dad.

"Wow! He must've been ancient!" giggled Noah.

Elijah snorted. "Fishing's cool, Grandpa. Can we invite Graydon to come with us sometime?"

Grey froze. He was not sure Emma would be cool with that. "Ummm, guess that's up to your dad." Grey glanced at Joe, looking for guidance. He thought it might be ok. But he didn't want to put Emma in an uncomfortable spot. He knew Graydon didn't have a grandpa, though, and that he might enjoy the outings with his friend.

"Let's run it by your mother," Joe suggested.

After much discussion between Lisa and Joe and Amanda, Joe's wife, they decided to run the idea by Emma.

"Mom, how would you feel if Graydon went fishing with Elijah and Grey?" Lisa watched her mom's face for a reaction. "Elijah's been going fishing with Joe and Grey and wanted Graydon to come along sometime. If it upsets you, I'll just say no."

Emma looked surprised by the question. She took her time answering. "Well, I guess it's okay. The boys have been friends for a long time. Grey knows him. And it really doesn't involve me anyway. Probably be good for Graydon to learn that 'manly' form of relaxation." She felt a little sad, though, as she thought back to their beach trip and how relaxing fishing had been for Grey. It was his form of meditation. She thought back to Samuel's words. *If only*, she sighed. *Guess I'm glad he's doing something fun and passing along the tradition.*

"Thanks, Mom! I think it'll be good for Graydon. Aaron isn't the fishing type. He hates worms and getting up early. And Graydon's been looking for some outdoorsy things to do. He'll be so excited. Just hope he doesn't sing the underwear song to Grey."

Emma rolled her eyes at Lisa. "Thanks for the reminder."

"Sorry, Mom. That was a long time ago. You have to admit, it was kind of funny. I mean, Grey was so shocked and embarrassed to see me."

"It was funny." But it didn't seem like such a long time ago to Emma, and she missed those days. "Let me know how Graydon likes fishing."

Lisa hugged her mom. "I will. And I'll let you know the lowdown on Grey too."

Emma shook her head. "Don't bother. He's moved forward and so have I."

*****

In April, the boys all went fishing. Grey had spoken to Graydon's dad, Aaron, and asked him if he'd feel more comfortable about the fishing trip if he came along. Aaron said no that he didn't like fishing, but he was fine with Graydon going. Then he suggested Steve might want to go. Steve liked fishing and didn't get to go much, since the girls were vegetarians like their mom. Grey hemmed and hawed and then decided, why not? Steve was a nice guy, and he might benefit from some male bonding time. He texted Emma and asked if she would share Steve's number with him. *Huh, wonder why he wants Steve's number?*

Emma: I guess so.
Grey: Thanks. How are you?
Emma: Fine. And you?
Grey: Getting better.
Emma: Glad to hear it.

Grey took a deep breath before he asked Emma what he needed to ask.

Grey: Ok if I ask Steve to come fishing with us next week? Graydon's coming with us and Aaron thought Steve might like to go as well.
Emma: ☺ Are you fishing a lot now?
Grey: It's helpful. And it reminds me of our beach trip.

Emma pictured him standing in the surf, waves crashing at his calves as he cast out and reeled the line in. He was so into the moment. So happy. A flash of anger shot through her. *Damn him! He leaves me but wants to take my son?* She took a deep breath in and out. *Anger doesn't solve anything. Non-attachment. Nothing I can do about the situation*, she thought. *Let go.* She repeated her mantra, *Let go, let go, let go.* Another deep breath, in and out, and then she replied.

Emma: Ok. Don't need to ask me. Steve's a grown man.
Grey: Right. Just didn't want to blindside you or upset you.

Emma snorted. *Now he's worried about blindsiding me?! That's rich.*

Emma: Bye. Have a nice time fishing.

She stalked around the house, cleaning with vigor. *Damn, damn, damn him*! She threw the toys the grandkids had left around into their baskets. She fluffed the pillows on the couch. She vacuumed vigorously. She tried to hate him. But she couldn't help thinking: *He was a nice guy. He invited her son and grandson to go fishing*. She knew how much he loved that sport. She dusted the bookcases and the tables. She knew he was trying to pass along the lessons his dad had taught him. *Argh!* She plopped onto the couch. *Damn him.* She saw through all that tough man exterior; she saw his true colors, his kindness, his strength. *Maybe someday he will see my true colors, how much I loved and needed him. How strong he had made me.*

Grey threw his phone despairingly on the table. He knew she was angry, even though her replies were cool. At least she still cares. Maybe not in the way he wanted, but …beggars can't be choosers.

He called Steve later in the afternoon. "Hi Steve, this is Grey Erikson."

"Uh, hi? Can I help you?" His voice was neutral but curious.

"Graydon, your nephew, is going fishing with my boys and me next week. Aaron suggested you might want to go because you like to fish, and he doesn't."

Steve was quiet for a moment. He rubbed the back of his neck as he thought it through. He did like to fish and hadn't been in years, since the girls were little. He and Graydon both liked outdoor activities, unlike his dad. Uncle and nephew had bonded over that. Aaron was more into video games and reading, quiet activities, while Graydon had that untamed boy energy that Steve identified with. But fishing with the guy who dumped his mother? This was a little awkward. He didn't want to be disloyal to Emma, but a little male bonding time would be nice. He was surrounded by women, and he loved them. He could play dolls and have tea parties with the best of them. But fishing, drinking beer, and just hanging would be great. He'd never had that with his dad.

"Steve, I understand if you don't want to go. Why not think it over? I mentioned it to your mom, and she thought it would be fine."

"You talked to mom?"

"Umm…well, I texted her. We do that occasionally."

Interesting. "Well let me think it over. I do like fishing. But…"

"No pressure, just let me know. We're going Sunday morning."

Steve hung up. *Huh, that was weird.* He talked it over with Emily, and then decided to mention it to his mom to see her reaction.

Emma just shrugged her shoulders. "It's fine. You're not being disloyal. Grey's a nice guy and it's good to bond with your nephew. I'll be okay. Tell him I wish him nothing but the best." It was true. She wanted him to be happy. She just wished he felt the same about her. *At least he's moving in the right direction.*

*****

The fishing expedition was a fun time. It was a beautiful spring day. The sun was warm, the air clear. The trees had started to leaf out, providing shade as they fished. Grey found groups less anxiety-producing when he was outside. Noah, Elijah, and Graydon fished a little and ran around a lot. Steve, Isaac, Joe, and Grey found they had a lot in common. They laughed and talked sports and workouts; but when the boys mentioned Emma, there was some unspoken tension.

He wasn't sure how Steve would handle being with him, but by the end of the day, they were more relaxed with each other. As they were leaving, Steve thanked Grey for inviting him. "Maybe we can do this again. That's if Emily lets me." He laughed. "It's nice to get away once in a while. Although I'm sure Emily will demand her turn."

As they shook hands, Grey pulled him aside. "I'm still a work in progress, but don't count me out of Emma's life yet. Maybe she'll have me back someday. But if not, I'm glad to have gotten to know you better. You're a great guy."

Chapter 16

Time by Hootie and the Blowfish

"Grey, you've met all your goals we set up," Celeste said with a smile. She stood up and offered her hand to Grey. He hesitated before taking it. It had been a long few months. It was June now. And he had worked extra hard since New Year's. She was proud of him.

"Are you sure?"

"I'm sure. Not that we can't have tune-up sessions. But I feel you have all the tools you need to handle your anxiety. You're like a butterfly that has broken out of its cocoon, fully formed and ready to fly."

Grey smirked. "Don't know if I've ever been compared to a butterfly."

"Don't you agree you're in a much better place? That strong emotions don't derail your everyday life anymore?"

"Yes." His voice was clear. "Now what?"

"Go live your life. Find love. Or," she said with a meaningful look, "go after the love you've already found."

"Not sure she'll still want me." He looked scared and sad. "I messed up so badly." His voice trailed off.

"Grey, if I know Emma, and I do, she'll be open to talking. She's a compassionate woman. And, this is off the record, she still has feelings for you."

A flicker of hope crossed his face. He missed Emma so much. Her laughter, her smart mouth, her kindness. The things that set his heart on fire.

"Think about it. What's the worst thing that can happen? If she is open to it…well… you know what to do. If she's not interested, you have the skills, the strength to move on. You've faced your past. You've made amends to those you hurt. It's time to move forward. Go find the one person who you need the most and make it right with her."

"Thank you. Celeste. You've saved my life."

"No, Grey. You saved your own life. Now go live it!"

As Grey drove to the gym, he thought about Celeste's words. Could Emma still have feelings for him? He hoped that a connection like theirs wouldn't just dissolve. Would she trust him enough to let him back into her life? That he wasn't sure of. He had hurt her and damaged the trust they once had.

It had been over eight months since he'd broken up with her. She still texted him occasionally, sending a picture of the flowers in her garden, or of her trip to the mountains for one of her workshops. She never said much other than *thought you might enjoy this*. He always answered. But the texts were short, like they were casual friends. Once, he had texted her saying he was thinking of her. She had answered back with a heart emoji followed by a sad face. Me too, she had replied.

Grey noticed she had gotten a new hairdo. Although she looked beautiful, he missed the soft, natural curls that framed her face. He hoped it didn't mean she was done with him… out with the old, in with the new. She radiated confidence, which was definitely attractive. And he noticed guys at the gym giving her second glances and talking to her after class. He was jealous, but knew he had no right to be. Luckily, she never left with any of them. At least as far as he knew.

Emma came to Core Connection often, but she prioritized taking Casey's classes now. She and Casey had bonded and hung out frequently. Casey was outspoken and fun, and she pushed Emma to try new activities. In April, he overheard them planning a zipline outing. Emma had been scared to try but Casey talked her into it. A few days later, he heard her teasing Emma about how she had screamed the whole way down. He had laughed, picturing Emma's face, wanting to join in, but knowing he couldn't.

He had caught Emma staring at him a few times, though. And, there was that memory of that one night. He wondered if she thought about it as often as he did.   But he was too scared to ask her. She looked a little sad whenever she saw him, but she always smiled and sometimes stopped for a very short conversation.

Maybe there's still a chance. He sat in the truck for a few minutes after therapy. Could he do this?

*****

"Isaac?" Grey asked, walking into the gym with determination. He would make this right.

"Yeah, Dad?"

"Can I teach your spin class tonight?"

"Ummm. I guess so." He paused. "You know Emma's usually in that class."

"I know," he said with a hitch in his voice.

Isaac narrowed his eyes. "Finally! Are you going to make a move? Do you have a plan?   She was the best thing you ever had. Well, except, of course for Joe and me. Well, and mom. But still."

"Maybe. I miss her so much. Not sure she can forgive me, though." He ran his hand along the back of his neck, gently massaging it, trying to soothe his anxiety.

249

"I think it's worth a try, Dad." Isaac said encouragingly. "Real love doesn't just disappear."

"How'd you get so smart?"

Isaac shrugged. "Born that way I guess." He grinned. "Plus, you're a good man who's had some bad experiences. Emma knows that. Open the door. Give her the opportunity to walk through it. At least you can talk to her about how you've been struggling and how far you've come. If I know her, she can't resist a good redemption story."

Grey reached out and hugged Isaac. "Thank you, son. I love you."

With tears in his eyes, Isaac hugged him back. "Me too, Dad. You deserve a break." Stepping away, he added with a sly smile, "Now can I get a raise?"

"Actually, I'd like to talk to you about that. Maybe tomorrow we can meet. You've been doing a fantastic job and I'd like to discuss a promotion."

Isaac fist pumped. "About time I got the recognition I deserve!"

Grey rolled his eyes as he headed to get ready for spin class. *That boy!* He scrolled through his playlist. He did have a plan, kind of a sappy one. But that's what always works in romance stories. Make a fool of yourself and end up with the girl. Maybe, fingers crossed, he could pull it off.

Chapter 17

Just Say Yes by Snow Patrol

Emma's brain was fried. Between teaching class, seeing her mom, and instructing private lessons, she'd had a busy day. She needed spin class tonight. Her stress level was high and spin class always made her feel better. She rushed around grabbing her workout clothes. *Damn,* she thought, *my workout bra is in the wash. Arrghh. Guess I'll wear this cami under my sleeveless tee.* No one would notice, *except Grey,* she thought sadly. She remembered the time she had purposely teased Grey about not wearing a bra. He had practically mauled her after class.

And on New Year's Eve, the look on his face as she had taken off her top. That brought a smile to her face. *I miss him so much. Wonder how he's doing?* Gwen had told her he'd been doing really well in meditation class; he was practically a pro, she said. *Good for him!*

She rushed into the gym. She was little late but, luckily, Isaac was teaching spin class tonight. Isaac's classes were always lively. He was very enthusiastic and funny. *Gotta love his dad jokes.* And she knew Isaac didn't care about tardiness, unlike his dad, who would've given her a hard time. She saw Isaac out of the corner of her eye still at the front desk. *Good,* she thought, *I'm not late after all.* She headed into the darkened bike studio, found her favorite bike, and started adjusting the settings.

"Can I help with that?" a deep familiar voice behind her asked.

Emma froze. Was that Grey? Turning around she ran smack into his chest. "Uhhh I thought Isaac was teaching tonight," she said with a tremor. God, he looked so good. She gazed up at his face.

"Isaac had something else to do. I'm subbing for him tonight." He noticed she didn't have a bra on. Damn that woman.

Emma gulped. She wanted to run right out of the room. But she couldn't. It was like there was an invisible hand holding her. His body was so close. His smelled as delicious as ever. She couldn't help but step just a millimeter closer to him and breathe in his scent. "Let me help you get the bike set-up since we're running late," he said with a lift of his eyebrows.

"Still the same stickler for time, I see. Remember though, we had a deal. I'd be late and you wouldn't say anything," she said, finding her voice again. "I can do this myself, thank you very much." She turned away from him, but he didn't move. The heat of his body right behind her was making her flustered. Damn, she wanted to turn around and kiss him. *What is he doing?*

"Emma, don't shut me out please." He leaned in closer whispering in her ear.

Her whole body was awake, on fire. "I'm not the one shutting people out," she managed to reply in a tight voice.

"I know I've made mistakes. But I've worked hard the last several months on healing and moving on. I miss you, Emma. Let me prove myself. Can we talk after class? Please?" People were staring at them now. Embarrassed, not wanting to draw any more attention to herself, she nodded quickly.

"Thank you." He said gratefully. Grey worked his way up to his bike in front of the class. He adjusted his microphone, started pedaling, and began checking out the other riders. Finally, he settled his gaze on Emma. He said, "Got a new playlist tonight, guys. More mellow than my usual class. Dedicated to an old friend. Someone who taught me that love and friendship are the keys to living a full life."

As the music started, Emma recognized "Midnight in Harlem" by Truck Tedeschi Band. She smiled, realizing the bluesy track was playing when the two of them had first met at the studio. Her heart thrilled. He winked at her as he saw the recognition on her face. "Let's take our warm-up nice and slow." He followed that track up with "You've got a Friend" by James Taylor and Carol King. *Oh my gosh*, Emma started. This was the song they listened to on their trip to Carolina Beach when they really got to know each other.

"All great relationships start out as friends, don't they?" Grey asked the group as he kept his gaze on Emma. There were a few nods and yeses from the riders. She closed her eyes as she thought of the beach and all that Grey had revealed to her. How they felt that strong connection. When she opened her eyes, she looked up at Grey and nodded with a smile and a few tears. He picked the pace up for a few songs and then took it back down by playing "Smiling Face" by James Taylor.

He hopped off his bike and walked around, encouraging, and motivating the riders. He stopped by Emma's bike and put his full focus on her. He covered his microphone and said, "My friend always had the best smile. The way her face lights up when she's happy or excited. It made my heart melt. Still does, Emma. I miss it."

By now, the other riders were looking at both of them. Casey shouted, "Go for it Grey. Emma! You know he loves you. And I'm pretty sure you love him." The others clapped in approval. Grey looked back at Casey, grateful, for once, for her directness.

Emma, embarrassed, confused, and hopeful, shook her head. *What is he doing?*

He got back on his bike. "The next song is one of my favorites." Looking directly at Emma, he said, "Hope it's yours, too."

The beginning strains of "Just say Yes" by Snow Patrol began to play. Slow and teasing, the song began to build up pace. Emma's heart beat faster as she realized what he was doing. He was asking her to say yes to him, to their relationship. She had done that before. Could she do it again?

His face looked calm, but inside, his stomach was churning, his heart pounding. He gripped the handlebars tightly. *Please Emma, give me another chance.* He mouthed, "Just say yes, Emma."

The words of the song dug deep into her soul. Her skin ached for his touch. Her body yearned to feel his heart beating next to hers. She pedaled a little faster. Could she do it again? Could she trust him? Could she let him back in her life? *Yes,* her heart was screaming. *No. Well Maybe,* her head was saying. Had Grey grown and dealt with his past? Could he handle loving someone without running? She couldn't take him leaving her again.

Grey saw the struggle play out on her face and prayed. And then, suddenly, her face was serene. She had decided. Grey steeled himself. He could handle whatever her decision was, but life would be infinitely better with her in it. She smiled up at Grey, nodded, and mouthed the word, "Yes."

Grey's heart was beating fast and not because of the workout. He was scared and excited. *She said yes!!!Please don't let me blow this, I need her.* "Let's finish the cooldown with a mellow Righteous Brothers song, 'You're My Soul and Inspiration.'

"Ooh, Grey, you're really going all out. Didn't know you had a romantic bone in your body! But you sure are trying," Casey said, loudly.

Everyone laughed, but Grey kept his face serious, his focus on Emma. "Sometimes songs can say what you can't."

After class, Casey came up to Emma in the locker room. "He loves you, Emma. I'm jealous, but you two were made for one another. What do you yoga people call it? You're the yin to his yang."

Emma reached out and hugged Casey. "Thanks for being a good friend. I value your opinion. We'll see what the future holds."

"Go play with his yang," Casey teased. She winked and walked away as Emma laughed at her.

"Emma!" Isaac called out eagerly to her as she sat in the lobby, waiting for Grey. "Can I speak to you for a second?"

"Sure."

"I just want you to know, Dad's worked hard on getting better. And he really took a big risk today. Letting his feelings out there in front of everyone. Didn't know the old grump had it in him to be so romantic. I think he took a page out of my book."

Emma blushed. "It was kind of romantic, wasn't it?"

"Will you give him a chance? Please?" Isaac looked earnestly at her. "He's a changed man. And he genuinely loves you. He's been lost without you."

"I want to Isaac. But … it'll take time. He hurt me. Let me see what he has to say."

Isaac came out from behind the desk and gave her a hug. "We're all rooting for you. And I'll kick his ass if he does anything bad to you again."

"You won't need to kick anyone's ass, son," Grey's voice boomed from behind him. "Emma, are you ready to go?"

Emma gulped and then nodded. "Yup. Where are we going?"

"How about Greek Guys Grille? We need dinner and that place holds some good memories, doesn't it?"

"I'll meet you there," she said.

"Why don't I drive? Your car is safe here."

"Umm… okay. Why?"

"Because I need you close to me. I don't want you to change your mind and go home."

Emma held his gaze. "I don't run. That's your thing."

"I deserved that," a chagrined Grey admitted. "But I've changed. My running shoes have been put in storage." He held out his hand to her. She took it tentatively and they headed to his truck.

Isaac and Casey cat called behind them. "I pray they work it out," Isaac said. "Dad's been a bear without her."

Casey concurred. "He's just been looking so sad. It's not sexy."

Grey opened the truck door for her and gave her a hand up. Just touching her hand was intoxicating. He smirked as she sat primly on the opposite side of the seat, as far away from him as she could.

The feel of his hand in hers had made her melt. It had been so long! She needed to stay strong though. *I'll listen to what he has to say, but I'm not jumping right back in. I need to know he's serious.* But the pull of his body was so powerful. She fought the urge to slide over next to him. The silence between them was awkward and fraught with tension.

"Emma?" His voice was quiet but reassuring.

"Yes," she answered with trepidation.

"I won't hurt you again. Let me tell you my struggles and my path forward. And then you can decide where we go."

Emma sighed, relieved. Those were the words she needed to hear. He wasn't going to pressure her. She gets to make the choice about their future. *If nothing else, maybe I can get closure.* She relaxed a bit and slid away from the door, closer to Grey. He reached out for her hand, and she gave it to him.

He glanced at her. Maybe there's hope. He gave her a hand a squeeze, then lifted it to his lips. "I've missed you, Emma."

Eleni excitedly shouted as soon as she saw them walking into the restaurant. "Where have you two been? We missed you."

Emma glanced at Grey with a grin. "Guess we hung out here a lot. I couldn't make myself come back here after we…well, you know."

He rubbed her shoulder lightly. "I'm sorry. Me either."

"The usual for you two? You paying?" She looked at Grey.

"Yes ma'am. Is that okay, Emma?"

"You invited me. So yes." She confirmed, "You damn well better pay."

"I see your smart mouth hasn't changed."

"Never will."

"Good thing. It's one of the things I like… *love* about you. I missed it."

Emma blushed. "What else did you miss about me?" she asked as they sat down at one of the tables.

"Everything. Your smile. Your sexy voice. Your laugh. Your compassion. The way you loved me. The way we made love. Especially that."

Her heart melted a little more. *Be careful Emma, he was always charming.* "Then why did you leave?" Her voice was forlorn. "If you liked all that, how could you leave? I loved you, Grey. I still probably love you. But you abandoned me. How can I trust you won't do it again?"

Grey took both her hands in his, intertwining their fingers. It was now or never. He was scared but Emma needed an answer. "I had to leave you, Emma. I was broken. I loved you more than I ever loved anyone in my life. The first time we kissed, the first time we made love, I knew you were the one. And you loved me back! The feelings were so strong, my mind couldn't handle it. I didn't believe I deserved to be loved. That I deserved someone as special as you. I have a dark side and it was winning again. I was struggling. It hurt so much." He took a breath. "And my natural inclination was to run away from the emotional pain. To deny. To not face my problems head on. I knew I needed to change if I wanted a life with you."

He stopped again. "No," he clarified. "I wanted to change. For you, but also for me. I can't live the rest of my life in fear."

Emma squeezed his hands as she searched his face. He was offering her his soul. "I know this isn't easy, but it's important we talk this through. So, what has changed? How do I know next time you get big feelings, you won't run again?"

"I can't lie to you. I will probably freak out a time or two. However, I have learned how to handle it. Celeste and I developed a game plan that we've been practicing. We talked about what I want out of life. I don't want to live in fear. To be afraid I'm not worthy of love. I know now what to do when those feeling surface, how to recognize them beginning to form. I know to rely on friends and family to help out when I'm feeling lost or challenged. And I know to come back to therapy when they get too big. We've worked very hard." He backtracked. "She would say *I've* worked very hard. And I have. On our last visit, she told me I was ready to live my life. She compared me to a butterfly breaking out of its protective cocoon."

"I love butterflies." She smiled. "You were always worthy of love. You just didn't see it." Emma stood up and walked around the table, sitting down next to Grey. She hugged him and then lifted her face to kiss his cheek. "I love your plan. I love your bravery for sharing. Most of all, I love you."

Their food had gotten cold as they talked. "That was a lot to take in," Emma said. "Let's bring this to my house. I can microwave it. And we can talk some more." Emma walked over to the counter and asked for some to-go boxes.

Grey packed their salads, souvlaki, and pita bread up, and they headed out. "Let's leave your car at the gym tonight. I'll come by and pick you up in the morning." He was emotionally exhausted. Their talk had taken everything out of him.

"Actually, well, I was thinking you could spend the night at my house. We might talk late into the night."

Grey's face brightened. "Oh my god, that would be great. I'm exhausted. Talking about feelings is hard. I can sleep on your couch."

"Nope." She grinned. "You are going to sleep in my bed. In my arms. We have a lot of cuddling time to make up."

"Is that a code word for 'make love?' 'Cause I'm so tired right now that, as much as I want to, I don't think I could."

Emma tucked her arm in Grey's. "Nope. I'm not quite ready for that yet. Maybe soon. But I have missed having your warm body around."

"I love you, Emma."

"I love you, too, Grey. Shall we go home?"

"Yes."

Epilogue

And I Love You So by Perry Como

As they boarded the plane bound for Italy, Emma said a little prayer, thanking God for all that happened this year, the good and the bad. She was grateful for the chance to finally see her grandmother's birthplace. She was grateful for her family's support. She was grateful for Grey. It had been a struggle, but they had pushed through the pain. They had taken their time re-establishing their relationship. She had needed time to trust him again, and he needed to open up fully to her. Couples counseling had helped.

Grey had decided to turn Core Connection over to Isaac and Joe. Isaac would manage it and Joe would do the finances. Grey would work part-time doing private training sessions and other classes as needed. Unsurprisingly, Casey had turned into a valuable asset. She was an excellent instructor, and she attracted a good crowd. Her unfiltered personality made for fun classes. And she had a head for business.

Now, he and Emma would be free to travel and enjoy life. They had decided it made sense to sell his house and live, together, in hers, which had more room and a bigger yard. They were still arguing about a few things. He liked clean empty spaces. She liked warm and cluttered spaces. Some things they still had to work on.

Grey had invested some of the money from the sale into Core Connection, allowing them to expand. He had also invested some into Emma's house – well, their house now-- updating the bathrooms with fancy new showers. Although, much to Grey's dismay, she still refused to make love in the shower.

And their honeymoon to Italy was all courtesy of Grey. They were starting in Milan and leisurely traveling up to Lake Como, staying in a small Airbnb in Bellaigio. Eventually, they planned to make their way to the Italian Alps, to Grosotto, Emma's grandmother's hometown. It was their dream trip.

Their wedding last month had been small and intimate. Cafe Amore had catered the luncheon. Emma's sister, Lizzy, had been matron of honor. Isaac had been best man. All their kids and grandkids, a few friends, and co-workers celebrated with them. Even Emma's mom had managed to make it through the day, although she kept calling Grey the pastry guy. For someone who had bad short-term memory, Emma thought, she sure remembered Grey and his pastry.

For their first dance, Grey chose 'And I Love You So'. Emma clung to Grey as he softly sang the lyrics, tears rolling down both their faces. At the end, Grey gently kissed her forehead. "I'll never leave you again."

"Nope, you won't. I'll never let you go." Holding hands, they turned to their friends and invited everyone to dance with them to "True Colors" by Phil Collins. Emma dedicated the song to Grey. "I'll always see your true colors, no matter what," she whispered.

Emma noticed Isaac and Anna danced together quite a bit. Fingers crossed; they would become more than co-workers soon. She knew Isaac had a bit of a history with women, and Anna knew too. She was being cautious. But Emma had a good feeling about them.

Casey, as usual, had been the life of the party. Surprisingly, she had made friends with Samuel, the newest yoga teacher at Half Moon Yoga. He was a little older than her -quiet and contemplative. Talk about yin and yang. But Emma had introduced him to her at a yoga workshop and Casey had seemed mesmerized. And Sam seemed equally captivated. She had seen him around at Core Connection a lot lately and they looked like they were into each other. *Hmmm maybe I have a second career as a matchmaker.*

Grey laid his head on Emma's shoulder as their plane sped through the clouds. "I love you, Mrs. Erikson. Thank you for not giving up on me."

Emma smiled. "Thank you for not running anymore."

"Best decision of my life." He squeezed her hand. "Asking you to marry me."

"Best decision of my life." She kissed his forehead. "Saying yes."

Emma and Grey's Playlist

*I included a playlist of some of the songs that helped me write Emma &
Grey's story. Most are the songs from 60's and 70's but a few more modern
ones are included. All songs that resonated with me (and my yoga people
because I played this playlist frequently before I taught my yoga classes.)
But the song Just Say Yes was the main driver of this story.*

*Midnight in Harlem - Tedeschi Trucks Band (Saw them live and they
are fabulous!)*
The First Time Ever I Saw Your Face – Roberta Flack
Everywhere– Fleetwood Mac
Hungry Eyes – Eric Carmen
Unforgettable – Nat King Cole
Can't Take My Eyes Off of You – Frankie Valli
You've Got a Friend – James Taylor & Carole King
Follow You Follow Me - Genesis
True Colors – Phil Collins
All of Me – John Legend
Can't Get Enough of Your Love – Barry White
Whenever I See Your Smiling Face – James Taylor
You're My Soul & My Heart's Inspiration- Righteous Brothers
Hello Again – Neil Diamond
Time is A Healer- Eva Cassidy
Time - Hootie and the Blowfish
Just Say Yes – Snow Patrol
And I Love You So – Perry Como

Acknowledgements

As with most books Just Say Yes would not have happened without the help and encouragement of family and friends. I had been mulling the story in my mind and actually started putting words to paper. But I'm a very private and insecure person. I told no one. Until one day I realized if I didn't tell people Emma and Grey's story would stay a secret. So, I gulped and then spilled my guts to my sister Sue (see dedication page). She encouraged me (just like she did when I started teaching yoga). And, she agreed to be my reader as the story went along. I will be forever grateful. And although she didn't live to see it published, her voice is reflected in every page.

Special thanks to John Stevens, Mary Clark, Kathy Beck and Janet Manzo for taking the time out of your very busy lives to be my first readers and copy editors, your comments and corrections were so valuable. Also, thank you to my sister Christine for sharing her friends, Kathy and Janet. And also sharing her take, along with my other sisters Adrienne and Jeanne, on the day to day living with someone with dementia.

Elisa Faison, my developmental editor, kept me from wandering off track from the essential point that Emma and Grey loved each other and each provided a piece/peace to their lives that was missing.

Thanks to my book cover designer Lynn Andreozzi for working with me to find a cover that represents this love story in a meaningful way.

The issues of anxiety, panic attacks and PTSD are real and common problems. I tried to deal with them in a thoughtful, realistic and compassionate way. Therapy, yoga and meditation are valuable tools for healing. With Emma and Grey we see how these issues affect both partners in a relationship.

And another special thanks to my sweet husband John who put up with my cursing at my laptop and even though romance isn't his preferred genre read every word of my book at least twice and told me he liked it. Also, I told my grown kids they weren't allowed to read it because they don't like to think their mama knows about sex.

****

If you liked Emma and Grey's story you'll love the next in the Half Moon Yoga and Core Connection series. Casey from Core Connection and Sam, from Half Moon yoga Studio, two opposites but so much alike, strike up an unexpectedly tender and spicy romance. See preview on the next page.

Please follow me on Amazon:
https://www.amazon.com/author/michellestevens2
Don't Forget to Review & Rate Just Say Yes.
Also review on GoodReads.com- (type in Just Say Yes by Michelle Stevens)

Follow me on Instagram- mischamarie2 or mmstevensauthor
Facebook ; (2) Facebook

Thank you!!!!

Preview of Show and Tell

Casey Huntington had never felt more naked. She never was shy about taking her clothes off but this…. She was panicking. Her heart racing, her field of vision closing She was an athlete and beauty queen. She was used to stripping down in front of others. People staring at her body, some admiringly and some jealously. She knew how to work the judges, how to work the show. She could look into a spectator's eyes and promise things that she would never deliver. She was a pro.   But … This was different. *Oh my god it's almost my turn. I've got to get out of here.* She looked wildly around for the exit.

"Casey, I believe you're the last one left." Samuel looked directly at her with a soft smile. He didn't look into her eyes like he wanted something. He didn't smile that knowing smile men often gave her. She froze.

"Uhh. Ummm…" Casey's voice wavered… "Not sure I'm ready for this." She lowered her eyes to the ground. Her heart about to explode out of her chest.

"That's ok. We'll check back later." His voice was kind and calming. Casey sighed with relief. "Thank you." She stammered. Her face red with embarrassment and shame. The woman next to her offered her hand to Casey. "It's ok." she whispered. "We've all been there."

"Okay everyone, let's take a short break and reconvene in fifteen minutes. There's some coffee and tea and some pastries and fruit in the room next door. Help yourselves. It's 9:30 now, see you back at 9:45."

Casey rushed out of the meeting room, almost knocking over the sign indicating the trauma informed yoga workshop and headed for the bathroom. She splashed water on her face and then looked in the mirror in despair. *Who are you?* She ran her hands over her wrinkles-not that there many –thanks to her regular botox appointments. Her blonde hair was neatly and stylishly coiffed. Makeup – what was left of it– carefully done. Everything in place, like a shield. A few soft wrinkles around the eyes, she needed some to look natural after all. *She was a babe- especially for age. Then why did she feel so ugly; so unworthy?* The tears streamed down her face. No man will ever want me again. Why am I so desperate for attention?

"Oh Casey, what's wrong?" Emma Griffen, a yoga teacher at the studio, came through the bathroom door and put her arm around her friend. "I thought you were attending the Trauma workshop today?"

"I am." she sobbed. "But I can't do it. Everyone was looking at me …I felt so exposed. I can't tell all those other people how stupid I was. I have an image to uphold. My mama would be ashamed if she saw me here.   And that man was so calm and kind. It rattled me. I can't …."

Emma gently rubbed her back, "Casey you weren't stupid. You were abused. Abusers manipulate you. Your husband took advantage of your insecurities, sucked you into believing you were weak, and you needed him. And your mama, well she was certified southern crazy!"

Casey stopped crying and gave a half-hearted laugh, "Yeah, she was a little over the top. But she was my mama. That's all I knew. She loved me. Just wanted the best for me."

"Let's get you headed back to the workshop." Emma gave her a big hug and a tissue. Casey wiped her tears and blotted at her remaining makeup. "OH, I don't think I can go back. I look a mess. And … It's too hard. That man was too kind. It was like he recognized my pain. You're the only person I've ever told about my ex. I don't share that part of my life with anyone." But to her it seemed like Sam already knew…..

Emma nodded. "That's Samuel's gift. He sees into your soul. Let him help you. I know he's a good man. And he's skilled at his job. That's why I recommended this workshop."

Reluctantly Casey headed back to the room. She re-adjusted her shirt and yoga pants, took one last swipe at her nose, paused at the door, *Head high, shoulders back, tits forward, Walk into that room as if you own it. Hide the real you at all costs. That's what mama would say.* She strutted back into the room, gave Samuel a nod and sat back down on her mat.

Sam watched Casey as she strolled back into the room. *Wasn't sure she was coming back.* She was an attractive woman no doubt. Tall blonde, all put together, no crack in her armor, yet. He felt a little stir of attraction. She knew how to sell herself. Not his type though - but he could feel her fear and pain. *And she was here for a reason.* He smiled warmly at her as he walked to her mat. "Glad you're back. Wasn't sure you would be."

"Frankly I wasn't going to come back. But my friend Emma talked me into it. You know Emma, right?"

He nodded his head. "Yes, Emma's the reason I'm doing this workshop here. I met her at a meditation retreat." He remembered meeting her and being drawn to her beauty and her quiet calmness, but it quickly became obvious she was in love with someone. He admired her courage in pursuing her love. She wasn't one to give up easily.

"She's very persuasive." Casey had put her protective shield back up. "She said you were skilled at what you do." She looked at him with a flirty look. Her voice low. Her body turned suggestively towards him. The only way she knew how to be with men. Dazzle them with her sexiness.

He kept his gaze on her face. "Casey, you're a beautiful woman with lots to offer to the world. You're here for a reason. Emma's right. I am good at what I do," he smiled confidently, "but you need to help me be good by being open to change. Let's work on that today and tomorrow." His voice was soothing and somewhat mesmerizing and completely professional.

Casey blushed as she dropped the sexy attitude. Her shoulders relaxed. *What is going on?* She felt safe in his presence. She never felt safe with any man, at least not since Dave her ex-husband destroyed her. No need to put that shield in place, to protect her vulnerability. No need to prove she was worthy. She was here for help. And he knew it. And she wanted help. She was tired of always being on guard. Tired of that walled off and empty place in her heart. She didn't feel embarrassed anymore as she found her mat and sat down. *Let's do this!*

By the end of the first day Casey had relaxed enough to share some of her story with group. No one acted shocked or looked at her judgmentally when she told how her husband Dave swept her off her feet when she was 19. A beauty queen, homecoming queen in high school, Miss Georgia Peach, Miss Atlanta, the homecoming court in college. She could dance and sing, walk across a stage and smile at everyone while wearing a bathing suit and stilettos. Perfect southern manners drilled into her by her ambitious mom. When she met Dave, a law student, with money, and political ambitions, her mom pushed her into his arms. She didn't resist. He was charming and good looking.

Their fancy southern wedding made the society pages, followed by a romantic honeymoon. Dave was loving and attentive.

They had lots of parties and hung out with the up-and-coming couples in their circle. Casey loved to entertain, and Dave loved showing off his beautiful vivacious wife. He made her feel special.

Her mother was ecstatic. It was everything she dreamed of for her daughter. But by the second year of their marriage Dave began criticizing her appearance, finding fault with her make-up, her hair, her clothes. He hired stylists to dress her 'more appropriately' for an important lawyer. He sent her to a plastic surgeon to enhance her breasts. "I need you to be super sexy, so my colleagues are jealous," he said. Casey was bewildered but she loved and trusted Dave, so she tried harder to make him happy. She wanted him to succeed. She fixed her makeup, bought the clothes he suggested; had the breast augmentation. She did look sexy, and it felt good to have other men admire her. She wanted children, maybe later Dave said, but Dave didn't want anything to ruin her figure. He was selfish. She was sad but figured there was plenty of time. Besides she still liked to party.

When she was thirty, she started botox at his suggestion. He looked sneeringly at her tiny wrinkles. 'Get rid of them. They make you look like a grandma. Not sexy.' At 35 he criticized her butt, even though she worked out all the time, spin class, pilates, tennis, personal trainer. Not an inch of her was flabby. 'Oh my god you are disgusting' he yelled when he was drunk. She believed him and worked even harder at maintaining her appearance.

That's where she stopped talking, leaving the rest to the group's imaginations. She sobbed quietly. She couldn't reveal the whole story to the group. It was too horrible.

When she was done with her story, Casey felt a sense of relief. Sam thanked her for sharing "I'm sorry for what you went through." His deep smooth voice was a balm to her soul. "That was hard to hear and hard to share. We're all here to help and support one another."

His deep brown eyes connected with hers. He held her gaze for a moment. He knew she wasn't telling the whole story to them. That she was far more shattered than she let on to the group. But it was a start.

"So today and tomorrow we're here to learn how to turn our trauma into power. It takes persistence, willpower and a commitment to change. Meditation is a key tool to help you along your journey. Remember you are as brave and strong as you believe you are. You've all survived trauma of some sort. So, I know you have the persistence, the willpower to survive. Do you have the commitment to change?"

His words resonated with her. She had survived, but the scars ran deep. Could she ever trust another man? Have a relationship that was based on more than her looks and sex? Not likely, she thought. It would take a special man to take her with all her edges. And she wasn't sure she wanted all the vulnerability that kind of relationship brought with it. But she hoped she could make peace with her past.

Casey gazed at Samuel. He was tall, lean and handsome. His brown hair had streaks of silver as did his beard that hugged his slender face. And there was something special about that face. He was definitely good looking, but it was more than looks. His eyes were compelling. But not in a come-hither way. No, she thought, more of 'let me give you a hug' way. In an 'I see the real you' way. So warm she could get lost in their depth.

No wedding ring she noted. *Wonder why.* His hands were long, and his fingernails were manicured. Casey remembered Emma telling her that Samuel was an oncology nurse. She didn't know any male nurses. *Wonder if he's gay?* She snorted; her radar told her he was most definitely not.

"Our thoughts create patterns, behaviors, and habits not always in a good way. When you've been traumatized even simple things can send your brain on a downward spiral." Samuel paused and looked around the room, his eyes resting briefly on each participant. He lingered for a moment longer on Casey. "My goal, *our* goal, is to get you to recognize the beginning of your downward spiral and give you the tools to stop those thoughts, those patterns in their tracks. Meditation, whatever form you chose it to be – and there are many different ways to meditate- can be the conduit to change."

"Fancy words for hard work" murmured Casey.

Samuel looked at her and then surveyed the group. "Indeed. Change is hard work and often painful. But is the pain, your suffering, now any worse?" he paused. "Can you see yourself hiding the true you for the rest of your life?"

Casey stilled. No, she thought, I need to move on. Emma told her she could do this, and she believed her. *I can do this. I am strong.*

The rest of the workshop was focused on learning meditation and learning to know what your body is telling you.

"Emma will come back, and we'll do some gentle yoga today and some yoga nidra. Come at these with an open mind. Change will come gradually with consistent practice. After this weekend I would recommend yoga and meditation classes with Emma, Gwen or myself here at Half Moon studio."

On Sunday afternoon as the weekend workshop concluded, they filed out of the room. Casey stopped to thank Samuel. "That was …amazing. I'm scared of what's ahead but at least now I have a path, a way out of the muck my life has been."

Samuel held her gaze. "It takes a strong person to survive trauma. To hold yourself together and to move forward requires intelligence and strength. Devote that intelligence and strength to healing yourself. You're worth it."

Casey blushed. "Thank you again." She turned to leave and then stopped. "Do you do other exercise besides yoga?"

"Funny you should ask. I was just thinking I needed to build up my muscles a bit. You know getting old you lose muscle mass." He looked ruefully down at his lean body.

"You should come workout at my fitness place." With a sly grin and a flirtatious glance, she added, "We can always use a good-looking man to brighten up the space. I teach a killer dance class. Do you like to dance?"

Samuel grinned and hesitated, "I do like to dance but I'm more of weights and spin class type of guy. Good for getting rid of stress."

"Ah yes, a more manly workout. Dancing can do that too. I feel free and more alive when I dance. It's how I stayed sane." Her eyes widened a bit as she realized she had accidentally revealed a bit more of herself to him. He was so easy to talk to. "But we'd love to have a new client. You know Emma's fiancé owns Core Connection. She comes regularly. And Grey and his son Isaac are fantastic coaches. Think about it. It's the least I can do- develop your muscles while you develop my coping skills."

"I will Ms. Casey. Thank you for the recommendation." He looked at her with a kindness that gave Casey pause. Her heart warmed in a way it never had. He sees me, she thought, me.

She blushed as she pushed it just a bit further. "I hope I see you there. Oh, and by the way, we give discounts to fitness professionals and to medical professionals."

"Well then that settles it. Can I get a double discount? I teach yoga and I'm a nurse."

"I'll see what I can do." She said as she walked away.

About the Author

Michelle Stevens is a yoga teacher who loves to write, read and workout. She has a BA in English and some graduate credits in writing but spent most her career in accounting. Retirement from the corporate world allowed her to focus on her passion for yoga, help with the grandkids and write the romance story that's been dancing in her head for years.

Michelle , like Emma hates cleaning, cooking and is a terrible dancer. She and her husband John live in Winston Salem, NC. She has four adult children, six beautiful and creative grandchildren. She's been a yoga and group fitness instructor for many years.

Just a note

This story reflects the effect that yoga, meditation, and exercise can have on anxiety and better health but in a fun and engaging way. They are not cures but ways to cope. The health issues Emma deals with are common issues most older women deal with. Anxiety, PTSA and body image issues have no age limit. And the idea that sex can be creative and exciting at any age is empowering to both men and women.